The Canterbury Question

The Canterbury Question

By

Jerilyn J. Tyner

Desert Breeze Publishing, Inc.
27305 W. Live Oak Rd #424
Castaic, CA 91384

http://www.DesertBreezePublishing.com

Published in the United States of America
Electronic Publish Date: May 2013
Print Publish Date: March 2014

Editor-In-Chief: Gail R. Delaney
Content Editor: Sherry Brinson
Marketing Director: Jenifer Ranieri
Cover Artist: Debbie Taylor
Photography Credit: Taria Reed Studios
Model: Alisa Sharoikina

Dedication

To Art Seamans,
with respect and gratitude for your influence on my life

Acknowledgments

Special thanks to my three siblings, Darlene, Ralph, and Ardis, for their encouragement and support, and to my friend Gia who patiently led me through the technology jungle. I also thank my husband Tom who kept telling me, "This story needs to be told."

Prologue

November 1818

Steam flared from the nostrils of the dappled mare pulling the small wagon up a gentle slope. The reins were held in the gloved hands of a gentleman who skillfully guided the horse around the crest of the hill and into a gradual descent to the town below.

The sound of a wailing infant behind him did nothing to disturb the driver's reverie. Andrew Judson was a determined man, focused on success in politics. For a man of his abilities, a bid for Congress was not out of reach. Yes, he had made some mistakes in his upward climb, but there were ways of making such embarrassments disappear.

It was a crisp day in early November. Autumn winds carpeted the road with leaves from blazing maples crowding the western side of the slope. Wisps of fog drifted aimlessly through the little valleys, waiting to be chased away as the sun climbed ever higher above the hills.

The horse soon reached the town, which was awake and bustling with activity. Slowing her gait, she pulled the wagon down the main street and came to a stop in front of the general store. The driver sprang from his seat, somehow managing to keep his well-polished boots from being splattered by muck from the road, and turned to tether his horse to the railing. He was a handsome man of thirty-four years. Although not overly tall, his frame was compact and strong. His thick brown hair fell over his forehead in a mass of curls. Creases radiated from the corners of his hazel eyes, set beneath a strong brow, furrowed, not from age, but from tension.

His task finished, he turned to watch the careful descent of the occupants of the wagon. The woman carried a small trunk in one hand and on her hip balanced a snugly wrapped bundle. Her full, cotton skirt impeded her movements, and the gentleman considered the possibility she might wind up standing in a puddle, but he did nothing to assist her. He would not humiliate himself by touching a colored woman here in town in broad daylight. She nearly slipped and landed in the mud, but kept her dignity and reached the street upright. He avoided looking at the young woman, but in spite of himself glanced at the baby. It was a sturdy, healthy infant, but the skin had a sallow, yellow undertone, not the rich, dark complexion of the mother. The eyes, still without lashes, were slits of darkness, mirroring the shame of its birth.

Rebecca, the gentleman's wife, had been alarmed at first sight of the child. "How queer she looks," she had exclaimed. "I am afraid, Andrew, that our maid has been with an Indian, for surely such coloring never

1

came from a pure race. It is shocking. No wonder she refuses to name the father. What will be said of me, the mistress of this house? That I permit low moral conduct in my own household?"

She had given Cassie shelter for a few months, but grew increasingly uncomfortable at the thought of having her own newly-born daughter reared on the same premises as this heathen child. Andrew readily agreed to Rebecca's demand that the housemaid, Cassie, be sent away. Today he had brought her from his home in Canterbury to Norwich where she would board a small boat taking her farther south.

They crossed the road wordlessly and approached the landing where a crowded barge awaited. Only then did Cassie speak. "I'm sorry," she whispered, staring down at the mud. Her dark eyes were moist; her full lips quivered.

He pressed a small bag of coins into her hand. "When you reach the harbor, other ships will be there. You have enough for passage wherever you want to go. There is much work in Baltimore. Perhaps you can go there. Wherever you want." He turned his head away, not looking at her. "We don't want to know where you go."

Without a word, she walked to the barge, her graceful head held high. There had been a time when he had been pleased by her fluid movements, but no more. He saw her for what she was -- a lure put in his pathway by Satan himself to tempt him at his weakest moment.

Now she was gone. Relief flooded Andrew Judson. He would return to his estate in the Connecticut town of Canterbury to enjoy his prime years as an honored citizen. He had been denied a commission in the second war with the British because he belonged to the wrong political party, but that had been before Rebecca Warner. After marrying her, he had been guided by his father-in-law's wisdom and changed his political loyalties. That had marked a change in fortunes for young Judson. Admitted to the bar over ten years ago, he was now one of the founding directors of the Windham County Bank. As husband of a respectable young woman who had recently presented him with a baby daughter, his personal and political futures looked secure.

A horse cantered past as he returned to his wagon. He did not look up at the rider, but down at his feet. He cursed. His boots were spattered with mud.

Chapter One

Summer 1831

Plainfield was behind her. The narrow, dreary streets lined with dreary, gabled houses. The Plainfield Finishing School, with its narrow windows, fusty parlors, and endless teas. At times it felt she would forever remain at Plainfield, teaching sewing and manners to half-hearted pupils who were merely waiting for their fathers to arrange suitable marriages for them. Pupils like Rosie Cooper. Poor girl. Reading the sublime verses of *Paradise Lost* with all the passion of a ticking clock. It was not her fault she was so unlike the flower she was named for, but -- oh! -- how she tried one's patience. As their teacher, Prudence had longed to challenge their minds and spirits, but being in the employ of Mistress Enroth, she must teach only the things assigned to her. This she did, for six years, with all the patience she could muster. Patience, she knew, was not her strong point. "I always tried, though, to do my best," she murmured.

Her brother Reuben, who was driving the carriage, looked down at her. "And thee did." was his solemn remark.

Her lips curved at his seriousness. She let the hood of her cape fall back from her head and inhaled the rain-washed air. Her honey-blond hair was done up in a simple knot, with short curls waved across her forehead. Her plain, gray dress, meant to be serviceable rather than fashionable, nevertheless accented the smoky color of her eyes. Anyone studying her face would have said her blue-gray eyes, framed with silky, dark lashes and sweetly arched brows, were her best feature. Her chin was a bit too pronounced for a classical beauty, but with her willowy figure, ivory complexion, and radiant smile, she was an attractive woman. Prudence, however, gave little thought to her looks. Cleanliness and tidiness were virtues she believed in. She had no time for vanity.

"I was only talking to myself. Thinking of all the years at Plainfield. I did not mean for thee to hear me. I sounded proud." Pride, of course, was a deadly sin, but not one to have a grip upon Prudence.

He shook his head. "Not proud. Only true. Thee truly has been faithful, and now way has opened for thee at last. I am happy for ye, Pru." The plain Quaker manner of speaking came naturally to their tongues when talking with family members, although they did not often use such speech with others. Brotherly affection was evident on his handsome young face. "Just think. Now thee is the schoolmistress, and shall teach what pleases thee."

"Also what pleases God, I pray." Prudence grew suddenly quiet. *I*

3

have always wanted to be completely on my own. But what if I fail?

In early May, a group of citizens from the town of Canterbury contacted her with entreaties to establish a school in their town. Mr. Judson, a lawmaker and spokesman for the group, shook a sheaf of papers under her nose. "We have numerous letters in hand describing your character and teaching abilities. They say you can teach anyone anything. From our own observation, they do not exaggerate.

"I assure you," he went on, "you will have the support of the entire town. There are at least a dozen families with girls who have finished the district school, and we will be forever grateful if you will establish an academy where they can pursue a higher education. My own daughter will be the first to enroll."

Prudence hesitated. "I am honored by the offer, but I must pray for guidance. I need to wait on the Lord to see if way will open."

"Way will open" was a Quaker expression, meaning a certainty that the hand of Providence was guiding, but it was evidently an unfamiliar idea to the expansive Mr. Judson.

"I would say the way is wide open," he insisted. "You have my personal guarantee that the Luther Paine house will be available to you at once. You couldn't hope for a finer house. It has room for at least a dozen boarding pupils. I myself will advance the funds. The merchants all agree to support the academy. Stephen Coit has a well-stocked store, and will gladly open a line of credit for you. He might even barter for his two daughters' tuition." He waved his hand with an authoritative sweep, dismissing all obstacles.

Prudence clamped her lips firmly together. "I dislike being rushed. I will give you my answer in a fortnight."

"I'm not sure," she said to her father after days of considering Judson's offer. "There is no Friends' meeting house in Canterbury, and since I would be teaching non-Quaker students, I'd be expected to go to their Sunday services and allow for non-Quaker thinking and customs."

Pardon Crandall leaned his elbows on the well-worn table and laced his capable fingers together. "Truth is truth, regardless of the dress it wears. I cannot think thee would forsake the ways of simplicity and service wherever thee goes. Perhaps way is opening for thee to let thy life speak in a new place."

Gradually, she came to sense the light within leading her to Canterbury. By June, the business details were settled, and she began planning for the first term in her own academy, The Canterbury Female Boarding School.

But what if I fail? The echo still plagued her, but it was muffled by excitement as the wheels of her brother's rig carried Prudence to her destination.

It was late afternoon when the carriage approached a bridge. Reuben slowed the horse as they clattered over a rushing stream. The frequent summer rains had kept the streams full, the fields lush, and the crops fruitful. He was a farmer. Not yet married, he worked the land with his father. Their property was northeast of Canterbury, only a few hours away.

Prudence was grateful for Reuben's help today, knowing there was much work for him on the farm. God willing, they would reach Canterbury by nightfall, and Reuben could be on his way home by early morning. They were almost ready for a second haying. A sideways glance told her he was only half listening to her enthusiastic plans as the small carriage turned southwestward and began picking up speed.

"I shall teach grammar, of course, history, and geography, and I think some of the older girls should learn chemistry and astronomy..."

"Chemistry and astronomy," marveled Reuben. "The fathers of Canterbury must be quite enlightened to suggest those subjects for their girls."

"They did not exactly suggest it," admitted Prudence. "I see no reason why girls should not study the same things boys do. That is why I disliked Plainfield. Girls were not challenged to do more than read and write. After all, there's more to learning than sewing and embroidery."

"So, thee convinced the town fathers their daughters should study science." Reuben squinted into the glare of the late afternoon sun. "What else shall thee teach?"

"Of course, we shall study moral philosophy... it is of the greatest value..."

But the value of moral philosophy was discussed no further. The downhill stretch of road turned sharply left, and at the very moment Reuben tightened the reins, a pair of turkeys fluttered up before the startled horse.

"Whoa!" He struggled for control. Plunging and rearing, the horse left the road, landing the open carriage in a ditch. Prudence went flying.

"Whoa!" her brother called again. Bringing the frantic horse to a standstill, he ran to Prudence's side.

"Oh, my, look at me-- oh my, how ridiculous of me. My ankle-- oh dear-- where are my books?" She was half crying, half laughing, and he could make no sense of her words.

"Pru, thee must have hit thy head. Hold still."

"No, no, my head is fine. But my books-- all over the road." Indeed they were. Making an effort to scramble to her feet to retrieve her precious books, she sank again into the ditch. "And look!" she raved. "The wheel is broken."

It was true. The carriage wheel lay splintered on the road, but Reuben's concern was for his sister. "Thee should be more worried about thy own limbs. Pray tell, is anything broken?" He bent quickly to examine her leg, and exclaimed in alarm when he saw the swelling of her ankle.

"I felt something pop," she admitted, "but at least I am in one piece. My ankle must be sprained. That is all." With help, she struggled to her feet, but even with Reuben's support she could not bear her weight on the injured foot. When he gathered the scattered parcels and returned them to the carriage, he found a dresser scarf among the packed linens.

"Hold still, Prudy. Let me wrap this around thy ankle."

"I can't-- I can't-- oh, Reuben, don't touch it." Tears sprang to her eyes, despite her determination to be brave.

"My books--" she began once more.

"Yes, yes. I have found them all, and put them in the carriage. But what do we do next?" They had met few travelers since leaving Plainfield, and both doubted any help would come their way this late in the day. "I'll not leave thee alone to go for help, so what is to be done?"

"I can ride," she assured him with more confidence than she felt. "Help me onto Dobbin, and lead him until we find a place..."

"What sort of place out here in the woods, Prudy? We haven't passed a settlement or even a house for at least an hour." The trees crowded against the primitive, rutted road, and the thorny underbrush forbade any exploration. His common sense cautioned him against walking off into the gathering shadows, but he had no other plan.

"I am sure, Reuben, that God sees all. We have to move forward and trust Providence to care for us." She bit her lip to keep from crying out as he boosted her onto the horse and took the reins in hand.

Clicking his tongue and speaking gently to the horse, he began walking toward Canterbury. "I pray we find shelter before dark. I doubt not there are animals in these woods."

"Thee did not need to remind me."

Before they had gone a mile, Prudence grimaced. Her ankle throbbed. How much longer could she endure the jarring gait of the horse? A short distance ahead, she could see another road intersecting the one they traveled. Perhaps there would be a fingerboard there, telling them how far they were from a town. At the crossroads, they would have a decision to make, and then she would ask Reuben to let her have a rest before continuing. *This is no tragedy*, she reminded herself. *Only an inconvenience. It will pass.*

Ignore the pain.
Think about the sweet country smells.
Ignore the pain.
It will pass.
Ignore the pain.
Listen to the contented sounds... the soft summer evening sounds... listen to...

Yes! There was a sound! "What's that?"

Reuben heard it, too. It grew more distinct until they were sure it was the fast trot of a horse and the whirr of wagon wheels. Reuben sprinted toward the crossroads, waving his arms urgently. The oncoming driver reigned in his horse, slowing to a walk as he took in the sight before him.

Prudence saw a bare-headed man of color whose white shirt, open at the throat, contrasted with his dark skin and revealed the muscles of a young man familiar with the hard labor of farm life. She was certain the rider was an angel sent by Providence. His voice was deep, and his words were as welcome as a song. "What's the trouble, sir? Can I help?"

"You are an answer to prayer, Friend. I am Reuben Crandall. My sister and I are headed to Canterbury -- she's to start a school there -- but we had an accident a ways back." He nodded toward the road from Plainfield. "We lost a wheel when our carriage overturned, and my sister was injured. Her ankle is sprained, or maybe even broken."

Seeing Prudence slumped forward on the horse, her brows drawn in pain, the man lost no time in helping her from the horse and transferring her to his wagon. As he tried to make her as comfortable as possible, he introduced himself. "My name is Charles Harris," he said, "and since you called me Friend, I take it you're Quakers?" Reuben's nod told him all he needed to know.

"I feel free then to take you to my father's place. Our farm is only a few miles away. On the way to Canterbury, matter of fact."

Soon, they were underway. Prudence lay in the wagon, her ankle carefully immobilized. Though still in pain, she was less miserable than she had been on horseback. Best of all, they would have shelter for the night, and surely this angel sent by Providence would help Reuben with the carriage wheel in the morning. Forcing herself to relax, she leaned back and closed her eyes, listening to the easy conversation between Reuben and Charles Harris.

When there was a lull in the familiar talk about farming matters, Charles asked his companion, "Have you heard of William Lloyd Garrison?"

"The publisher of the *Liberator?* The abolitionist? I've heard reports of the speech he made at Park Street Church in Boston a couple of years ago. He has stirred up quite a controversy, so they say."

Charles made a sound of agreement. "I've just met him. I'm on my way back from Massachusetts, and I've brought bundles of the *Liberator* to give out in this county."

Prudence had noticed the twine-bound newspapers surrounding her in the wagon. She could just make out the masthead, *The Liberator.* She, too, had heard of Garrison.

"I left half my copies with Reverend May in Brooklyn. He's a great friend of our cause."

Again Reuben questioned, "You mean, he's an abolitionist also? Not too popular a cause, I think."

"I'd say Quakers aren't too popular around here, either, Friend.

7

Most people use the words Quaker and abolitionist in the same breath." Charles Harris chuckled. A deep, musical sound. "I've spent some time listening to Garrison, and reading his papers. I don't think 'abolitionist' really describes the man. True, he hates slavery."

"People say he favors immediate freeing of the slaves, regardless of how it affects the economy of the South. I agree, the slave trade should be outlawed in all the states."

"That, Friend Crandall, is only part of the problem. Garrison is one of the few who understand emancipation is only the beginning. Even here in New England, most of our people are poor and live like outcasts. Most folks hate social change of any kind, and true freedom for us is a long ways down the road. Garrison hopes education will lead the way down that path." Harris' face was solemn. "Do you know he prints his newspaper at his own expense? He has sacrificed much for the cause of freedom."

"It sounds as if he is your hero, Charles."

"I'm just glad to be part of his mission. Even if I'm only passing out papers."

"What would you say is his mission? His message?"

"Equality for all men is guaranteed by our Constitution. As a Quaker, Reuben, don't you believe that, too?"

Reuben hesitated only a moment. "As a man, definitely, and as a Quaker, too. Brotherhood is a part of our faith, but I guess I have devoted myself to farming more than philosophy. Here I am in the presence of an apostle."

Charles chuckled again. "Just a paper boy, Friend. Just a paper boy." He turned to Prudence with a gentle smile. "We're almost home now, miss. Sorry about all the bumps and rattles."

The road lay before them like a narrow, brown snake. Charles was familiar with every twist and turn and negotiated the curves expertly. Twilight deepened as they rode, shadows lengthened into night, and just as the moon arose, the Harris farm came into view.

Prudence sighed when the horse came to a stop before a tidy clapboard farmhouse. The door opened, light poured out of the house, and three people hurried to greet them.

Charles bestowed a brotherly peck on the cheek of a young woman who rushed to hug him. "My sister, Sarah," he introduced her. "This is Reuben Crandall and Miss Prudence Crandall. I found them on the road in need of a place to stay tonight."

Mrs. Harris stepped forward, her dark eyes snapping in a friendly, broad face. She promptly took charge of the situation.

"*Land o' Goshen,*" she exclaimed when she saw Prudence's ankle. "Just you look how puffed up your foot is. You musta had a powerful jolt to bring on such swelling. It's broke for sure."

"Oh, no," objected Prudence. "I think it is just a sprain. See? I can move it a little."

"Sprained or broke, we can fix you up good's new." She turned to her daughter. "Sarah, we're goin' to need cold water -- as cold's you can get -- and some clean towels for a soft splint. A shame we ain't got ice. Be quick, now. You can just call me Sally," she murmured, taking Prudence's arm.

Over her shoulder, she called to her husband, "And William, get them horses to the barn afore you come inside."

William and Charles Harris remained with Reuben in the yard, busying themselves with the horses and wagon as the mother and daughter assisted Prudence into the house.

Soon she was resting in a small room off the kitchen, where Sally applied a cold compress to the injured ankle and used thick towels to wrap her foot. "There, now." Sliding a folded quilt under the leg, Sally propped it at an angle which eased the pressure and pain. "Let's get you into some nightclothes and scare up a bite to eat. You look peaked as can be, miss."

Soon Sarah was at the door. "Try this, please, Miss Crandall. Here's fresh bread, milk, and a cuppa tea. It'll help you sleep."

It had been hours since she and Reuben had eaten, and Prudence's hand trembled as she took a bite of the nourishing bread. Pain and nausea overcame her, and she put the bread aside. It was all she could do to sip the fragrant herbal concoction in the teacup. As Prudence drank the tea, Sarah removed a few things from the wardrobe. "You'll sleep here in my room tonight, Miss Crandall, and I'll stay in the parlor. It's got a settle that's comfy as any bed."

Prudence protested. "I could not think of taking your room, Sarah. Just help me to the parlor. I can rest there." But Sarah was insistent about her plan, and Prudence had to accept it. Besides, she was too tired to do otherwise. The herb tea had its effect, and at last she relaxed. She heard Sally in the kitchen, preparing a late supper for the men. Listening to the murmur of Reuben's voice, she fell asleep.

Morning came. Prudence woke to the sound of singing. The alto voice flowed, rich and free as the lyrics themselves.

"Immortal love, forever full,
Forever flowing free,
Forever shared, forever whole,
A never ebbing sea..."

It must be Charles's sister. What is her name? Oh, yes... Sarah. She looked around the cozy room, remembering how she got there. She sat up, stretched her arms overhead, then tossed the bedclothes aside and inspected her ankle. The bruise looked ugly, but at least the swelling had not increased. However, when she swung her feet to the floor, she groaned.

Immediately Sarah hurried to her side. "Oh, Miss Crandall, don't try to get up by yourself. Let me help you, please." She was wearing a calico dress of yellow and brown beneath her white apron and a white mob cap on her head. In the daylight, Prudence could see she was a pretty girl with luminous, dark eyes, flawless skin, and a softly rounded figure.

Giving a shaky smile, Prudence accepted Sarah's help. "What is that wonderful aroma?" she inquired once she was upright. "Do I smell bacon?"

"Yes, Miss Crandall," Sarah beamed. "There's biscuits and eggs, too. Do you like blueberries? There's fresh cream to go with -- just brought in this morning."

"Oh, my dear, you needn't have gone to such trouble."

Her hostess grinned. "What's the fun of having a guest if you can't fuss a little? But I hope you won't mind eating in the kitchen. It's only you and me here now."

"I am not used to being the last one out of bed," Prudence said. "Where is everyone else?"

Sarah bustled about, bringing Prudence all the necessary items for her comfort, including linens, a wash basin, and a fresh, daintily embroidered chemise. Prudence glanced at her traveling clothes, folded on the chair beside the bed. Someone had tried her best to sponge off the dirt, but still her dress was a sorry sight. It would have to do for now.

"Well, Charles and Mr. Crandall got up with the rooster. Soon as they had a bite to eat, they set off to fix the carriage. I think they took Toby along. He's 'most as good a hand as a wheelwright for fixin' wagons.

"My papa is doing chores -- milkin', I s'pose -- and Mama and Daisy are washing the clothes. Daisy's our hired girl, but I get to stay here and take care of you," she concluded.

"Now you wash up and dress, and I'll be back to help you to the table."

Soon Prudence was seated in the cheery kitchen. A bouquet of yellow flowers set off the embroidered tablecloth and enhanced the mellow ivory tones of the china. Fragrant steam rose from the teapot, tempting her senses. With ravenous pleasure, she bit into a tender, buttery biscuit.

When the nourishing breakfast was gone, Sarah helped Prudence into the parlor and made her comfortable on the settle. "Mama said to keep your foot up and keep the compresses cold as we can." Sarah fitted actions to her words, and when her patient was comfortable, brought in two fresh cups of tea and sat down for a visit. Her eyes sparkled as she spoke. "I heard Charles talking to your brother last night, Miss Crandall. You are a teacher?"

Prudence nodded, sipping the invigorating beverage.

"How wonderful." Sarah went on. "Teaching girls to read must be the most exciting thing a body could do. Why, if a girl can read, she can learn anything a'tall -- history, mathematics, the Bible, about the stars... what is that called?"

"Astronomy." Prudence set her teacup on the saucer. "Yes, I plan to teach all those things in Canterbury. I am to open a school for young ladies there."

"Canterbury." Excitement rose in Sarah's voice. "I've been there often. The district school is just south of town."

"Then do you know where the meeting house is? The school will be right across the Green from the meeting house. It is known as the Luther Paine house. He built it twenty-five years ago."

"I know the house," responded Sarah. "It's in a beautiful spot. I've never been inside, though," she added.

Prudence placed her empty teacup and saucer on the side table. "The girls will study grammar and history, and we shall have astronomy, geography, and French. My sister Almira will join me soon to teach music and to help with the younger classes. She has a wonderful way with children. Sometimes I am not so gentle..."

Sarah's huge, dark eyes were fixed on her with longing. *She looks like the puppy at Plainfield. How often that little beggar sat under the table by the girls' feet, even though Mistress Enroth forbade the girls to give him treats. Sarah has the same hungry look.*

"I am going to charge twenty-five dollars a term for each girl, and books, stationery, and other supplies will be added." Sarah's interest did not wane with this information, as Prudence had expected. On second thought, why would it? The well-set table, nicely furnished rooms, and quality of Sarah's clothing showed William Harris was prosperous. He was a free Negro who farmed his own land and hired men to help him and Charles with the work. That much she learned from the conversation between Reuben and Charles last night. Sally also had household help, as Sarah had said earlier. Probably William would be able to afford schooling for his daughter as easily as many of the Canterbury fathers. Prudence shifted her weight in the chair and dropped her gaze.

"Have you been to school, Sarah?"

"I finished the district school five years ago," she replied. "I love to read, and I have a few books. I can figure some, too. But, of course, I couldn't go on from there." An unspoken question hung in the air, and there was no answer except silence.

A slight breeze lifted the curtains at the window, calling their attention to a carriage not far down the road. Sarah sprang to her feet. "It's Charles and Mr. Crandall. They have fixed the wheel already, praise be to Goodness."

Before long, a smiling Reuben came through the door. "The wagon

11

is fixed. They had an extra wheel just the right size. The job went smooth as butter thanks to Toby and Charles."

"Great news, Reuben. And did thee find all my belongings? My books..."

Reuben laughed. "Yes, yes. Thee cannot be at rest without them. They are all packed in the carriage, safe as chicks under the mother hen."

"It's only four or five miles to Canterbury," Charles interjected.

"If thee can travel, Pru, we will have thee in thy new home today."

She answered his enthusiasm with a wry smile. "That may be easier said than done, Reuben. It will be weeks before Almira can come to help with the school, and I don't think I can manage alone with this bad ankle."

He sat on the edge of the settle and reached for her hand. "It may take a month for your ankle to heal. Even then, thee will need help running the household... it is far more than thee and our sister can handle. Charles has a wonderful idea." He glanced toward the doorway, where Charles stood politely."

"I hope you think the same, Miss Crandall. Your brother told me about your school, and I know that even if you had not smashed up your ankle yesterday, you would need help with the cooking and cleaning and such."

Prudence had to agree. She had expected to have recommendations from Mr. Judson in hiring help, but she was willing to hear what Charles had to say. "Do you have someone in mind?"

"A young woman named Marcy Davis. She lives near Brooklyn, and I know for a fact she's healthy and strong and has good character." His smile widened. "You see, she is my fiancée. If she is agreeable, I could fetch her today and bring her to Canterbury." He went on to name her many virtues -- efficiency, thrift, cleanliness, honesty -- but it was hard to say how objective he was in describing the woman he loved.

"Indeed," Prudence said, "I am sure she is all you say, but will she agree to come on such short notice? How long will she be able to stay? What salary will she accept?" Even while voicing the questions, Prudence knew she had little choice but to accept this Marcy Davis as a Providential answer to her need. She only hoped the lady would be half as agreeable as Charles said. If the arrangement did not work out, she would consult Mr. Judson, as she had first planned.

"Tell her she will not be expected to do all the work of the household. I plan to hire a man for the heavier jobs. Besides, I grew up on a farm, and my father would be ashamed of me if he thought I would not do chores. He trained us well."

Reuben nodded in agreement.

"As for my students, I expect they will learn the virtues of physical labor as well as mental discipline."

So Charles eagerly headed his wagon northward to find Marcy

Davis and bring her to Canterbury. With the help of Sally and Sarah, Prudence was outfitted with a sturdy walking stick and prepared for the last of her journey. From the seat of the carriage, Prudence smiled down at the Harris family.

"I cannot thank you enough for your hospitality. If ever someday I can return your kindness, do not hesitate to call on me."

The day for that promise to be fulfilled would come sooner than any of them dreamed.

Chapter Two

Winter 1831

The footprints on the frosty path showed Prudence had cut across the town green from the meeting house where she stopped to pray. She was in the habit of taking solitary walks in the early morning when the world was fresh and undisturbed. She found the morning the best time to meditate and commit the day ahead to the Creator. Pausing, she looked up at the house directly ahead -- her house, home of the Canterbury Female Boarding School.

"It still seems like a dream -- my own school." A sigh of thankfulness and satisfaction escaped her. It had taken nearly two months for her ankle to heal completely after the carriage accident. "Another opportunity, I suppose, to develop patience," she murmured, "but I would never have managed without Marcy and Almy."

Of the eighteen girls enrolled, eight lived at the school. There were the Graber twins, Abby and Angelina, lively twelve-year-olds with freckles and bouncing curls. Lucretia Jackson, who shared their room, had a sober temperament which provided some balance to the twins' antics. Hannah Pearl was the shining star of the group academically, and Prudence hoped her success in the classroom would help overcome her innate shyness. Leah Comfort, Kate Hyde, and Susan Lyon came from the same neighborhood and chose to occupy a room together. They were amiable, hard-working girls who gave Prudence little trouble and much joy.

At age seventeen, Margaret Hough had the status of being the eldest pupil and was therefore privileged to share Almira's room. Prudence sometimes heard them giggling together as they practiced the French lesson Monsieur Narcisse Fournier had given them that day. Prudence suspected her sister had a romantic fancy for the French teacher, but most likely it would pass. Almira was only nineteen herself, and couldn't be expected to be serious all the time, even though she taught music and assisted with the reading and arithmetic classes.

Prudence expected her ninth boarder sometime today. That had been the focus of her morning prayer. "Elizabeth Madeline Philleo." She pronounced the syllables thoughtfully. "I wonder what she is like. She's close to the same age as Hannah, so I'll assign her to Hannah's room. It would be wonderful if they became friends and not just roommates. But then, if they are both shy... Oh, dear, I cannot decide." All she knew about Elizabeth Philleo she had learned from her father's letters. A widower who had lost his wife three years ago, Calvin Philleo was doing his best to be mother and father to Elizabeth. He was a minister -- a Baptist, as she recalled -- who had settled in a parish in Suffield. Seeing to his thirteen-year-old daughter's education was a duty he would not neglect, and after corresponding with Prudence about the academy, he had decided to enroll Elizabeth. Prudence intended to do her best to see he would not be disappointed in the quality of the Academy.

As she ascended the steps of the school and opened the door, the smell of breakfast surrounded her. Marcy was a gem. A petite, spunky woman with skin the color of coffee, she reminded Prudence of a buzzing bee intent on her tasks. Prudence smiled to see her often climbing on a stool to reach the high cupboards. Charles Harris had done her a great favor in suggesting she hire his sweetheart to work for her.

Almira was, as usual, the first to come down the stairs. With her white cap resting on wavy, light brown hair and her blue dress swathing her slender frame, she was a pretty sight.

"Good morning, Prudy. I see thee has been walking as usual. Shall I ring the bell for breakfast?"

"Yes, indeed. I can smell the biscuits now, and you know they are best fresh from the oven."

The girls soon assembled around the table, subduing their chatter and giggles as they bowed their heads to say a silent grace. Not a word was spoken as the moments of silence descended upon the new day and each person communed with the Creator in her own way. The simple, wholesome food was then passed around, and Angelina helped herself to a generous serving of oatmeal. "You know," she confided to Lucretia, "I never ate breakfast a'tall before I came here. Abby and I stayed in bed as long as we pleased and ate cakes in our room when we did get up."

Abby joined the conversation. "We had ever so many sweets, too. But I never truly felt hungry as I do now."

"Did you ever drink so much water?" asked Susan, reaching for a blue and white mug. "I don't know why Miss Prudence thinks we need so much water. I feel like a fish, I do," she laughed.

Prudence hid a smile behind her napkin. It was true. Samuel Thomson, a pioneer in herbal medicine, had convinced her of the value of adequate amounts of water in removing toxins from the body, and she saw to it the girls drank plenty of pure water from the deep well on her property. She hoped by following his methods, her pupils would have little need for the expensive services of a doctor. So far, they had responded well to the discipline of healthy diet, consistent schedules, and daily fresh air and exercise.

The clock in the parlor sounded, informing the pupils they had only fifteen minutes until time for morning meditation. Conversation faded away as they finished breakfast and began clearing the table. By the time Prudence and Almira finished their tea, the pupils from town had arrived one by one and joined the others in the schoolroom.

15

Morning meeting, as it was called, was not a formal prayer time, but rather a time of silence, where each person was expected to reflect upon her actions and listen for divine guidance for the day ahead. However, this morning the fidgeting child in the third seat broke the silence with an unrestrained sigh. It was Catherine Judson.

"Miss Prudence," she hissed in an exaggerated whisper. "Can I be excused to fix my hair? The pins are so tight they are giving me a headache."

The number of pins securing her unruly hair gave her the appearance of a hedgehog, and Prudence did not doubt her discomfort, but she hated to disrupt the meditation. She felt the bench she was sitting on begin to vibrate and glanced at her sister. Almira's lips were pressed tightly together, but her sides quivered with suppressed laughter.

"She ought to say 'May I be excused,' oughtn't she, Miss Crandall?" piped up Lucretia, turning to Catherine with a baleful stare.

By this time, Eliza and Phoebe were whispering in the back of the room, and even Hannah had looked up from her prayerful posture and stared at Catherine with wide blue eyes. The meeting would have ended abruptly had Prudence not maintained her repose. Her hands lay open on her lap. Her face betrayed no emotion but peace. Her gray eyes swept over the room, meeting each girl with a sobering glance. Last of all, she looked at Catherine. Giving her the smallest of smiles, she spoke two words. "Soon, dear."

At that, the only sounds left in the room were the ticking of the schoolroom clock and the breathing of twenty-one young ladies. At nine o'clock, the meeting over, Marcy picked up her apron and returned to the kitchen, the serene girls gathered their materials for class, and Miss Almira Crandall took her place in front of the schoolroom to begin the music lesson. Prudence kindly and efficiently loosened Catherine's hairpins and brought her wiry locks into submission. A new day was underway at the Canterbury Female Boarding School.

Classes continued until 11:30. Then, at a signal from Miss Prudence, the pupils closed their daybooks, blotted the ink from their pens, and returned them to the holders. With grateful sighs, they stretched their spines and filed from the schoolroom. Prudence smiled to hear their friendly chatter as they gathered their cloaks and bonnets. To tell the truth, the daily walk was nearly her favorite time of day. She was raised on a farm, and even though she was no longer a girl, she still preferred outdoor activities to the confinement of the schoolroom.

Eagerly the eighteen girls and their two teachers emerged from the house and at a brisk pace began their trek through the town of Canterbury. Two by two they passed by a row of painted wooden homes shaded by oak trees. Their voices chimed in girlish conversation as they marched up the cobblestone street, passed Mr. Coit's store, and crossed the Green. Nearby, they could see the gracious brick home of Mr.

Judson, Catherine's father. The cold wind brought the color to their faces and they stamped their feet and swung their arms to keep from shivering. At last, they circled the meeting house with its gleaming white spire and headed back toward the school.

"It's snowing!" cried out Jane. The gusting winds powdered their upturned faces with flake after flake as they watched the snow icing the bare tree branches with white. Some of the girls glanced longingly at the wooded area beyond the meeting house. It would be a wonderful place to spend an hour at play, but their teachers were resolutely moving toward home, knowing Marcy would have dinner on the table at 12:00. They would have to wait until Friday to have their free time in the woods. If only the snow would last until then.

An appetizing aroma wafted from the dining room, encouraging them to make haste to the table. The main meal of the day was hearty, but by no means rich. Plain food graced the table in abundance, beginning with a smooth and flavorful onion soup. Fricasseed chicken, accompanied by biscuits, hot slaw, and roasted carrots quelled their appetites. As she began clearing the table, Marcy smiled with satisfaction to see the girls had done justice to her meal.

The pupils waited for their teacher to dismiss them for their hour of rest, but instead, she began to speak. "Girls, we will receive a new student this afternoon. I do not know for sure what time she and her father will arrive, for they are coming from some distance, and the snow will most likely delay them."

"How old is she?" interrupted eleven-year-old Mary. "I hope she is my age."

Prudence continued. "Her name is Elizabeth Philleo. She will be a boarding student, and I believe I will ask Hannah to share her room with the new girl. She is your age, Hannah."

Hannah's smile told Prudence she need not have worried about the new pupil's acceptance. "I have plenty of room, Miss Crandall. We can study together."

"Coming at this point in the term," Prudence went on, "she will need some catching up, and I cannot think of anyone better to help her." Miss Prudence was not given to compliments, and Hannah flushed with pleasure at the sincerity of her teacher's words. The girls were dismissed from the table, and with much discussion and anticipation of the new girl's arrival, they left the dining room. Some wandered into the parlor and curled up near the fireplace with books and studies, a few picked up their sewing, and others went to their bedrooms to peer out at the transformation of their world under the falling snow. Almira and Prudence looked forward to this hour to themselves each day and made it a practice to lay aside their work for a time of quiet rest.

Removing her shoes, Prudence sat on the bed and sighed. A flash of orange fur and a soft meow told her Whittington had come for his daily

17

conversation. Smiling as he rubbed against her arm, she stroked his neck. "Where hast thee been, thou vagabond? Thee hasn't dragged anything up from the cellar, I hope. I think I shall make a place for thee in the schoolroom so I can keep my eye on thee. Maybe thee will learn something besides catching mice and chasing birds. Perhaps thee will learn to meow in French if thee pays attention to M. Fournier."

Whittington leapt from the bed, as if the suggestion of learning French did not please him. Prudence laughed. She had assured Marcy and Almira the reason she let the cat have the run of the house was because he was a superior mouser, but in reality, she was foolishly fond of the orange tomcat and often confided her private thoughts to him.

She picked up the cat, and reached to the dresser for a packet of envelopes. "Look at this stack of letters, Whittington. All from Mr. Philleo. All about his daughter. It seems she is the apple of his eye, and all he has left to remind him of his wife, Madeline. I wonder what he is like. He says almost nothing about himself, yet he seems to have a sense of purpose and firmness. I hope he will find my school up to his standards. We will meet him soon. I confess I am curious about him... curious, in fact, as a cat."

At this point, Whittington appeared bored, rather than curious. He escaped from his mistress and with a yawn curled up on her pillow. Encouraged by his example, Prudence stretched out on the bed and allowed herself the luxury of falling asleep.

Her nap ended when she heard Almira and Margaret swishing past her room. As usual, they would be the first ones back in the schoolroom, always eager to greet M. Fournier with their well-practiced, *"Bon jour, Monsieur. Comment allez-vous? Tres bien, merci."*

Prudence chuckled. Their accents, she was sure, were not Parisian, but after all, Narcisse Fournier was from Quebec, and it was providential she had found a French teacher at all. Her own mastery of the language was weak at best. She rose from her bed, shooed the cat from her room, and tucking a wayward curl behind her ear, made her way to the day room to read over her students' latest compositions.

Scarcely had she finished marking Abby's composition when she heard a disturbance from the schoolroom. It sounded like a stampede of small feet racing to the window, and she deduced from the excitement company had arrived.

The Philleos' chaise drew up to the gate as Prudence sent the gawking girls back to the schoolroom. It would not do to have Miss Philleo met with twenty pairs of curious eyes, and what would her father think of such lack of order? Prudence, eager to make a good first impression, stepped onto the porch to welcome the newcomer, but the young girl in the gray cloak held her focus for less than a minute before the tall man beside her captured Prudence's gaze.

Ascending the steps with his daughter on his arm, Calvin Philleo greeted the schoolmistress with a smile that lit up his rugged features. Despite the cold, the man held his hat in hand. Snowflakes stuck to his head, their white brilliance contrasting with the rich auburn hair secured at the nape of his neck with a dark brown ribbon. The hand engulfing hers was warm and dry, and in its grip, her own fingers felt powerless. Wordlessly, she nodded a greeting, but feeling Marcy behind nudging her elbow, she at last found her voice.

"Mr. Philleo and Elizabeth. Do come inside by the fire. We have all been expecting you, and the girls are eager to meet Elizabeth. I am Miss Crandall, and this is my assistant, Marcy Davis."

"I'll take your wraps." Marcy held out her arms, but before giving her his cloak, the gentleman reached down and shook Marcy's hand.

"How do you do, Miss Davis? May I introduce my daughter, Elizabeth?"

Elizabeth smiled self-consciously and struggled to remove her cloak. Underneath the cloak, she was dressed in a dark green traveling frock trimmed with black velvet. In the chill of the hallway, she shivered. Marcy put a friendly hand on the girl's shoulder.

"What weather to be travelin'," she exclaimed. "Dear chile, you must be chilled t'the bone. A cuppa tea is what you need." So saying, she hurried off toward the kitchen with their wraps, leaving Prudence to usher her guests through the double doors into the parlor, where a fire burned on the grate. With the high ceiling and tall windows, the heat did not reach far into the room, so Marcy had drawn four chairs near the fireplace. Inviting the Philleos to make themselves comfortable, Prudence also sat down, choosing the farthest chair so she would not encounter Calvin Philleo's long legs, which he stretched gratefully toward the heat.

Instead of taking a chair, Elizabeth sank onto the footstool by her father's feet and placed her hand on his knee. He covered her hand with his own.

"This is a lovely home, Miss Crandall." His eyes took in the warm hues of the carpet, framed paintings, and carved mahogany chairs. "It is just as I pictured from your letters."

"I was fortunate to obtain this house for our school. It suits our needs perfectly." She turned her attention to Elizabeth. "I hope you will be comfortable in the room I have chosen for you. I know you will like your roommate, Hannah. She is just the same age as you and a very good student."

These assurances did nothing to ease Elizabeth's anxiety. Though she held her head high, her lip quivered. Fearing the young girl might burst into tears, Prudence hurried on.

"Do you like learning, Elizabeth? What is your favorite subject?"

She looked to her father to speak for her, but he merely smiled and squeezed her small hand. "I... I sometimes study in the library... with my

19

Papa... and I like to read, but his books are not very interesting. I would rather draw and paint. My mother used to draw. She was an artist. And I like to sing."

"My sister, Miss Almira, will be happy to hear that. She likes to sing, too. You will meet her soon."

"Tea's ready," announced Marcy. Entering the room with a tray of tea cakes, china cups, and a steaming teapot, she proceeded to serve their guests. Prudence took advantage of the lull to study Elizabeth more closely. Her hair was the same rich color as her father's, and her expressive eyes were the same gold-flecked brown. She was, however, small and dainty, in contrast to his ruggedness. A sprinkle of freckles dusted her charming little nose, and Prudence could guess she would be a beauty when she matured. *I imagine*, thought Prudence, *she will look like her mother. She was probably a beautiful woman.*

"I am pleased, Miss Crandall, with the studies you offer here. You seem to have a fine balance of classical subjects and the practical arts. The people of Canterbury are fortunate to have such opportunity for their daughters."

Prudence smiled. "I am fortunate -- blessed, truly-- to have their encouragement and support. This is an ideal location. I suppose you might consider it a typical New England town. A 'land of steady habits,' as they say. You passed the meeting house, of course? We worship there every week."

He nodded, awkwardly setting his empty teacup on the tray. His white cuffs contrasted with strong, tanned hands. He had such big hands to be holding the little china cup. "So, you do not have a Quaker meeting house here?"

"No, there is none nearby. I do miss the Meeting for Worship, but I have learned much from attending services with my Canterbury neighbors." She stopped looking at his hands and continued describing the church services. "The minister, Mr. Hobbes, is a polished speaker."

"I would like to meet him. I'm sure we would have much in common. How old is the gentleman?"

"Oh, quite old, compared to you-- I mean-- I am sure you have much experience-- but he is, well, gray-haired and rather elderly-- not very strong--"

"But Miss Crandall," Elizabeth interrupted, "Papa is quite old, too. In fact, he is nearly forty years old. He has been a minister for ever so long. He knows 'most everything about God."

Her father laughed as he hugged her to his side. "No, my dear, I'm afraid I am not even close to that kind of wisdom. All I can claim is I am a seeker and a servant. She is right, though, about my being 'old.'" He gave Prudence an amused grin. The twinkle in his eyes made him look anything but old.

Prudence reached for another tea cake, and set it on the plate beside

20

the first cake, which she had not touched. In an hour or so this man would be gone, leaving his daughter in her care. Surely there were things she ought to be discussing, and things she ought to be paying attention to other than the traces of silver at his temples, size of his hands, and length of his legs. Though he was a Baptist minister and a widower, he was not yet forty, though why this piece of information should matter to her was not quite clear.

A gentle knock at the parlor door gave her a reason to excuse herself. It was Almira, with a cluster of eager girls behind her.

"Excuse me, sister. The girls want to meet Miss Philleo. Is she ready to be shown to her room?"

Warm and kind, the young ladies welcomed the new scholar without overwhelming her with enthusiasm, and Mr. Philleo smiled in approval of their good manners. Elizabeth visibly relaxed as each girl greeted her. Hannah was last of the group to be introduced.

"I am so happy you are going to share my room, Elizabeth. I have acres of space, and you can have the bed by the window if you want. You can see all the way to the creek, and sometimes deer come there in the evening. Shall we go up now? I'll help you settle in before supper."

Elizabeth let go of her father's hand, smiling shyly at Hannah and looking up the wide staircase with curiosity.

Over the girls' heads, Mr. Philleo caught Prudence's eye and beamed with approval. She smiled back at him, then placed her hands on Hannah's shoulders. "Thank you, Hannah. That's a wonderful idea. Miss Almira can go along to help. The rest of you, go back to the schoolroom, and Marcy will bring in your tea.

"Mr. Philleo, let us go to the parlor and finish our business there." In the presence of her pupils, her earlier discomfiture vanished, and she was the schoolmistress once more, ready to put aside her self-consciousness and send this man on his way.

Back in the parlor, she crossed the room and took a receipt book and some other papers from her desk. "Here is the itemized list of charges, Mr. Philleo. I explained them all in my letter, but if you have any questions--"

"Your charges are fair and reasonable, Miss Crandall." He placed a small purse on the desk. "And I would like to leave some extra money with you for an allowance for Elizabeth and enough to cover any unexpected expenses, such as a doctor's fee or clothing. She is growing fast and may need some new frocks before I see her again. I am afraid my duties are going to keep me away for months."

Prudence counted the money and wrote a receipt. "I am sure this will be more than enough. You will probably have a refund at the end of the second term. Will we see you before then? Suffield is not so very far away."

"It's a full two days' journey, but I would not hesitate to leave my work and come any time my daughter's welfare was at stake." His voice grew earnest as he spoke. "Miss Crandall, I have a special favor to ask of you. Will you continue to write to me?"

"Of course. I shall let you know at once if Elizabeth is in need. I also send regular letters about the school and the progress of each girl."

"I was sure of that. However, what I am asking is more personal." He hesitated before taking her hand. Prudence felt her face warming when their eyes met. "I have enjoyed our correspondence more than I can say. I want to know more about you, of course, because you will be caring for my daughter... but also because the things you write interest me. I feel we share many of the same views, but often I find myself looking at things in a new way after reading your letters, seeing a new light challenging an old way of thinking."

Prudence withdrew her hand and lowered her eyes. "I am grateful if you have found my letters interesting. I only write ordinary things, I am afraid. I will continue to correspond with you if you wish."

"*Capital.* I will write back. Perhaps I will send you one of my sermons, and you can tell me what you think of it. Are you a student of the scriptures?"

"Not really. I do read my Bible daily, but I am not much learned in theology. It seems to me it does more to cause arguments among men than to edify them. It would be well if they talked less and listened more for the still, small voice."

He laughed. "I see you are not shy about speaking your mind."

"That is the Quaker way. I believe plain-speaking prevents many a misunderstanding."

"Then may I plainly say I am glad Elizabeth will be under your influence, Miss Prudence. I already feel I made a wise choice regarding her care and education."

She did not miss the casual way he had addressed her by her first name. *A bit too personal for such a short meeting.* She looked away. "Speaking of Miss Elizabeth," she said primly, "I ought to find her and see how she is doing. I do hope she will adapt to our ways. We follow a quiet, disciplined pattern here and live by the rule of simplicity."

She hesitated a moment, then went on in a softer voice. "Mr. Philleo, would you like to stay for supper? It might help Elizabeth to feel more at ease, and Marcy always prepares plenty of food."

He shook his head. "I appreciate your offer, but I need to be on my way. It is some fifty miles back to Suffield, and I must get on with my journey. I see the snow has stopped and shall make the most of that good fortune. I hope to reach the inn at Henderson Crossing before dark. You will give me a few minutes alone with my daughter before I leave?" He folded the receipt Prudence had given him and tucked it in his pocket.

As they emerged from the parlor, Elizabeth was coming down the staircase. She hurried to her father and wrapped her arms around him.

Prudence took Hannah by the hand. "I believe we are needed in the schoolroom, Hannah." She tactfully withdrew, leaving Calvin Philleo and his daughter to say their goodbyes.

Chapter Three

Autumn 1832

Indian summer swept through the town of Canterbury, spattering the hills with vibrant color, then brushing the trees bare and leaving them shivering in dread of the coming winter.

The new term was well underway at the Canterbury Female Boarding School. For over a year, the school had been running smoothly. Increased enrollment and steady income enabled Prudence to repay Andrew Judson for loaning her money to buy the Paine estate. By frugal management, she also had enough money to hire Fredrick Olney as a handyman and his wife Nerissa to help Marcy run the household. The colored couple moved into the small caretaker's house behind the school, so they were close at hand without sacrificing their privacy.

Prudence's early fears of failure faded as she watched her pupils blossom and heard the townspeople describe the school as "an ornament to our fair town." Week followed week in a pleasant pattern until one day the autumn winds blew up a tempest in Prudence's soul.

The Crandall residence had settled into its customary Sunday afternoon tranquility when Prudence headed for the parlor. She came softly down the stairs, wishing her heart reflected the peace of her surroundings. At her desk, she spread out several sheets of writing paper and thoughtfully began writing a letter to Calvin Philleo. Their correspondence had flourished since he brought Elizabeth to the school last year. He wrote vividly about people and places around Suffield and often included humorous happenings he used as sermon illustrations. She had come to appreciate his practical faith, and often thought he would get along well with her brother Reuben. Answering his letters had become a welcome addition to her Sunday routine, and it was satisfying to share her thoughts with him whether she was in a cheerful or pensive frame of mind. She began her letter:

Dear Mr. Philleo,

She chewed the end of her pen. "Dear," of course, was proper etiquette. Not personal. She assumed he would realize that. She continued:

We have enjoyed another blessed Lord's Day, with all the girls in good health and able to attend the Sunday meeting. Elizabeth will probably write you today, and we shall post our letters together. She continues to make wonderful progress in her studies and has an unexpected aptitude in mathematics. Does she get her ability from you? Also, my sister says her voice is beautiful and clear, and as she matures, her confidence will grow. In a way, I am sorry to think of 'my girls' growing to maturity too soon. Their sweetness and purity are precious jewels, and I am privileged to have the opportunity to polish these gems. I am glad for their influence on my own life.

I must confess, this evening my heart is not entirely at rest. I had Sunday dinner at the Judson home with a group of our leading citizens, including Captain Fenner and his wife, the Frosts, Rufus Adams, and some others I believe you met last year, and though the company was pleasant and the food wonderful, some of the topics of conversation disturbed me.

Do you remember Mr. Judson? I know you met him when you brought Elizabeth here at the beginning of the term. He is quite the most important man in town. Not only a lawyer, he is founding director of the Windham County Bank and also of the fire insurance company. Just before I came here, he was elected to the state senate from this district. So, as you may suppose, he is not hesitant about stating his opinions. I usually can tolerate him, but today he was particularly offensive.

Have you heard of Arnold Buffum? He belongs to the Society of Friends. He is a good man, speaking out on behalf of the downtrodden and calling people's attention to the plight of our colored neighbors. His name came up in a discussion regarding the tradition of having a separate gallery for seating Negroes in the meeting house. Buffum has opposed this and many other practices, on the basis of the text in the epistle of James, 'God is no respecter of persons.'

Well, Mr. Judson loudly took up railing against Buffum, calling him a radical of the worst sort who would soon be wanting to lift all restrictions 'necessary to maintaining proper and decent separation of persons of color.' The most irritating thing about Mr. J. is he makes himself sound so pious. He said, 'As a Christian man, I do not approve the institution of slavery, but neither can I reconcile myself to the heresy that the colored race should co-exist peacefully alongside the white citizens of Connecticut.'

When one of the guests asked, 'What, then, is the solution?' J. came out with the most outrageous comments. He is a leader of a movement called Colonization. They believe since 'these people' were brought here against their will, the freed black slaves should be sent back to 'their benighted homeland' to a place called Liberia. He said, 'Let us send them back to Africa to Christianize their countrymen, for doubtless this is the sovereign plan of God for their race.'

Can you imagine the impossibility of such a plan, not to mention the hypocrisy of such thinking. It is nothing more than a ruse to get rid of free blacks in the country and perpetuate the evil of slavery. It's bad enough to realize slavery is still legal in Connecticut even at this date. I truly had to bite my tongue to hold back an outburst. I would not be so rude as to argue with him under his own roof and before his guests. Besides, I know his stubbornness. He will not even yield his opinion in a matter so small as his daughter's hairstyle. (There's a story I should tell you some day.) Perhaps the best way to deal with Mr. Judson is to ignore him and hope other people have enough sense to do the same. I must remember that without his influence, I would probably not have my school today.

Now that the subject has come up, I am curious as to your practice in Suffield. I never thought to ask you before, but do you require the colored worshipers to have separate seating in your meetings? I hear some churches actually have the colored section, as it is called, boarded over so no one can see they are there. There is a peep hole for them to look into the main meeting. It is one of those things a person accepts without thinking until it is brought to one's attention, and then one has to ask the question, 'Why is it so?'

It is getting late and time for me to close this letter. I hope it finds you well and happy. I know Elizabeth misses you, but she is doing quite well. This term is flying by, and you may expect a report of her accomplishments soon.

Although I know your duties in the Suffield parish are demanding, it would be wonderful if you could spend a few days with us in December. Almira and I are not accustomed to celebrating Christmas, but since my students are not of the Friends Society, we will close the school for a few days to allow them time with their families. I would be happy to entertain you and Elizabeth. Although I can promise you only a modest celebration, there will be good food and good fellowship. There are any number of neighbors who would welcome you as a lodger, including Levi Kneeland, the Baptist minister in nearby Packerville. Please write when you have opportunity.

With kind regards,
Miss P. Crandall

Carefully, she blotted the signature, smiling to herself. She knew when he wrote back, he would not address "Miss P. Crandall," but "Dear Miss Prudence." Oh, well. She was beginning to consider him a friend, but certainly never a suitor. He did not share or understand the Quaker beliefs, and at the age of twenty-eight, she was an independent woman who would never be content to be ruled by a Baptist minister. *Yes, a friend. That is the best policy,* she thought. She could not succumb to silly notions, no matter how appealing his brown eyes and rugged looks. She had a calling here in Canterbury nothing would deter.

She folded the pages and slipped them in the envelope, leaving it unsealed so she could add Elizabeth's pages later.

Outside she heard the sound of a wagon pulling out of the yard. It must be Charles Harris. He often came to see Marcy on a Sunday afternoon. Moving the curtain aside, she could see Marcy by the gate watching until the wagon was out of sight. She let the curtain drop and sat on the sofa.

Soon Marcy slipped in to tend the fire. Her face had the soft glow of a woman who has been tenderly kissed moments before. Prudence lowered her eyes and did not comment.

"Charles was here," Marcy offered.

"Yes. I heard him leave."

"He brought the wagon. He's got bundles of papers to deliver."

"*The Liberator,* I suppose."

"Yes, Miss Prudence. Here's a copy for you. Did you have time to read the other one I set down in the schoolroom?"

"I have read part of it. I would prefer you leave it here rather than in the schoolroom. I'd rather the girls did not see it. Some call its message violent, you know."

"Do you think it's violent, Miss Prudence, to want to be free?" Afraid she had spoken too boldly, Marcy covered her mouth with both hands.

Prudence answered gently. "I am against slavery, Marcy, and I wish freedom and justice for all, but I fear the process we must go through to achieve it."

"I hardly ever think you could be 'fraid of anything," Marcy replied. "Sometimes I'se 'fraid for Charles, but I'se mighty proud he's working fer the cause."

"I once heard him say," mused Prudence, "that emancipation alone would not bring freedom. I remember him saying education would lead the way down the path of equality."

"*The Liberator* is part of education, fer sure." Marcy was elated her employer would remember Charles' words. "When did you hear him say that?"

"Before I met you, Marcy. Remember when Reuben and I had the accident on our way here and spent the night at the Harris' farm? Mrs.

27

Harris and Sarah took such good care of me. Pray tell, how is Sarah? Have you seen her lately?"

"She stopped in with Charles 'bout a fortnight ago. We had a good gossip. She says she's bein' courted by a blacksmith named George Fayerweather." Marcy chuckled. "Maybe someday we'll have a double weddin'. She already seems like a sister to me." Marcy paused and studied the cuffs on her muslin gown. "Miss Prudence, what do you think of Sarah?"

Though the question took her by surprise, Prudence answered quickly. "She seems like a lovely, well-mannered young lady."

"She is," Marcy went on, "and she's smart as a steel trap--" Marcy stopped mid-sentence. She knew her employer did not like her to use slang, but in her enthusiasm about Sarah, she'd forgotten. She went on in a quieter tone. "She was the best reader in the district school. Nobody could keep up with her. An' you ought t' hear her recite. Why, when she goes to say the Declaration, it 'most makes me tingle. It's too bad she's gone 's far 's she can."

Prudence wondered where all this talk was leading. Aimless chatter disturbed the peace of the evening, and it was unlike Marcy to disregard the quiet Quaker customs Prudence lived by. She waited patiently for Marcy to get to the point.

"It seems to me... I mean to us... Sarah and Charles and me... that with her wit and all she oughta... well, she oughta have more schooling. She'd love t' be a teacher and teach other girls like herself t' read. Trouble is, there's no place for her t' go. Do you think a way would open?"

"My dear Marcy, I've never encouraged such a roundabout way of speaking. I can make no sense of what you are saying. Speak plainly, if you please."

Marcy drew a deep breath, lifted her chin, and blurted. "Sarah wants t' be a teacher. I know she could do it, and it would mean a heap to our people t' have their chil'ren get an education. Is there any way you could take in Sarah as a student so she could get a bit more learnin'?"

Now it was Prudence's turn to take a deep breath. She sat straight on the sofa, her hands lying still in her lap. Was there any way she could admit Sarah? It was a good question. From the first meeting, she had sensed an intelligence, a quickness in Sarah. Sarah's smile was warm and genuine, and an inner light shone through her eyes. Her father would have no problem with expenses, and since they were members of the Congregational Church, there could be no doubt as to their faith or respectability in the community. Moreover, Prudence had no doubt Sarah would prove an excellent pupil. What then was the root of her discomfort? Why did she have no answer ready for Marcy?

If there had been any spiders in the room, one could have heard them spinning, so complete was the silence. Of course, there were no spiders. Marcy's housekeeping wouldn't have permitted it. So Marcy merely stood by the wing chair, holding her breath as she awaited an answer.

At last, Prudence rose from the sofa and walked to the desk where she picked up a morocco-bound book. The gilt edges were dulled by frequent use. "I do not know, Marcy, whether it would be possible or not. I need to think more about it before I can answer. Are you certain this is what Sarah wishes to do?"

"Oh, yes'm, it is." The relief in Marcy's voice expressed her gratitude. "We can wait for an answer. I'se so glad you jist didn't say no right off."

"You know that is not my way." The rebuke was soft. "Your request deserves serious thought. Sarah deserves it. I would like to speak with her, too. When do you expect to see her again?" Book in hand, she crossed the room and sat down near the fire.

"I 'spect Charles in town mid week to get things fer the farm, and I'll leave word fer him to come by. I'll ask him to tell Sarah you want t' see her. Fer sure she'll come right soon."

Marcy fairly danced from the room, leaving Prudence alone with her conscience, her Bible, and her cat. Whittington had dashed into the room as Marcy left, and leapt into his mistress's lap. The late afternoon sun surrounded them both with a pool of golden warmth as she searched the scriptures and struggled with her own heart.

Much later the silence was broken by Prudence's own voice. "The spark of the divine... it dwells in every human being. There is that of God in every man." Whittington had left her lap and lay curled at her feet. He raised solemn yellow eyes as if receiving from his mistress a lesson in Quaker wisdom.

"Man or woman, slave or freeman, Christian or savage. It doesn't matter. I know it doesn't matter. We are all from the same Creator, who loves us all. So why should Sarah Harris not attend the academy? Prudence, it is thy pride... only thy pride." Regret tinged her soft whisper, which sank again to stillness.

The last rays of sun disappeared. Whittington stood, arched his orange and white body, and meandered to the fireplace. The last burning log fell into a heap of ashes, and the room grew colder. He meowed piteously, but Prudence did not react, so he burrowed into her shawl which had slipped off her shoulders and to the floor.

The clock ticked monotonously as Prudence sat with bowed head and closed eyes. At last, a knock sounded at the door. Without waiting for an answer, Almira stepped into the room. "Prudence, is thee not coming for supper? We all have finished our meal ages ago, and I wondered why thee did not come or send word to us. All Marcy said was, 'She's not t' be pestered.' Is thee unwell?

"Brr. It's past candle lighting, and cold in here. The fire is out, too. Shall I stir up the embers and add a log?"

Prudence was as barely aware of the cold, and the questions with which Almira had been pummeling her seemed to come from far away. She rose from her seat with a radiance on her face which made Almira forget the lack of heat.

"What is it?" asked the younger woman. "Has thee heard good news?"

"Good news, indeed." Prudence's arm encircled her sister. "I have heard from heaven, dear Almira, and now I know what I must do. Our school is getting a new pupil."

"Someone special, I believe from thy happiness."

"Yes, a very special person, and thee shall hear in good time." It was not uncommon for the sisters to lapse into the familiar speech of their childhood when they were alone. The language of the Friends, which sounded odd to their Canterbury neighbors, was sweet on their tongues and to their ears. It brought memories of precious hours in the gray meeting house and recalled faces of loved ones they saw too seldom now. It was their private way of expressing the bond between them. It was more than a bond of family. It was a bond of faith.

"Now," continued Prudence, "I suddenly feel very hungry. I missed supper, Almy, and thee did not call me?"

Almira opened her mouth to protest, but seeing the teasing smile on her sister's face, she hugged her instead, and they left the room together. "The soup is gone, I'm sure, but there will be cold veal left. Do tell me about the new girl."

Instead of answering, it was Prudence's turn to question. "Where is Marcy?"

"Why, she's finished the washing up and has gone to her room. She was anxious at suppertime. Shall I call her to fix thee a plate?"

"I can feed myself. Let Marcy rest. Besides, I have much to tell thee before I speak to Marcy."

At that, Prudence proceeded to tell her sister about Sarah Harris's wish to become a teacher and how Marcy had pled her cause.

Almira'seyes widened.

"Oh, thee can't be serious about letting her come. It would be too... shocking..."

Prudence nodded. "Yes, I understand. I was against it at first," she admitted, "because I know there will be many who will disagree with my actions. It could affect the whole of our school. I told myself I had no right to make a decision which will put others in a difficult position, for the way I am choosing will not be an easy one."

"What about Mr. Judson?" Almira objected. "He is certain to close the school if there is a colored pupil. He will foreclose the loan."

"Mr. Judson does not own my school," she answered tersely. "He only loaned me the money for the property, and thanks to our father's generosity and the income from the students' families, I have repaid my debt to him. So whatever he may think, he does not run this academy."

"Have thee considered Mr. Frost, Mr. Adams, and the other men on the Board of Visitors? They have trusted thee with their daughters' learning and supported us in every way. Shouldn't thee ask them?"

"I cannot think everyone in this town is as narrow-minded as Judson. There are people like Mr. Philleo, for instance. Fair-minded people of honor."

"It is the people here in Canterbury which concern me, not Mr. Philleo. I can guess what thee are going to say next, Prudy. I must call thee Prudy, for Prudence never was thy true character, only thy name."

"Thee knows me too well, sister, and I see thee has guessed my secret. I must own my decision was not easy. God showed me my heart this afternoon, and it is as full of pride as Mr. Judson's."

"Oh, no," Almira objected. "That cannot be. Thee has cared for me like a second mother since I was born, and I know the goodness of thy heart."

Prudence shook her head. "Truly, all my thoughts when I started the school were filled with fear that I should fail. I have been too jealous for my own reputation and standing in this town. Too full of my own success. I would hate to become an object of scorn to my neighbors. I like being accepted in the society of the Adams and the Hydes. I enjoy having the deacons and their wives smile at me on the street and hearing Mr. Coit boast about his daughters learning French in my school." Her voice dropped to a near whisper. "It pleases me when Mr. Robinson waits on me and walks home with us on Sundays."

"We have worked hard-- *thee* has worked hard, Prudy, to teach the girls well. It is not wrong to enjoy the reward of hard work." Almira continued in a rush, "The Bible says it is right and good to rejoice in our labors, to enjoy the fruits of diligence. I would hate to lose all we have worked to build for the sake of one girl."

"Ah, yes." Prudence linked her arm through her sister's and drew her toward the silent kitchen. Whittington, probably enticed by the warmth radiating from the stove, ran ahead of the two women. "Should anything become more important to us than serving God? Are we not called to lift up the downtrodden and walk humbly before the Creator of us all?"

She opened the stove and fed three sticks of kindling into the firebox. The flames leaped up as if fanned by her zeal. "The sweet taste of man's approval will turn sour in our stomachs if we put our own comfort and safety ahead of doing what is right." She looked earnestly into Almira's eyes. "Is it not right that a young girl like Sarah Harris should be free to pursue her desire to learn?"

Almira pondered her sister's words before answering. "I will stand by thee, Prudy, no matter what. I know it makes no difference to God that Sarah is colored, and I am determined it shall make no difference to

31

me."

Prudence smiled. "Sarah Harris has knocked at the door of education, and we will open it to her. Now, Miss Almira, will thee brew the tea?"

So there was nothing for Almira to do but reach for the kettle. She could tell from the weight it was more than half full of water as she placed it on the front burner.

Why is Prudy always so stubborn? What makes her so sure of herself?

She reached for the canister of tea, measuring the pungent leaves adeptly.

Why do her words have the irritating habit of echoing in one's head until they start to sound convincing?

Sighing, she took down the gleaming cups and set them on the table.

I've given Prudence my word I will stand by her. So I might as well reconcile myself that the spark of determination in Prudy's eyes will soon have the whole town aflame with indignation.

The water had started to boil.

Chapter Four

November 1832

George Fayerweather had the best horses in the county. This morning, he had chosen his favorite bay mare to pull the buggy in which he was driving Sarah Harris to Canterbury. He was quite sure Sarah was as nearly as fond of him as he was of her, but it never hurt to put in a little extra effort to impress a young lady. He had been courting Sarah for a few months, and it was his good luck he could oblige her by driving her to school on his way to work at the blacksmith shop in Canterbury. It didn't bother him a bit when a drizzle of rain caused Sarah to huddle close beside him. He glanced sideways at his companion, admiring her slim figure, fine eyes, and abundant dark hair peeking out from under her cap. Her face showed both excitement and fear.

George took the reins in one hand and reached over to touch her hand. "Don't be scared, Sarah. I'm sure everything's gonna be jist fine. Didn't you tell me Miss Crandall is a fine Quaker lady, and she invited you to come to her school?"

"It's not Miss Crandall who worries me, it's all the others -- the girls and their families. I'd feel awful if my being there caused any trouble for Miss Crandall."

"Thought you said you knew the girls, Sarah. Didn't you go to the district school with some of 'em?"

"Mmm, well, yes. That was some time ago, though, and there are others there from the town and some from farther away who live at the school. I don't know them at all. Since I'll be there early, maybe the other Miss Crandall, Almira, will let me in the schoolroom before the others see me, and I can stay in the background. I'd rather not be noticed."

George chuckled. "How could you not be noticed? I'd sure notice you."

She poked him. "Don't be silly. Girls notice different things than boys. Do I look all right?" She glanced down at her attire, a plain, nutmeg brown dress, smocked across the bodice and from there hanging in narrow pleats to the floor. The only ornamentation was a darker ribbon around the neckline. She sighed.

"The best I can hope for, I guess, is they will be polite to me, but even if they ignore me or say cruel things, it will be a small price to pay. I have wanted to be a teacher since I was twelve years old, George, and now, thanks to Miss Crandall, I finally have a chance."

"Why, Sarah. I didn't know that was your aim. Who would you

teach, for goodness sake?"

"You know Charles' work with Garrison and the *Liberator,* don't you, George?"

George nodded. "He's doin' a great thing for the cause, takin' the message around the country and helpin' people understand our pain."

"Yes, but emancipation is a long way off, and even if it gets to be a law, our people will never be equal if they can't read and write. So education would be my part in the cause. That's who I would teach. Girls like me -- and boys, too. Maybe even you."

George winked at her. "I say, you'd be my favorite school ma'am."

*****

The fence around the academy was now in view. George gave his attention to the horse and brought the wagon to a stop in the front drive. Sarah sat motionless, her gaze traveling up the steps to the front door. The fan-shaped window above the door looked like an all-seeing eye of judgment. Today she was taking the first step to making her dream a reality. George saw her safely from the carriage and gave her arm an encouraging squeeze. She responded with a tremulous smile. "Thank you, George. I'll see you this evening. Come to the back door to find me. I'll be waiting with Marcy." With a deep breath, she climbed the steps and reached for the knocker.

To Sarah's dismay, it was neither Marcy nor Almira who answered her knock. The door was flung open by none other than Catherine Judson, the saucy, blue-eyed daughter of the town's best known alderman.

"It's Sarah Harris," she exclaimed. "What are you doing here?"

"Did you bring something from the farm for us?" Angelina Graber peered at her.

"She's here to see Marcy, of course," Jane White, the tanner's daughter, pronounced airily. She craned her neck to look out the doorway. "Who is driving the wagon you came in? Is it your beau?"

Sarah was frozen to the spot and could not utter a word. She might have stood there an age while rain blew into the hallway and the girls stood staring at her, had not Miss Prudence Crandall herself appeared. Brushing the inquisitive pupils aside, she drew Sarah into the house and closed the door. "Sarah will be joining us in the classroom today. Young ladies, please finish your morning duties. We meet in less than half an hour for our morning gathering." At her matter-of-fact manner, the girls had no choice but to return, curious but silent, to their chores.

Relieved, Sarah followed Miss Crandall into the schoolroom. Her eyes opened wide as the teacher led her around the room. The district school with its rickety stove, rough benches, needlepoint hanging of the ABC's, and slates hung on pegs around the room could not compare to the sight before her. An upright, rosewood piano stood along one wall, opposite a cheery hearth. There were tables for each student, and large maps on the walls. Shelves of books beckoned to her, and the smell of chalk and floor polish filled her senses. She had often imagined herself in this very room, but never had she realized it would be so splendid. There were even windows, overlooking an expanse of lawn.

Miss Crandall was filling her arms with supplies and guiding her toward the last row of tables. "This will be your seat, Sarah, between Hannah Pearl and Jane White. They know our routine very well, so follow their lead if you are in doubt. We always begin with a quiet time of meditation, so you will have time to center yourself and prepare for this new challenge."

*****

Challenge was the word uppermost in Prudence's mind this morning. As pupils filed into the room, many a fleeting look was cast in Sarah's direction, but discipline prevailed, and they took their places with scarcely a ripple. Though her heart was beating fast, the teacher's words were measured and solemn when she faced her class.

"Many of you have met Sarah Harris before, and she is joining our classes today. Having finished the district school, she will be in the upper classes and follow their schedule. We will begin, as usual, with our quiet time, and I ask each of you to remember a time when you were a newcomer in a strange place and determine to follow the Golden Rule with our new scholar. That is the rule of our school, as well as Christ's commandment for society."

Some of the girls soberly nodded their heads, but Prudence was not surprised a few cast knowing glances at each other and dared to roll their eyes. Ignoring them, she bowed her head, and at this signal, the room became silent. Another day had begun, but it was bound to be anything but ordinary.

By eleven-thirty, the gentle rain had become a steady downpour. Almira nervously approached her sister.

"I think," she began, "perhaps we should stay indoors today instead of taking our usual walk."

Prudence looked up from her work and stared grimly at the rain. "We have galoshes and cloaks, Almira. The girls need at least a short break."

"Couldn't we have some games instead?" Almira pled. "We could have a spelling bee. Everyone likes that. Besides, I don't think Sarah has any galoshes."

"So, that is what is bothering thee. Sarah's galoshes. I see. Well, I suppose we can save ourselves a drenching and keep Canterbury from seeing our new scholar for one more day, but mark my words, it will make little difference in the long run."

So Almira doggedly tried to interest her charges in spelling polysyllabic words, though it was clear they would much rather question Sarah Harris. The strained atmosphere at the midday meal which followed left even Prudence at a loss. Marcy came and went with the serving dishes while the girls whispered to each other or stared at their plates. Finally, Jane White boldly broke the silence.

"It was certainly a surprise to see you here today, Sarah. I swan, I never expected to be in class with you again." She stuffed another biscuit dripping with honey into her mouth and continued. "Remember in the district school when I had such a horrid time drawing the map of Europe? All we had to look at was that old globe? I don't think I'd a ever got it if you hadn't helped me."

"You learn fast, Jane, once you get started. I'm glad you're sitting near me in the schoolroom here. It's nice to see you again," Blushing, Sarah took a sip of water and laid her napkin beside her plate.

"Well, I've never heard of a colored girl at a finishing school," Franny Ensworth interjected.

"Me neither," Catherine Judson chimed in.

Franny went on. "I'm not sure it's ever been done. Where'd you get the idea to come here? Where'd you get the money?"

Several girls gasped at Franny's rudeness. Smiling sweetly at Franny, Almira rose to the occasion. "The desire to learn knows no barriers of color, Franny. All the girls who know Sarah from district school can tell you she is an excellent pupil. So, of course, she wants the best possible education, just as all you girls do."

Elizabeth Philleo smiled across the table at Sarah. "Are you good at writing, too? Maybe you can help me. Miss Crandall is having us write an allegory for our composition this week, and I can hardly tell the difference between an allegory and an alligator."

Sarah could not help but laugh, and the girls around her joined in. Soon conversation had resumed its casual tone, and by the time Marcy brought in a tray of bread pudding, Sarah had ceased to be the focus of attention.

"Pudding." squealed Abby. "It's been ages and ages since I've had dessert, Marcy. Could I please have that piece in the middle? It looks so lovely."

Not even Prudence had the heart to correct her manners, it was such a welcome return to everyday matters. Nevertheless, she did not let her guard down through the rest period or the afternoon classes, and by the end of the day, she felt a headache coming on. She dismissed the boarding pupils first, asking them to leave quietly for their rooms, and then excused the others as their parents or companions came to collect them. When Sarah left the room to join Marcy, Paulina, the youngest girl, approached the teacher's desk.

"Miss Crandall," she asked, "should I tell my Mum and Dad we have a new pupil?"

"Why, you may if you wish, Paulina. Don't you usually tell them what happens at school?"

"Oh, yes, but not everything. I won't tell them that... that Sarah is... colored. Would it be a lie not to tell them?"

"To omit a truth that should be told is a lie, Paulina. Why would you not want to tell them the whole truth?"

"I am not sure they would like it so much. We don't have colored people in our house. They are... well... different from us. Mum says they are dirty and ignorant."

"Is it true, dear? Does Sarah look dirty? Does she seem ignorant to you?"

Paulina's round face turned pink and she studied the floor. "No, I guess not. Mum doesn't know Sarah. She will think she's like all the other darkies... I mean coloreds."

"I think you need to let your mother make up her own mind, Paulina. Maybe she will decide Sarah needs a chance to learn, too." Watching the youngster gather her wraps and head out the door, Prudence tried to let go of the fear in her heart that Paulina was probably right. She was well aware Paulina would not be the only student carrying home the shocking news of a colored girl taking a place at the Canterbury Female Boarding School.

At last, the girls were gone. Prudence straightened her desk and made one final trip around the room to make sure all was in order. She met Marcy in the hallway.

"You ready fer tea, Miss Prudence? I c'n bring it any time."

"Thank you, Marcy. I believe I will just have a cup in my bedroom. No biscuits or cake, though." She rubbed her temples and closed her eyes.

"Yes, miss." Marcy was all concern. "You'se had quite a day. Go on up, and take a rest. I'll be jist a jiffy with the tea. Sure you don't want a bite to eat?"

Prudence shook her head and mounted the stairs. It would be a relief to take off her cap and shoes and stretch out on the bed for an hour or so. The day had gone as well as could be expected, but what the rest of the week would be like, she could only guess. Some of the girls accepted Sarah's presence, a few appeared hostile, but most of them had not quite made up their minds. Would they take their cues from her and Almira, from their own mothers and fathers, or from Franny and Catherine? Elizabeth and Jane, at least, had been friendly to Sarah.

She must have dozed for twenty minutes or so when a tap on the door awakened her. She sat up suddenly and grabbed the bed post as a wave of pain and nausea swept over her.

"Miss Prudence?" It was Marcy. "I'se jist sorry as c'n be to wake you,

37

but there's a gen'leman downstairs t' see you. Shall I send him away, and say you'se sick? You look pale as whey."

"Who is it, Marcy?"

"No one so grand you need t' come down. He c'n wait 'til tomorrow, whether he wants to or not. He says it'll only take a minute, but I jist don't b'leeve that. He's a talker."

"Who is it?"

Marcy threw up her hands. "Oh, it's Mr. Judson, Catherine's daddy. Says what he has to say can't wait 'til tomorrow."

"He wasted no time traipsing over here, did he?" Prudence was not surprised to learn he had come. Even though she had a miserable headache, nothing would be gained by delaying the meeting. If she refused to come down, he would surely believe she was avoiding him. "Lord, help me," she muttered. Pulling herself to her feet, she smoothed her skirt and replaced the cap on her head. "Show him into the east parlor," she instructed Marcy, "and close the door. I don't want anyone else to see or hear him. I'll be down as soon as I wash my face and rub some lavender oil on my forehead."

Quashing apprehension, she made her way to the parlor. Mr. Judson's back was to her as he stood staring out the window, rocking back and forth from his heels to the toes of his shiny boots. At the soft click of the door closing, he whirled to face her. He forced a greeting through large, yellowed teeth.

"Miss Crandall, I am sorry to call without letting you know ahead of time, but this is urgent business. I won't take too much of your valuable time. Shall we sit down?"

Prudence had grasped the back of a chair to steady herself. "Perhaps we had best stand thus, Mr. Judson, and say what must be said."

"I am here to offer you my apologies, my dear."

Prudence could not have been more surprised at his words. "What? I am afraid I don't understand..."

"Miss Crandall, you are such an example to your fair sex of common sense and discreet behavior... prudent... yes, that does describe you... that I have overlooked the fact you are a single female with no husband to rule or guide you. I apologize for not offering you the benefit of my services to advise and counsel you in certain matters." His florid face was perspiring, and he removed a large blue handkerchief from his pocket and wiped his brow. "Decisions of a delicate nature, you understand, which could harm your success. I regret I have not thought of it before."

"Why, Mr. Judson, I assure you, an apology is wholly unnecessary. Though I am unmarried, I am not without counselors. My brother Reuben and I often discuss matters, and my father is also near at hand. Most of all, I depend on the inner light -- the still, small voice of conscience which guides us all."

"Yes, well, that is all well and good in most cases." Judson paused and cleared his throat. "But in the matter at hand, if you will be guided by my wisdom I assure you it will be for the best."

Prudence felt her face grow hot, but she spoke mildly. "I cannot think of any matter at hand, Mr. Judson, in which I have asked for your involvement. Pray, to what do you refer?"

"I understand," he said, "you had a visitor... an outsider...come to the school today, and you are entertaining the thought of admitting her as a scholar."

"You were misinformed, I fear. There was no visitor. However, I have admitted a new pupil, a young lady named Sarah Harris. Do you know of the Harris family? Their property is just outside Canterbury. They have a prosperous little farm, don't they?"

Judson's brows shot up his forehead. "Yes, I know where their farm is. That is not the point. You cannot possibly put this colored girl in the same class as Catherine and the other girls in our school. Do you think we brought you here and helped you establish your school in order to cause trouble in our town? None of the Board of Visitors will tolerate such amalgamation, I assure you. My wife nearly fainted when Catherine came home today talking about the colored girl eating at table with the rest of the girls. Such a mixture of races is unnatural by God's law."

"What law would that be, pray tell?" Prudence could not resist the question.

"There are laws of propriety... unwritten laws which govern our civilization, and despite your Quaker notions, young woman, they are the laws we live by in this county."

"That which is not just is not law. What about the written laws, sir? Every girl in my school, including your daughter Catherine -- including Sarah Harris -- knows our Constitution, knows the Declaration of Independence, the self-evident truth 'that all men are created equal, and are endowed by their Creator with certain inalienable rights, and among these are life, liberty, and the pursuit of happiness.' Surely the pursuit of an education is the right of every citizen in this country."

"Ah, there you have it. Every *citizen*." He rapped his cane on the floor to punctuate his pronouncement. "No one can be so misguided as to think a black man, a black woman, or child is a citizen alongside our European stock. I have made known well enough my efforts to return the freed Negroes to Africa, where they belong, and I will not countenance a Negro girl being taught under the same roof as my daughter."

Andrew Judson's words were a foul smog in the room. Though Prudence braced herself on the frame of the chair, she almost collapsed. Judson noticed her ashen face and stopped his tirade. "Miss Crandall, I have no wish to be your adversary. I see we are both becoming agitated, and lest either of us has cause to regret our words, let us call a truce. I know you are a good woman, and you have a woman's impulsiveness. No doubt your feelings led you to make a hasty decision, but it is not too late to remedy the error in your judgment.

"The hour is growing late, and I can see you are weary from the labors of your day. My wife and I will call upon you tomorrow evening, and we will help you set things right."

Prudence gathered her last bit of strength and pulled herself to her full height. Her eyes blazed. "I have always been grateful, Mr. Judson, for your help and support with the school, but if excluding Sarah Harris from this school is your idea of setting things right, I must decline your offer. My decision was not made on a whim or an impulse as you suppose, but by clear thinking and soul-searching. My conscience tells me God has a special work for me to do in righting the wrongs our colored neighbors have endured so long, and Sarah Harris's education is where I shall begin."

It was now Judson's turn to pale. His jaw clenched into a hard line and the hand in which he held the ivory-headed cane became a fist. "You would oppose me, then? You will see this venture of yours fail completely if you do not stop this nonsense immediately. I am not a renegade committee of one, young woman. I am a leader in this town, and I know my fellow citizens well enough to be certain I speak for them as well. We are all Christian men. We do not hold with slavery, and we tolerate the Negroes in the district well enough. They know their place, and there have been few outrages as long as the distinction between races is honored. You must listen to reason and dismiss this girl before the day is done tomorrow, or *upon my word* it will be the *last* you will see of my daughter."

With that, he snatched his cloak off the bench and strode to the door. He turned to face her once more. "I will give you one day. One day to consider the consequences... talk to your brother if you wish... we will speak again tomorrow." He nodded tersely. "I take my leave of you, Miss Crandall."

Stung by his rudeness, she made no effort to delay his going, but sank onto the brocade chair. *So, it has begun.* Her trembling fingers smoothed the tucks of her bodice and she licked her dry lips. *Where is Marcy with the tea? I could certainly use it now.*

Well, Mr. Judson, I will see you tomorrow, then, but be prepared for disappointment if you expect me to change my mind. I am even more determined to uphold the validity of this cause. I cannot believe everyone in this town... all the parents of my dear girls... will be as bigoted as you. Surely some of them will stand by me. I must tell Almira what has happened...

At that moment Almira herself crossed the threshold and closed the door behind her. "I thought I heard voices. A man-- he was angry-- Sister, is thee all right?"

"Thee heard right, indeed, Almy. It was our distinguished neighbor,

Mr. Judson. Thee can guess why he came."

"Oh, no. He wasted no time, did he?"

"Just exactly what I thought. I suppose we should have expected his visit and had Marcy bake a cake for the occasion."

"Laugh if thee will, Prudence. I am sure his visit brought no good will. What did he say?" She sat down on the sofa and leaned forward, a frown creasing her young face.

"About what one would expect from him. Blacks are not citizens, should not be in school, on and on. I am too tired to repeat it all."

"What about our school? Can he force us to make Sarah leave?"

"Well, he thinks he can. He has given me an ultimatum to change my decision by tomorrow, or else..."

"Or else what?" Almira's pretty brows knit together in anxiety, and alarm crept into her voice.

"He will remove his daughter. Oh, Almy, I didn't want it to come to this."

"I feared this would happen. He is such an influence on the others. They will follow his lead..."

Seeing the agitation on Almira's face, Prudence sat beside her and put her arms about her trembling shoulders. "Now, sister. Remember the Word. 'Sufficient unto the day is the evil thereof.' Let us not worry ourselves about what hasn't happened. It is enough for now to know we have taken the right path. God will sustain us."

"Maybe God has given us this chance to reconsider. We have tonight to think it over, and perhaps... perhaps find some compromise. Maybe I could teach Sarah. Give her lessons when she comes to visit Marcy. I am sure she would understand."

"I know thee mean well," Prudence answered, "but even if Sarah understands, I would not understand." She stood again and walked to the fireplace. "We knew-- I knew this would not be easy, but I believe good will come of it. Who knows, we may be on the brink of a great change in our history. Or, on the other hand, admitting Sarah to the school may be a small stir which is soon forgotten. After all, I am just one ordinary woman, and I am sure the people of Canterbury have more important matters to spend their time on."

"Nay, Prudence," Almira solemnly shook her head. "Thee may be an ordinary woman, but thee has raised a question of human rights. I doubt there are more important matters in all the land."

Chapter Five

"That is why, Miss Crandall, we must withdraw our Lydia from your school. We are certain if you consider our position, you will understand." Mr. Fowler's mutton chop whiskers quivered self-righteously as he took his daughter's hand.

Prudence tucked a determined blond curl under her cap and succeeded in looking unruffled despite a prickle of irritation. No, she would not understand Mr. Fowler's position, so there was no sense in considering it. She was certain neither the unimaginative Mr. Fowler nor his mousey wife would have thought to remove Lydia from school without the interference of Rebecca Judson. Not only had she withdrawn her daughter Catherine from the school, but Rebecca took up her husband's cause willingly, spreading gossip and encouraging spiteful actions from the people of Canterbury.

As a result, faceless enemies had pelted the fence surrounding the school with mud and rotten eggs, and every time Prudence or Almira had ventured out shopping, they had been overtly snubbed by the community.

Knowing the thought of the Judsons would only disturb her, she turned her attention to Lydia. "Well then, Lydia," she patted the child's hand, "Miss Almira will help you and Mrs. Fowler collect your things from the schoolroom. The other girls will miss you, I am sure, as will I. Don't forget the lessons you have learned here -- remember to always do good to others."

"I will try to, Miss Crandall." Lydia's face puckered and a tear slid down her cheek.

"Come along, dearie," Mrs. Fowler called to her daughter as she picked up her full skirts and followed Almira from the room.

Prudence patted Lydia's shoulder one last time before returning to her desk. Mr. Fowler was waiting for her to refund his money for the remainder of the term.

Less than two weeks had passed since Sarah's first day and already the hue and cry against her reverberated through the town. The first time she went out with the other girls for their customary walk, a group of jeering boys dogged their steps, beating on drums and chanting, "Baa, baa, black sheep, have you any wool? Yes, sir, yes, sir, three bags full. One for my master and one for my dame, and one for the Nigger gal who lives down the lane." The young ladies held their heads high and pretended to ignore the taunts, until at last Jane White stopped in her tracks and whirled upon them.

"Quit following us!" she shouted. "Don't you have anything better to do? Go home and help your mothers, you little brats!" Her strident tone and imposing size had the desired effect, and the youngsters scattered like rats.

Abby and Angelina cheered Jane's performance, but some of the girls began to cry. "Oh, Miss Crandall, I'm scared. Can we go back inside?"

"We will finish what we set out to do, girls. We cannot let ourselves be frightened by some ill-mannered boys. If you would like, you may walk with me and hold my hand." She offered them her gloved hands and a warm smile of encouragement, and they were on their way again.

She only wished the mothers and fathers were as easily dealt with as the children. She knew the parents were the source of the boys' hateful behavior. True to his word, Mr. Judson brought his wife along to confront Prudence the day after his previous visit. Seeing the futility of changing Prudence's mind, he next rallied the men of the Board of Visitors to present her with an ultimatum.

"This has gone far enough," Mr. Frost declared. "We have invested our time, our money, and our good will in your school. Most importantly, we have trusted you with shaping the morals of our daughters. Yet you repay us by placing a child of an inferior race in their midst."

"I cannot agree with your assessment," she protested. "I believe in the Quaker principle of Universal Brotherhood. Whatever the color of the skin, it is God-given, and in His sight, if there is any superior status, it is because of one's obedience to Him, not due to one's outward appearance."

"O-ho," answered Judson. "So you would elevate your own opinions over those of *men* far wiser than *you*, who have determined the Negro race will never rise above their menial condition. They are meant to be laborers and servants, not to exercise themselves in the higher branches of learning. Besides, we are straying from the matter at hand. What do you intend to do about this colored girl? Do you choose her above our daughters?"

"I say to you all, gentlemen, Sarah Harris is fully able to pursue a higher education, and mentally she is on equal footing with any of the other girls. As for her character and deportment, she does not give the least offense. She is a model pupil in all respects, and my conscience will not allow me to make her color a factor in her presence in this school." Though the tone of her voice was mild, her cheeks flushed and her eyes flashed with anger. "Perhaps I was wrong to come here. I could move my school to another town where there is a better opportunity for growth."

"Now, now," Captain Fenner joined the fray, "I beg you not to be hasty. We do want your school here. You are doing a wonderful job of teaching our daughters the refinements. We only want you to be reasonable about this issue of color. We -- and I speak for myself,

43

especially -- have nothing against the Harris girl. From all I have heard, she is a good girl, the kind who would make a valuable servant, but you must understand, in the eyes of many people, it is insulting to put her on equal social footing with the daughters of our leading citizens. I might not mind so much if it were only me," he went on in an oily voice, "but I feel a responsibility to my neighbors to keep the social division unmistakably clear for the sake of future generations."

"It is precisely *because* of our responsibility to future generations that we must take a stand for what is right. Do you want our country torn by a bloody conflict? Do you want your daughters' and sons' lives scarred by the horrors of a civil war? We owe it to them to dismantle the lies of racism responsible for the immoral institution of slavery before it turns brother against brother and leads to open warfare. We must stand against the deplorable treatment of the Negroes even here in Canterbury. Admitting a colored student is only one small advance toward enlightenment, but it is one step, and I am determined to take it."

The men drew back, stunned by the passion of this usually obliging woman. Clearly, they valued the services of her school, and they had never expected to encounter such stubborn resistance. Smoothing his thinning hair, Judson spoke up once more. "Tush, Miss Crandall. We must be careful of imbibing the philosophy brewed by that poisonous paper, the *Liberator*. It is full of radicalism and exaggeration. Let us take a stand for moderation and agree to live in peace here in Canterbury. I see no reason why proper division of the races should cause offense."

"*Proper*." Prudence tossed her head in indignation. "I see we are unable to agree on the meaning of the word. This discussion is useless, gentlemen. Until we can look at the issue without prejudice, we have nothing more to say to one another." She reached for the bell to summon Marcy, then let her hand fall. "You may see yourselves out. I believe you know the way." She turned her back to them and walked to the window.

Mumbling and protesting, they at last departed. Marcy had been waiting for the men to leave, and she made sure the door was shut fast. Sniffing in disgust, she swept up the dirt they had tracked into the hallway and encountered Prudence by the stairs.

"Oh, Miss Prudence," Marcy burst out. "I can't help thinkin' this is all my fault. I got you into this mess by passin' on those copies of the *Liberator* Charles gave me and talkin' you into bringin' Sarah into the school." Her eyes clouded with tears.

"Well, yes, you may take the blame for that." Prudence's eyes held a subdued twinkle. "Blame or credit. Whichever way you view it, you certainly were the instrument God used to bring me to my senses."

"I'll tell Sarah what happened," Marcy offered. "I know she'll understand. She won't blame you a'tall."

"Blame me for what?"

"Why, that she has to leave the school. It's clear by now the folks

44

won't put up with her bein' with their daughters, and it's jist as clear you can't run a school if all the other girls leave. Sarah will understand that's jist the way it is. At least you tried your best."

"Marcy, if you have been eavesdropping -- which is a very bad habit, by the way -- you heard my answer to the Board of Visitors. I have no intention of telling Sarah to leave the school. We shall carry on as we have been this past week. Perhaps if we behave as usual, the townspeople will settle down and accept her presence."

"Already we lost another pupil," Marcy replied. "You even gave him back the money he planked down for the rest of the term. We can't afford that..."

Prudence laid her white hands over Marcy's dark ones. "The quarter is more than half gone. I don't think eleven dollars is going to be the cause of a financial crisis."

"The grocer's bill--" began Marcy.

"We have enough for that," Prudence assured her, "and the merchants have always been generous with giving us credit. Try not to fret about the grocer, Marcy, when greater issues are at stake."

*****

Despite her brave words to Marcy, Prudence knew the way ahead would be difficult. For certain, Lydia Fowler was only one of many girls who would be withdrawn from the school, and since Mr. Coit's generosity at the grocery store was due to the fact he had bartered supplies for his daughters' tuition, once they were gone from the school, he would expect immediate payment.

After Sarah had been in attendance for exactly two weeks, two more families had withdrawn their daughters from the school. Sarah approached Prudence at the end of the school day.

"Miss Crandall," she began, "My family is coming to fetch me today." Her eyes were downcast, and she held a quivering lip between her teeth. "We've been talking about the problems here at the school and have decided I am to leave. This will be my last day. My parents want to talk with you when they come, if it's all right."

Prudence placed a gentle hand on the young woman's arm. "Oh, Sarah, do not be hasty in making your decision. I know this has been hard for you -- for all of us, in fact -- but we can't give in so easily to pressure from a small band of people."

Sarah shook her head. "We have not been quick to decide. We've talked about it a lot, and even Charles agrees it's the right thing to do. They'll be here soon."

The conference with the Harrises took place in the back parlor where there would be no chance of interruption or of being overheard. The usually quiet William Harris took charge of the meeting.

45

Twisting the hat in his hands, he delivered a well-rehearsed speech. "Miss Crandall, our whole family 'preciates the chance you gave our Sarah. You're a true example of a fine Christian lady. But we ain't wantin' to be the cause of trouble to you. Much as Sarah wants to learn, this can't be the only way. My daughter won't be back after today. You c'n keep the rest of our payment as thanks for what you've done. Sarah told us about the girls leavin', an' we feel it's our fault."

Sally Harris stepped to her husband's side and took his arm. "We don't want to endanger you and your sister any more. When I think of those young hooligans following you and the girls around town. Shameful."

"Yes, it is shameful," Prudence agreed, "but I can't consider those boys a danger -- more of a nuisance."

"Nuisances have a way of becoming dangerous," Charles put in, "and a handful of young boys can grow into a full scale mob. Like Mr. Garrison says, racial prejudice spreads like wildfire. People's emotions get stirred up and run ahead of their brains, it seems."

"Once I am gone," Sarah added, "things will go back to normal. They will soon forget I was here, and school will go on as usual."

Prudence crossed the room, adjusted the pillows on the settle, and sat down, inviting them all to join her. "I am afraid that is not true," she said. "Things will not go on as usual."

She did not speak for the space of a full minute and then resumed her explanation in a voice full of conviction.

"You see, this whole matter has given me pause to think about my purpose in being here and the opportunity afforded by this spacious home. As soon as I decided to admit Sarah as a student, I began to feel the certainty inside of Providential leading. Then when I faced opposition, my commitment did not waver in the least. In fact, it grew ever stronger. I now feel assured that I am to dedicate the rest of my life to doing whatever I can to benefit people of color."

Charles drew a deep breath. "How will you do that?"

"In the best way I can. Mr. Harris, you just said a minute ago this can't be the only way for Sarah to learn. What if it is the only way? I know of no school in our country for young ladies of color. What if I was to start one?"

"Sarah would be your first pupil," Sally was immediately enthusiastic.

"You can't have a school with just one girl," Sarah pointed out. "Where would you find enough colored girls in Canterbury to fill a school?"

Prudence clasped Sarah's hands and looked into her eyes. "The Lord will provide, Sarah. There must be other girls like you -- bright young women who want to learn, with families to support them. If I only knew where to look."

Charles's face lit up with excitement. "In the cities around New England." He snapped his fingers in delight. "There are many good families of means with daughters just the right age for your school. I know just the person who can help you find them."

He looked at his father who returned his huge smile. "William Lloyd Garrison."

Prudence gasped. "Of course. Why didn't I think of that? Charles, you could help me, too. Tell me where to find him. Give me letters of introduction. Let him know about what has happened with Sarah. We must begin right away." She jumped to her feet, ready to race to her room and begin packing immediately for a trip to Boston.

"What about the girls here now?" Sarah brought her back to reality. "Jane, Hannah, Elizabeth, and the rest. You can't just go off and leave them, can you?"

"No," Prudence quickly agreed. "The fact is, for financial reasons, I will need this school to continue for the rest of the term. Meanwhile, I can write letters and go see Mr. Garrison. Almira can take over my duties for awhile, and when I am sure I have enough colored girls to begin anew, I will announce I am closing the school and then reopen as soon as I can."

"I'll make you a new sign for the gate," William promised. "What'll it say?"

"I think I will name it 'Miss Crandall's School for Young Ladies and Little Misses of Color.' I can just *see* it."

"You'll have to plan carefully," Sally said. "I'd be tickled pink to go along with you as a traveling companion. People -- people of color, that is -- will more likely accept you if I'm alongside you."

Prudence smiled. "I had not thought of that, but you are right, of course. What reason would they have to trust me? I am glad you would be willing to vouch for me. Now, listen. This whole plan depends on utter secrecy. No one, not even Marcy, must know what I am planning to do. If anyone got word of the true purpose of my trip, they would no doubt take steps to ruin all. Only Almira will be in my confidence."

"What'll you tell the townsfolk about Sarah leaving school?" asked Mrs. Harris.

"Tell them? I shall make no announcement at all," Prudence declared. "They will see she is not here, and assume whatever they wish. I cannot lie and say I dismissed her, but I can let their foolish minds mislead them until they learn the truth, which they will know 'in the fullness of time' as the Bible puts it."

*****

The next Sunday arrived. The cold shoulder the Crandall contingent received at the Sunday meeting did nothing to dampen Prudence's resolve. After sundown, she called Almy to her room and disclosed her intentions to her. Almira was especially sad to learn Sarah had left the school, but gave her sister her solemn word to keep her secret and support her plans to find "little misses of color" for a new start.

She did, however, have one serious question for Prudence. "What about Elizabeth Philleo? Has thee thought about what it will mean to lose her as a student? I mean, personally."

Prudence's face grew warmer. "Of course, we have grown especially fond of Elizabeth, and it will be a great loss to see her go. But personally... well... I cannot afford the luxury of letting my personal feelings get in the way of what I must do."

"Has thee written to Calvin-- I mean, Mr. Philleo? To tell him what thee plans to do?"

Prudence picked up a handful of scribbled sheets of paper. "Oh, Almy, I have tried all evening to write to him. It is so hard to put on paper the struggle I am in. Listen to this. How does it sound?

"Dear Calvin,

"Or maybe I should say Dear Mr. Philleo. Anyway...

"Dear Calvin,

"Forgive my tardiness in replying to your last letter. I did enjoy your story about the family with the pet pig and your humorous observations about how we will indulge and pet even our worst faults."

She looked up from the paper. "Did I tell thee that story, sister? Remind me to do so sometime. He is such a good storyteller. Where was I?

"As you have no doubt heard from your daughter, we have been through some interesting changes here at the school.

"Next, I just tell him about Sarah coming into the school and, of course, your support of me. Listen to this part -- it's right after I tell him about Jane scaring off those ruffians.

"I am pleased to tell you Elizabeth has also been kind to Sarah. You'll be glad to know she shows much compassion and in many ways is mature beyond her years.

"My dear sister has been a great comfort to me during all the opposition. She has been firm as I in her conviction that Sarah's color

has no bearing on her suitability as a student. Almira is a wonderful model of respect for the girls to follow."

"More credit than I deserve, I am sure," Almira commented. "Thee has said nothing about students leaving the school, nor about Sarah leaving--"

"I am coming to that. It is the hard part. I can't get it to come out right.

"By the end of this past week, four of my dear girls, including, of course, Catherine Judson, had been removed from the school, and more threaten to follow suit. Their parents consider it an insult to have Sarah in the class, and I have refused time and again to bow to their demands to exclude her. I sometimes feel it would be easier for everyone if I went along with their wishes. I know it can't be pleasant for Sarah herself to be the center of such meanness.

"On Friday, however, the decision was taken out of my hands. The Harris family came to me on their own and took Sarah out of the school. I could not talk them out of their decision, for they insisted they did not want to be the cause of trouble.

"This week I will go forward with school as usual, and continue til the end of the term in February. It remains to be seen if the girls who have left will ask to return. I must tell you I am contemplating some changes here. Whether it will involve moving to a different location I am not certain, but as you are not only a parent of a boarding student but a friend as well, be assured I will try my best to cause you the least inconvenience possible. At this point, I am not free to discuss plans with anyone. You know how people are. If they hear I am thinking of getting a cow, they will soon be spreading the word I am starting a dairy."

She paused again, looking quizzically at Almira.
"Now, does that sound like I think he is a gossip?"
Almira shrugged. "I don't know. I wouldn't take it that way, but then, thee is my sister, and I know thee would say it straight out if thee thought so. It will certainly make him curious. What does a cow or a dairy have to do with thy plans?"
Prudence nodded. "I see what thee means. I'll just strike it out. Now I must rewrite the whole page. It wouldn't do to send him this mess. Going on...

"I am not free to discuss plans with anyone. I will tell you only the changes will require some traveling on my part. Almira, Marcy

49

Davis, M. Fournier, and the Olneys will take care of the school in my absence. I will let you know as soon as I have anything else definite to say.

"Meanwhile, keep me in your thoughts. The Green is frozen now. I look out at the oak trees bordering the drive, a few brown leaves clinging stubbornly to the branches. Soon the November winds will force them to give up their place and bring them to an anonymous end. I feel a bit like a leaf myself, struggling to hold on to what I know is right and wondering how long I can last against the buffeting of this town. Please, Calvin, pray for me if you think of it.

"I am happy you have accepted the invitation to spend a few days here in December. I will tell you more of what has happened then.

"Until then, yours truly,
Miss Prudence Crandall"

She folded the sheets of paper and laid them aside. "Though I don't like to think of it, most likely when I send Elizabeth back to him, I will never see him again." Rising, she walked gracefully to the window and looked across the field.

"Is thee growing fond of him, then?"

"No, it isn't that." Her answer was a bit too quick. "He is pleasant to talk to. He likes my letters. We seem to have many things in common, but enough differences to make for interesting conversations. Each time he has visited, I feel... I feel... something good has come into my life."

"Thee is growing fond of him."

"I respect him. He is a good man with a sweet daughter. I can still write to him, even when Elizabeth is no longer my pupil. Anyway, I am almost certain he will look with favor on the task I am undertaking and will be the one person outside of my family I can count on for approval.

"Now, dear Almy, we must prepare for a full day tomorrow. How many of our little charges do thee suppose will show up for class?"

"Thee is changing the subject," Almira teased, but she gave her sister a warm hug and a kiss on the cheek, then made her way to her own room.

When Prudence at last got into bed, her thoughts did not dwell on the gigantic task before her but rather on a long-legged Baptist minister. She pulled the quilt up to her chin. "I must not let Almira put silly notions in my head," she said, drifting off to sleep.

Chapter Six

Christmas 1832

"Elizabeth!" Prudence's usually composed tone held great excitement as she called up the stairs. "He's here. I see your father just turning into the drive. Come at once."

She did not wait for Elizabeth's appearance, but tossed a cape over her dress and dashed out the door. There was no snow, but the ground was frozen solid.

The wind whipped at her hair and brought color to her cheeks.

Wearing a broad smile, Calvin Philleo dismounted his horse.

"Miss Prudence. How wonderful to see you." He caught her by both hands and pulled her to him. "You're looking fine, in spite of all you've been through. You must be cold, though, out here with no cloak."

Indeed, she was anything but cold. She could feel the warmth radiating from his broad chest as he held her ungloved hands over his heart. The faint, masculine smell of his shaving soap encircled her, making her light-headed and rendering her incapable of doing anything but blushing as she smiled up at him.

Mr. Olney appeared on the scene, ready to assist with the horse. Calvin released her hand and introduced himself and his horse, Jackson, to the handyman.

Olney gave a snort. "Mus' be some reason you named yer horse after the Pres-y-dent, but I ain't goin' to axe whut it be." He grinned and wagged his grizzled head.

"Sometimes he's as unmoving as a stone wall, but just give him a good rubdown and your best oats, and he'll give you no trouble," Calvin laughed.

Elizabeth came swooping out of the house and rushed upon her father.

"Oh, Papa! I am so glad you are here. Wait 'til you see what we've done in the parlor. Miss Almira and Hannah and I. We'll have the best time ever now you've come. Leave the horse to Mr. Olney and come inside at once."

"Well," he responded with a chuckle, "how my quiet little miss has changed. Will you listen to her giving her Papa orders? Ah, well, what can I expect when I go off and leave her with a bunch of strong-minded women?" Giving her a quick hug, he obeyed her commands and headed for the house with Prudence beside them.

Scarcely had he removed his wraps when his daughter propelled him to the parlor. "Look, Papa," Elizabeth crowed. "See what Miss

51

Crandall let us do?"

The girls had decked the mantel with greenery intertwined with
white candles in silver holders. Cheerful red berries peeped from a shiny
holly arrangement on the side table, and even Miss Crandall's desk was
festooned with green and white bows.

Miss Crandall looked a bit sheepish. "We are usually very plain,"
she explained, "but I couldn't see that a few simple things from nature
could be out of place. It does brighten up this dark room, don't you
think?"

"Oh, no. Whittington is in here again." Elizabeth made a dash
toward the cat, who had not waited for an invitation to slip through the
open door. "*Stop*, Whittington. Leave those bows alone. He thinks we put
them there for him to play with," she lamented. "Hannah. Come help
me."

Her roommate, Hannah Pearl, who lived too far away to go home
for the holiday, rushed into the room and made a futile grab at the cat as
he leapt from the desk, dislodging two festive bows. He pranced
gingerly across the mantel, then shot onto the side table, creating a
shower of holly berries. Squealing and giggling, Elizabeth chased after
the animal until he darted behind the sofa. At last, the girls captured
Whittington and carried him off where he could do no further harm to
their adornments.

Still laughing at their antics, Calvin and Prudence sat down by the
fire. "It does my heart good to see my daughter playing and laughing as
a girl her age ought to," Calvin said. "For too long after her mother died,
she was a very sober little child. Your school has done wonders for her,
Prudence."

"She is in all ways a very satisfactory girl, Mr. Philleo. You have
trained her well. You've met her roommate, Hannah. They have become
dear friends, and Almira, with her love of singing, has earned Elizabeth's
admiration and trust."

"Your wisdom has made it all possible. You are too modest,
Prudence. Please, call me Calvin. Surely we know each other well
enough by now to use each other's given names. Especially since I will be
spending the next two days here."

"All right," agreed Prudence, "at least when the girls are not with us.
You know you are to spend the night at Levi Kneeland's, of course. Mr.
Olney will show you to his house, and then he'll spend the night there as
well and bring you back tomorrow."

"Does Mr. Kneeland have a family?" Calvin rubbed his hands
briskly before the crackling fire. Even though the shutters had been
fastened shut, the strong wind forced its drafty way into the room.

"He is married -- his wife's name is Deborah -- but they have no
children. They have ministered at the church there for about four years,
and the congregation has grown since his coming. I have never heard

him preach, but he seems to be a good man. I have invited them to join us for dinner tomorrow."

"Capital. I look forward to getting to know them." He turned from the fire and settled himself on the sofa. "Now, let me hear what you have been up to. I know you made a trip to Boston. Am I to know the mysterious purpose of your journey?"

"It's not so secretive as all that," Prudence smiled. "I thought I told you I was going to pick up some furnishings for the school."

"I know there is more to it than that. Since when did new desks and maps make you look like the cat that licked the cream?" Calvin teased.

"Well, since you insist on knowing all my business, I will tell you I met the most interesting person in Boston. You know how you hear about someone and have an idea what he will be like, and then when you actually meet, all your notions must be put aside? That was my experience. I met William Lloyd Garrison."

"Really." exclaimed Calvin. "How interesting. I have often wanted to meet him myself. What is he like? Loud and bombastic and Elijah-like?"

Prudence shook her head. "Just what I was expecting from the things I've read in the *Liberator*. Really though, he's not at all so. To begin with, he's much younger than I thought. About my age, in fact, and not yet married, though he is betrothed. He doesn't look like a fiery old Elijah or Moses. He has a high, intelligent forehead and wavy, dark hair. His hairline is just starting to recede a little. Maybe he will be bald in a few more years. He wears spectacles -- suppose he's worn his eyes out by much reading, for he certainly is a scholar. Anyway, his glasses make his eyes look even bigger. They seem to bore right through a body. Oh, yes, he has fine eyes."

"Just like a woman to notice all those external details," Calvin grumbled. "You seem quite taken with him. I'm glad to hear he is already betrothed. What is his character? Is he as excitable as his words seem in his newspaper? How did you happen to meet the gentleman?"

She was beginning to enjoy keeping Calvin in suspense, so she dragged on the description a bit longer. "He is quite impressive-looking, really, but his manner is humble as can be. You can tell he is a man of strong convictions and his speech is thoughtful and deliberate. No shouting or arm waving. Don't you hate it when someone is so dogmatic you feel you are being lectured just as a not-too-bright child? He treated me as an equal to him, though I'm not sure I deserved his high opinion. In fact, he treats everyone that way. It is what inspires my confidence in him, I must admit."

"Was meeting Garrison the purpose of your journey, then?"

"I suppose you could say that, but it goes a little beyond merely meeting him. You see, I went there to ask his advice and also to ask him for help."

"Advice from Garrison?" Calvin looked a bit perplexed.

"Maybe I should start at the beginning. I seem to be muddling the story." She rose from her seat and paced the length of the room before standing with her back to the fireplace.

"After Sarah Harris left the school, I wrote a letter to Garrison. Now remember, Mr.-- Calvin, what I am telling you is confidential.

"I asked him if he thought the time is right to begin a secondary school for colored girls -- free blacks who had an elementary education in the district schools and wanted more learning." She ignored Calvin's widened eyes and went on. "Charles Harris took the letter to him, and also told him what happened with Sarah in the school here. When I asked if he could help me find some colored pupils, he not only assured me he would be glad to do so, he volunteered to assist me in starting such a school and getting support from others he knows through his work. One of whom is Arnold Buffum, the very man I once told you about in a letter.

"So, I made the trip to Boston to meet Garrison and get more information. Oh, yes, I did get supplies for the school, but the main purpose was to get names of young ladies in Connecticut and adjoining states who could come to my boarding school. Sally Harris, Sarah's mother, was my traveling companion, and together we visited three homes with prospective students."

Calvin's usually unruffled manner was becoming decidedly ruffled. He was incredulous. "I don't know what to say, Prudence. What do you mean to do, then, about your school here? Is it not going well? I am under the impression the girls here, my Elizabeth included, are getting an excellent education and your success as a teacher is spoken of all over the state. The people of Canterbury cannot want to lose an institution that is such a credit to their town. They boast about it all the time."

"Well, you do know the shine on my halo has dulled since I had the nerve to defy the board and enroll Sarah, and even though Sarah is no longer in attendance, my enrollment is still down. I cannot operate the school unless I have full enrollment." She paused and sat down beside Calvin again. Allowing him to take her hand in his, she kept her eyes lowered.

"Do not think I've lost my reason, Calvin. I would never take such a drastic step on a mere whim. I have thought much about all that has happened since the day our rig left the road and I was thrown into the ditch. Meeting the Harrises, having Marcy work for me and bring me the *Liberator* to read, the behavior of the people in this town -- Providence has been leading me down a new path of service."

He lifted her chin and looked deep into her expressive eyes. "Dear Prudence," he murmured, "Forgive my outburst. I was so surprised I spoke without thinking. I could never think you would do anything out of caprice. You are far too sensible and conscientious for that. You have more reason in you than ten people. I will be quiet, and you tell me what is in your heart."

Encouraged by his tenderness, Prudence talked on about her vision for the future, teaching colored pupils and being part of the abolitionist mission. "I know my role is only a small one," she said, "but Mr. Garrison pointed out to me that the success of any great moral enterprise does not depend upon numbers. Even if I teach only a few dozen young girls, I am part of the whole work of liberation."

"I feel the same way about my calling," Calvin confided. "My parish may be small, and the people very ordinary, but if I can bring light into darkness, I am serving God in the best way I can."

"Of course," Prudence answered. "I have always believed in the ocean of light washing away the ocean of darkness in this world. I'm so glad you feel that way, too."

"Better to light one candle than to curse the darkness, eh?"

"Oh, I am sorry to close the school and say goodbye to the girls here now. I have truly loved my work here. When I first agreed to open the school, I was so afraid of failing and losing everything, and now the school is a success, and I am giving it all up."

Calvin frowned. He dropped the hand he was holding and ran his fingers through his thick, auburn hair. "There's the rub, Prudence. I admire your courage in taking such a step, but are you sure you want to do this? Is it truly your desire, and the voice of your conscience, or are you being influenced by those who would use your sincerity to advance their own agenda? Much as I agree in principle with emancipation, the abolitionists often overlook the well-being of individuals for the good of their cause. They are not above sensationalism, and I would hate for you to be caught up in a public spectacle."

"All these things I have thought of, Calvin, and I appreciate your reminding me of them. At each step of this path I have waited for clarity, and at each step, way has opened so quickly I cannot doubt Providence is guiding me."

"Then I must be resigned to what is to be. Can you tell me, then, when you expect to make this change? When must I take my dear Elizabeth back to Suffield?"

She looked at Calvin's face, and seeing his sorrowful expression, her own eyes became moist. She scarcely trusted her voice to give an answer. "The term will end in February, and I will make my plans known then. The month of March will be spent interviewing new students and preparing for their coming. If all goes as expected, the new school will open in April.

"Oh, Calvin, it must be a well-kept secret until March. Then, I'll do my best to explain to my pupils and their parents why I am closing the school."

After a moment of thought, Calvin again took her hand. "Then I shall be silent as the Sphinx, but I know not whether to ask in my prayers that all goes forward well, or that you are beset by such difficulties you change your mind."

Prudence smiled. "Only ask that I do what is right. That is my prayer. Let us not let the future cast a shadow on these next few days."

"Miss Crandall." It was Elizabeth, peeking in at the parlor door. "Marcy is making us a plum duff for dinner tomorrow, and she is out of eggs. Would you and Papa like to go with me and Hannah to gather some? We have the finest hens in the neighborhood, don't we, Hannah?"

"Of course we would," Calvin answered. "Is there a rooster in the barnyard, too?" With that, he and Prudence collected their outdoor wraps and followed the girls outside. They wound their way to the south side of the house, passing the carriage house and the barn. The chicken coop was a small structure, but well built and adequate for the flock of speckled hens who roamed the yard at will and laid their treasures in the nest boxes in the coop. Hannah carried a small basket, and Elizabeth cautiously reached for the eggs in the boxes.

"Papa," she called, "you should come in here, too. See if the hens will let you take their eggs. They are not much used to gentlemen, so be careful."

Calvin did as she asked, but when he reached into the last box, he did not see the biddy in the nest. He got a sharp peck on his hand and dropped the fresh egg on the floor. The three ladies who witnessed his dismay, broke out in peals of laughter.

"Well," said Elizabeth, "that's the last box, and we have enough now. The hens don't lay as many when it's so cold. We can't risk you dropping any more eggs, Papa, so come along, and beware of the rooster if you bother his hens again."

As the girls headed back to the kitchen, Prudence asked, "How would you like to walk across the Green to see our meeting house? Perhaps Mr. Hobbes and his wife will be in, and you can meet them."

Arm in arm they crossed the Green, Prudence's full skirt billowing like a bell as they bent their bodies and leaned into the force of the gale.

"Mr. Hobbes!" she called out breathlessly as Calvin swung the unlocked doors inward. "Mr. Hobbes!" She lowered her voice to a whisper. "I suppose I shouldn't be shouting in the sanctuary," she chuckled. "It's irreverent."

"Let's go in," Calvin urged. "Maybe he's by the altar." Further search turned up no trace of the reverend as they explored the meeting house. Calvin was impressed by the size of the place. With galleries on three sides, above and below, there was surely room for all the residents of Canterbury. "A good place for a town meeting," was his remark. "Much bigger than my little church, but then the Baptists are not as strong in this area as the Congregationalists."

"I've never seen it over half full," Prudence said. "Though the Congregationalists may be a strong presence in the area, they aren't necessarily a strong presence on the Sabbath."

Calvin smiled. "It is more important the presence of the Lord is here." In a change of mood, he stepped into the chancel and ran his hand over the intricate carving. "Beautiful craftsmanship." he commented. "All in all, this is a handsome structure, a fine setting for worship."

"Come down," Prudence remonstrated. "What if Mr. Hobbes comes in and sees you in his place?"

Obliging her, he took a seat in the front pew and drew her down to sit beside him. Prudence was sure it was only because of the penetrating cold that he sat shoulder to shoulder with her, but the cold could not be responsible for the attentive look on his face.

"I'm glad we can be alone here, Prudence," he began, "because I have something for you, and I don't know quite how to give it to you."

Her heart began a fast rhythm inside her chest.

"I am so grateful for your care for Elizabeth... but it's not a thank you gift. I find the letters you write me full of encouragement and humor... but it's more than a gesture of friendship." He reached inside his overcoat and withdrew a prettily-wrapped parcel.

Her hands began to perspire. Never had she accepted a gift from a man. The implications -- she could not let him think-- but on the other hand, how could she be offended by the hopeful, almost boyish look on his face? Yielding, she allowed him to put the package in her arms. From somewhere inside her heart she found the words and heard her voice echo in the room, "Let's call it a Christmas present. I hear people do give them this time of year."

It did not take her long to remove the wrappings and discover a beautiful shawl within. The shades of blue and deep rose were like the streaks in the sky just before the sun slips from view. "Ohh," she breathed, tracing the tear-drop pattern. "A Kashmir shawl."

"Do you like it? I thought of getting a china crepe one, but in the winter, Kashmir will be more practical than silk. My sister-in-law says the Paisley pattern is all the fashion now."

"It is lovely, Calvin. Both practical and beautiful. You chose colors I love." She grew warm as he draped the fabric around her slim shoulders.

"I could imagine you in those colors," he said. "The blues will match your eyes," and he found himself looking into those beautiful gray-blue eyes. He was tongue-tied. Prudence, also, was silent, scarcely breathing as his head bent closer.

The wind, which had been gusting when they crossed the Green, had not abated. In the hushed room, they became aware of the whistling around the meeting house. Suddenly, a shutter banged above their heads, releasing them from the spell of the moment.

"I think we shall not meet Mr. Hobbes here in this weather," Calvin said. "We had better get back to the house before they all think we got blown away."

57

Prudence folded the shawl and tucked it away in her cloak before they secured the door and returned to the beckoning lights of the house across the Green.

After partaking of another of Marcy's savory suppers, Prudence, Almira, Calvin, and the girls retired to the schoolroom. A merry fire was burning, and the girls eagerly performed for Calvin on the piano. Almira played for the girls' duets, then Elizabeth and Almira each sang solos while Hannah accompanied them. When Marcy and Nerissa had finished their work, they called Mr. Olney inside, and they all gathered around the piano and sang. Even Prudence, who claimed she had a voice like a crow, joined in the merriment.

"Wal," Mr. Olney drawled when the last chorus ended, "I 'spect we better get over to th' Kneelands les' they think we ain't comin' an' lock the gates."

So Calvin bade goodnight to his daughter and the rest, and sending a special smile over his shoulder to Prudence, he followed Mr. Olney's lantern out into the darkness.

"Good night, dear Papa," Elizabeth called after him. "I will see you tomorrow -- Christmas Day."

Such a Christmas Day it was to be for Prudence! Always before, December 25 had passed as any other day in a Quaker community. Shopkeepers kept shop. Farmers did their chores. Wives and daughters cooked and sewed. Little was made of the holiday. Because of its reputation for pagan excess, the Friends wanted nothing to do with it. This year, she was in a new setting, and she could not bear disappointing Elizabeth and Hannah. Even Almira was looking forward to the holiday.

She had discussed her reservations about the celebration with Reuben, who said, "Do as your conscience tells you, Prudy. If you do not keep the feast, it is for the Lord that you do not keep it; but if you do keep a feast day, keep it as unto the Lord, and give thanks for it."

So, although it seemed to Prudence a great departure from tradition, in reality the celebration was to be a simple one, with company for dinner and a festive basket on the table with a gift for each person in the household. It had not been easy to select a gift for Calvin. She had finally chosen a slim volume of poetry by Robert Southey. Though the British writer was hailed as a romantic, many of Southey's poems had spiritual themes and deep meaning Calvin would surely appreciate.

She arose early December 25, taking pains with her hair and attire. She wanted to wear the shawl, but everyone in the house would know it was new, and it would be embarrassing to have someone call attention to it. "I'm going to wear it anyway," she resolved, slipping into a blue velvet dress with long puffed sleeves and draping her shoulders in the Kashmir shawl. She looked at herself critically in the mirror, something she seldom thought to do, and remembered what Calvin had said about her eyes. Her eyes were nice, she admitted to herself, but not so nice as

Calvin's brown ones. She saw her mouth go soft at the thought of him, and turned away from the mirror. *I am being ridiculous. Just get me a new shawl and I lose my common sense. Vanity of vanities.*

With that, she whisked out of her room and went to see if Almira was dressed yet. As she passed by the Palladian window, a random thought breezed through her brain. *I wonder what Calvin will think when he sees me in this shawl.* She could not prevent the tiniest flounce in her step.

Chapter Seven

Prudence strode up Manton Avenue in the city of Providence, Rhode Island, with Sally Harris in her wake. Under a voluminous black cape, Mrs. Harris wore a full-skirted frock with wide, leg-o'-mutton sleeves. She had stylish pattens on her feet to keep them above the slush, and wore a wide-brimmed bonnet trimmed with shiny, black plumage. Even though Miss Crandall walked in front, Sally had the air of being in charge of the expedition and felt as important as she looked. She was taking Prudence to meet with Mrs. Hammond and her two daughters, prospective students for the new school.

Prudence wore a somber blue cloak, and her trim ankles were covered with leather half boots. Her mind was not on her attire, but on her mission. Since December, she had been exchanging letters with William Lloyd Garrison and his friends, compiling lists of possible students in the New England states. Three days ago, she left Almira in charge of the Canterbury school and traveled to Providence to begin her interviews there. Arthur Tappan, a wealthy silk merchant who was a strong abolitionist as well as a philanthropist, put her in touch with the Hammond family. Sally Harris had been born in Rhode Island. Being acquainted with the Hammonds, she was keen to share her inside knowledge with Prudence.

"I know you're goin' to like Mrs. Hammond. She's a real lady. Born and married right here in Providence with genuine city ways. She knows how t' set a table that'll beat all for style.

"'Tis a pity her husband took sick and died so young, when her youngest was just a baby. She's done real good in spite of it, and raised them young 'uns to be fine young ladies."

"Mr. Tappan told me she has two daughters," Prudence commented. "I recall Ann Eliza is the oldest and her little sister Sarah is barely nine years old. I wonder if she is old enough for boarding school."

"Oh, I s'pose she'll be fine if her big sister is with her. I say as long as there's family alongside, a body can get through anything. Oh, look, here's their house right in front of us. Do you want to go first, or shall I knock and do the introductions?"

Before Prudence could answer, the front door was flung open by a bright-eyed, dark-skinned girl with a smile from ear to ear. "They're here!" she announced to the world in general. "Everybody come. Here they are!"

Opening the door wide, she beckoned them to come in. "My name is Sarah Lloyd Hammond an' I'm nine years old." She dropped a small curtsy. "Are you Miss Crandall, ma'am?"

By that time, "everybody," or at least quite a few faces filled the hallway, and a tall, dark woman with upswept hair led the way. She wore a violet half-mourning gown, though her husband had been gone for over eight years. The empire waist, though no longer in style, suited her generous proportions. "Ladies, do come in. Forgive my daughter. She is so excited to meet you, she's been watching the front door all day. I'm Elizabeth Hammond." She glanced first at Mrs. Harris, but addressed herself to Prudence.

"Miss Crandall, I can't say enough how honored we are by your visit. Sally, how good to see you after all these years."

Mrs. Harris smiled with pleasure at the acknowledgement and looked inquisitively at the other people in the hallway. Prudence was also curious about their identities. Nothing had prepared her for meeting anyone other than the mother and her girls.

"Let's all go in the parlor and get acquainted," Mrs. Hammond said. "Ann Eliza, be a dear and take our visitors' wraps." So saying, she led the way into a small parlor furnished in the regency style which had been in vogue when she was a bride. Now the chairs and sofa formed a slightly shabby but intimate grouping in front of the fireplace.

Mrs. Harris spoke first. "You all know, of course, this is Miss Prudence Crandall of the Canterbury Female Boarding School, and I'm Sally Harris, who used to be Sally Prentice, born here in Providence. It was when Miss Crandall admitted my daughter, Sarah, to her school that all the ruckus started."

Mrs. Hammond shook Prudence's hand, then nodded toward the white men beside her. "Miss Crandall, I hope you don't mind, but I dared to invite these two gentlemen, Henry and George Benson."

The two men, obviously brothers, stepped forward to take Prudence's hand in turn. "A privilege to meet you, Miss Crandall," said the taller man. Reddish blond hair waved back from a broad forehead, and his smile was pleasant even though it revealed a row of slightly crooked teeth. "My brother Henry and I are part of the Anti-Slavery Society. I'm hoping to help the school by writing about your project for the *Liberator*."

Prudence looked alarmed. "Oh, sir, I am glad for your good will, but having publicity about the school at this time could mean the end of it. I beg you not to write anything."

"Do you not intend to advertise for scholars?"

"In good time. I will give an advertisement to Mr. Garrison to put in the paper when I am reasonably sure of success, but there is much groundwork to be done before the academy is announced to the public. My first task is to talk with prospective families to see if my plans are even feasible. That is why I'm here today -- to meet Mrs. Hammond's daughters."

George Benson nodded gravely. "I understand your position, and give you my word I shall write nothing without your permission. Remember though, you have our wholehearted support. There are others, too. The preacher Samuel May who is your neighbor in the town of Brooklyn, and our friend Arnold Buffum are both prepared to give whatever aid they can, including finances."

"I trust the school will be self-supporting from the first, Mr. Benson, but I appreciate your kindness." She looked toward the doorway, to see the young woman who had taken their cloaks re-entering the room. Mrs. Hammond took her daughter's arm and guided her to Prudence's side.

"Here is my Ann Eliza, Miss Crandall. She, too, has been eager to meet you."

In contrast to her younger sister, Ann Eliza was demure and soft-spoken. Tall and long-limbed, her pleasant smile and expressive eyes brought a glow to her otherwise plain appearance. She appeared to be around seventeen years of age. Prudence was not surprised to learn she had finished the district school a few years ago and had hopes of becoming a teacher.

The last person in the gathering to be introduced was a colored woman named Hattie Doud. "My neighbor and dear friend," Mrs. Hammond introduced the small, dark woman. Her eyes were bright in her wrinkled face, and her body bore the marks of a lifetime of hard work. Prudence could imagine she had a story worth hearing, and after everyone was comfortably seated around the tea table (which was, indeed, set in style) the hostess urged her to tell Prudence about her life.

"Oh, I don't know," Hattie demurred. "There's lots o' folks been through more trials than I has. I'se jist an ordinary lady."

"Nonsense," said Mrs. Hammond. "You have more spunk than ten ordinary ladies. Go ahead and tell..."

"All right, jist a little bit, then," Hattie consented. She went on to relate how she was born as a slave on a Virginia plantation. She had worked hard to buy her own freedom, and then she came North to live in Providence. She worked as a farm laborer, a housemaid, a laundress, and any other work she could find, spending as little as she could and saving and scrimping year after year until she had enough money to purchase freedom for her two sisters.

"Happy as we is to be free, we is allus goin' t' be jus' workers. None of us never had a chance t' learn... t' get the kind of schoolin' you, Miz Crandall, is makin' possible fer these girls.

"I knows how much it'll mean t' them t' be able t' teach others, an' tha's why I wants t' help by givin' money for Ann Eliza an' little Sarah."

Prudence and the Bensons were overwhelmed by the generosity of this dear woman. How little she had, yet how much she gave. Prudence noticed George Benson jotting down notes which would probably be used in his writing for *the Liberator*.

As they rose from the tea table, Prudence embraced the small colored woman. "I am humbled, indeed, Miss Doud, by the many people who are willing to help begin this work. I assure you, your investment in these girls' future will not be a loss."

"We'll be prayin' for ye," Hattie's countenance was wreathed in smiles. "You'll be needin' all the prayers ye can git."

The prayers of many well-wishers seem to follow Prudence and Sally Harris in the days which followed. They visited six more homes and were always received with enthusiasm. Soon she had promise of seven young ladies, all from homes of moderate or substantial means which were able and willing to pay the required fees and come to live and study in Canterbury.

The night before they were to return to Canterbury, Prudence received a letter which brought even greater elation.

"Mrs. Harris," she called. "Come in here and listen to this."

Sally hurried in from the adjoining room. Since Sally had been refused lodging at the hotel, the two women had found a place to stay with Jonathan Hunt, a Friend Prudence's father had known for many years.

"It's a letter from Mr. Arthur Tappan himself. Remember? He's the silk merchant. He has sent me the names of ten prospective pupils living in New York. We must arrange a trip to visit them. Just think, counting your niece Mary, your Sarah, and the girl from New Haven, Harriet Lanson, our school will be full."

"Hmm." Mrs. Harris raised her eyebrows and studied her cuticles. "Harriet Lanson. It's kinda odd, ain't it, a white pastor of a big church like that having charge of a colored girl?"

Prudence nodded. "Well, it is a rather strange circumstance. He explained to me the Lansons came up from Baltimore a few years back, and their maid, Cassie, had a little girl. Cassie, as a matter of fact had come to them from Canterbury."

"That so?" Sally interjected. "What a small world."

Prudence went on. "When the maid died, the Lansons adopted her girl. They were childless, you see, and though they were in their later years, they loved Harriet and wanted to protect her."

"What happened to them?" Sally inquired.

"They both passed on. I think Mrs. Lanson had been in ill health for a long time, and when she died her husband lived less than a year. A heart attack, I believe. Before he died, he had arranged for Reverend Joycelyn to be her guardian. It's not easy to find someone willing to take on a mixed race child."

"That's for sure," Sally sighed. "Well, he must be a good man, that reverend. I thought you said Harriet didn't have enough money to come."

"Reverend Joycelyn is going to help support her, and I have decided to allow her to work for us to earn the rest of the money herself. Oh, I am truly amazed the way everything is working out."

"It's a beginning, Miss Crandall. Just a beginning. We have a long ways yet to go."

"Of course," Prudence said. "For starters, we'll plan a trip to New York soon. March isn't the best time of year for travel, I know, but we'll have to hope for an early spring. There's no time to be wasted if I intend to open the new school in April."

*****

Three days later, Almira cried out in joy when she looked out the window of the schoolroom and saw Prudence and Mrs. Harris emerge from their coach. "Girls, they're back, and they're safe, thank the Lord."

Several of the pupils rose from their places, anxious to rush into the yard, but Almira prevented them. "I believe Miss Crandall would be pleased to find you at your studies, rather than making a mad dash outdoors. Keep your seats, young ladies, and continue with the reading. Angelina, please go on -- page ninety-two."

Angelina obediently stood and read about Marco Polo and the wonder of his discoveries, but neither the pupils nor Almira were concentrating on his genius. It felt like a long time, but in reality it was only a few minutes later when a smiling Miss Crandall entered the room.

Then not even Almira could keep them at their task.

"Miss Crandall, we've missed you," burst out Paulina, and other girls chimed in.

"Welcome back,"

"Have you brought more new books?"

"How big is Providence?"

"Did you have a good trip?"

"Did you stay at a real hotel?"

Prudence looked at her students with affection. "Girls, girls. I am glad to be back, and yes, we had a fine trip. I'm relieved to be out of that coach. My bones have been bounced more than an India rubber ball."

She smiled at her sister. "Now, it looks like Miss Almira has a lesson to finish, and I need to freshen up after my journey, so we will talk later, and I will tell you all about it."

They did talk about the trip over a delicious meal prepared by Mrs. Harris and Marcy, but Prudence was not able to tell them everything about her trip, for the purpose of the journey was still known only to Almira, Calvin, and the Harrises. With mixed emotions, Prudence stepped back into the routine of daily lessons and activities, while she continued her correspondence and preparations for the new school. Parents came and went with their daughters, smugly observing the continued absence of Sarah Harris and having no suspicion of Prudence's intentions.

The month of February brought a muddy thaw, followed by a hard freeze and six inches of snow. Several of the girls caught colds, including Paulina, who spent a week home in bed until she was over her cough. The month seemed longer than its twenty-eight days, but at last it drew to a close.

On the twenty-eighth day of February, a sober Miss Crandall brought the day's lessons to a close. "Girls," she addressed her students, who were laboring over the day's composition assignment, "please finish the sentence you are writing, and then put your work aside. I have something important to say."

The girls did as they were told and turned their attention to Miss Crandall, sensing something momentous was about to happen. Almira slipped back into the schoolroom and took a seat in the back.

"Of all the books we study," Prudence began, "the Bible is our first text. It has lessons for every decision we face in life. Who knows what the book of Ecclesiastes says about time?"

She was not surprised Elizabeth Philleo was first to raise her hand.

"It says there is a time for every purpose under heaven. A time to be born, and a time to die..."

"Yes, Elizabeth, you are right. It also tells us there is a time to plant, and a time to pluck up what is planted. The time for planting has passed, and it is time for us now to pluck up what was planted. It is time for our lessons here at the Canterbury Female Academy to end. It is not only the end of the day, it is the end of the month, the end of the term, and I am sad to tell you, the end of our school. After today, this school will be closed."

"Closed?" Jane repeated the word in disbelief.

Leah's hand flew to cover her open mouth.

Franny and Hannah shook their heads and frowned at each other in confusion. Audible gasps traveled up and down the rows.

Prudence continued. "I believed when I came to Canterbury I was planting a school that would last for many years, but it seems God had other plans for me I did not know at the time. Now I can see the lessons I taught you all have grown to bear fruit in your lives, and it is time for a change in plans... time to close the school. The things you have learned about grammar and mathematics and science and philosophy are well worth knowing, and I hope you never forget the knowledge you have gained, but there are more important lessons, to be sure. The virtues of courtesy, kindness, modesty, honesty, and charity far surpass any book learning a woman can possess, and these are the lessons I hope you will take with you from this school.

"The day pupils will take their things with them as they leave today, and the boarding pupils will pack this evening and be prepared to leave in the morning. Your parents have been notified of the school's closing, and arrangements are made for each of you to be picked up by stage or by a family member."

Seeing the apprehension on her students' faces, Prudence was forced to lower her eyes. She needed to swallow, but her mouth was too dry. Her voice trembled.

"Though I will no longer be your teacher, you will always remain in my heart and in my prayers, and when we meet again, may it be as friends."

The room was silent except for the insistent ticking of the clock.

At once, the Graber twins jumped to their feet. Running to their teacher, they threw their arms around her and dampened her neck with their tears. Like a dam breaking, the other girls followed. Almira joined in the crush of hugs and outpouring of emotions.

"Have we been bad, Miss Crandall? Don't you want to teach us anymore?"

"Please don't send us away. We love you. We want to stay."

Squelching her own emotions, Prudence admonished them. "Girls, one of the lessons we have tried to practice is self-control. I know this is unexpected and upsetting, but I am not free right now to explain everything to you. Soon, I promise you will know what has caused this change, and though it seems sudden to you, I have very carefully considered the decision, and my conscience tells me it is the right thing to do. Will you trust me, and do as I ask?"

Gradually, the students dried their tears and accepted their teachers rule. Gathering their belongings, they straggled from the schoolroom, lingering in the hallway for parting embraces and promises of everlasting friendship.

Supper that night was a solemn affair. Both Prudence and Almira were emotionally spent, and more than one girl dabbed her eyes and nose with a soggy hanky during the meal. Marcy, who had just heard the news, came and went with soup and bread, her features so glum one would suppose she was serving the Last Supper.

Once the girls had been sent to their rooms to begin packing, Prudence called Marcy into the east parlor.

"I got my dishes to do--" began Marcy.

"That can wait, Marcy," Prudence assured her. "It's high time I let you in on what is going on. I am sorry I haven't been free to share with you before, but secrecy was key to my success. Now that the public will know, I want to tell you everything."

Marcy sat, looking at her friend and employer with a puzzled frown. Her expression changed from disbelief to wonderment to excitement as Prudence explained the project she had been developing since Sarah Harris left the school.

"Mercy me. I would never have guessed that was what you was up to, Miss Prudence. You do cap the climax... yes'm you surely do beat all. I'se sorry as I can be that I was huffy cuz you didn't tell me what you was up to. This is the best news I ever heard, and I just bet we're goin' to be famous. Here I was worryin' you wouldn't need me no more, but I 'spect I'll be busier than a cranberry merchant, and I better get back to my kitchen and get to work." With that, Marcy was off, leaving a smiling Prudence sitting in the parlor.

"Marcy is like a spring tonic," she told Almira as they ascended the steps to prepare for bed. "Her enthusiasm is contagious."

The feeling of enthusiasm did not last for long. Prudence had just let down her hair and was giving it a thorough brushing when she heard a timid knock at her door and opened it to find Elizabeth.

"Can I... may I come in Miss Crandall," she said between sobs. Seeing the child's distress, Prudence's throat tightened, and she drew her into the room and wrapped her arms around her.

"Oh, Miss Crandall," she cried, "what's to become of me? Where will I go, and what can I do? Hannah's parents will send her to another boarding school, and Margaret says her parents have already arranged a good match for her. She's planning to marry this summer. The Grabers will find a governess... and I will miss them all so. I'll never see them again."

Prudence made no attempt to stop the flow of words. She held Elizabeth close and stroked her soft hair. Her own heart was aching when she thought of parting from this dear, motherless girl. At last, her sobs and hiccoughs ceased.

"I need a hanky," she managed to whisper.

Prudence pressed a clean cotton hanky into the small hand and placed her hands on Elizabeth's shoulders.

"You will see us again, Elizabeth. Suffield is not so very far away, and if you can't come to see us, Almira and I will come to see you."

"Can't I stay here anyway? I don't need a big room. I'll take Margaret's place with Almira... or even set up a cot in the back parlor..."

"I'm afraid that won't be possible. Think of your father -- how much he has missed you. He will be so glad to have you by his side again, and I am certain you'll have many interesting times traveling with him. Nothing is more educational than travel, and nothing more satisfying than serving others.

"Your father knows about the school, and he has promised to be here as soon as he can. I expect him tomorrow, in fact. It would not do for him to find you with a blotchy face and swollen eyes, would it? Let's bathe your face in some cool water, and I will tuck you in tonight. Things will seem better after a good night's sleep."

Prudence and Almira made the rounds to every room that night, making sure each young lady was settled in. With soothing words and gentle touches, they assured the girls God would help them adjust to the changes before them.

Everyone was grateful when the first day of March brought

sunshine and blue skies. The household was a beehive as girls finished packing their trunks and said fond goodbyes to their housemates of the past year. More than a few tears dimmed their eyes, but anticipation of going home and seeing loved ones again overcame their sadness. Mr. Olney, Nerissa, and Marcy were, indeed, busy as the proverbial cranberry merchants, carrying trunks, making sure nothing was left behind, and saying their farewells to all. Some of the Canterbury girls also walked over to the school to observe the excitement of departure and give their friends a send-off.

By afternoon tea time, the house was almost empty. Prudence could hear her footsteps echo as she walked down the hallway and into the dining room. How grateful she was Marcy had anticipated her need and prepared scones with gooseberry jam to go with a cup of hot tea. Almira soon joined her, and the two sat without speaking, finding consolation in each other's company.

Finishing off the last crumbs of her scone, Almira rose from the table with her plate and teacup in hand. "I don't know why people say, 'parting is such sweet sorrow,'" she sighed. "I don't see anything sweet about it. It is sad to see everyone go their separate ways when we've all had such good times together. Even M. Fournier has gone back to Quebec."

"Don't worry," Prudence assured her. "We'll soon be so busy with our new pupils, thee will not have time for sadness."

"When will that be?"

"The first ones have promised to be here by April 1, so that gives us barely a month to prepare. In that time, I must make another journey -- to New York this time. Would thee like to come with me?"

"I would indeed," Almira replied. "When would we start?"

"After Elizabeth leaves us, I suppose." Prudence also gathered up her plate and cup and started toward the kitchen. "Her father is to be here today or tomorrow. I am not ready to receive him looking like this. I'm as bedraggled as a gypsy." She ran a nervous hand through her hair.

Almira smiled as her sister brushed through the kitchen door and headed toward her room with the cat cavorting in front of her. Interesting that Calvin Philleo's arrival should cause Prudence a sudden concern over her appearance. "I wonder how close they have become," she murmured to the clock on the wall. "Perhaps his visit will bring some changes to Prudy's plans."

It was not long before Calvin arrived in the front yard with his horse and buggy to find his daughter waiting for him.

"Papa!" she greeted him with a combination of kisses and tears. "Are we leaving right away, or can we stay another day? Oh, Papa, I wish you were a pirate instead of a minister."

"*What?* A pirate? Do you have a sudden longing to put to sea?"

"No. I read a book about pirates kidnapping a high-born lady and taking her far away to become a governess. I just wish we could kidnap both of the Miss Crandalls and take them with us to Suffield. Don't you think they would be fine governesses?"

"Oh, yes, they are both fine, high-born ladies, but I am afraid kidnapping is out of the question. There are laws, you know."

Elizabeth sighed ruefully, "Yes, I know, and you are not a pirate."

"You must be satisfied with me, anyway." He kissed her cheek soundly. "Now, let's go in and find the Miss Crandalls. I am sure they have no idea of the danger they have escaped.

"Here's Mr. Olney, just in time to take care of Jackson." Calvin greeted the hired man kindly and turned over the horse and buggy to him.

"You should not seem so cheerful," she admonished him as they entered the house. "This is a sad day. I can't believe the school is closing for good. Do you know why, Papa?"

"Yes, I believe I do, but I don't think it is my place to tell you. Prudence-- Miss Crandall will explain it to you when the time is right."

He smiled to see Prudence descending the stairs. She was wearing the Kashmir shawl he had given her at Christmastime over a light rose-colored dress, and the bright rays coming through the window backlit her blonde hair. She answered his smile with outstretched hands.

"Calvin, how was your trip?"

"Muddy. The roads are all but impassable, and if I had a less worthy horse than Jackson, I don't believe I would have made it here today."

"Then you must not attempt to start back tonight. We have plenty of extra beds available, so you need not put up at the Kneelands this time. You have your pick of the empty rooms. Perhaps the one next to Elizabeth's will do."

"I'm sure it will be just fine. I have a special outing planned for tomorrow." Calvin grinned mysteriously. "You'll need to be ready early in the morning. Dress warmly."

Elizabeth exclaimed in glee, "Oh, Papa, I can't wait. Where are we going? Can Miss Almira come too?"

"I hope both the Miss Crandalls will go with us," he replied.

Prudence looked doubtful. "Oh, Calvin, I have so much to do. I don't think I have time to take a day off."

"That is why I insist. You and Miss Almira have been working much too hard, and since you have no classes now, you have earned a holiday. I assure you, you will not regret it. Besides, I have already made all the arrangements."

"May we not at least know where we are going?"

"No, indeed. That would spoil the fun. As I said, we'll leave right after breakfast and be back well before dark. We will need Mr. Olney to go with us, too."

At that moment, Almira joined them. "Where are we going?" she asked.

Elizabeth ran to her side. "We don't know. We're to wear our warmest clothes and be ready to go after breakfast. My father is taking us on a mysterious journey. No work for tomorrow. Hurrah." She turned to her father. "Oh, Papa, perhaps you are a pirate after all."

The prospect of the mystery outing banished the last traces of gloom and the evening meal was a pleasant time. After supper, Almira and Elizabeth went upstairs to finish Elizabeth's packing and get their clothes ready for the morning, leaving Prudence and Calvin alone in the parlor. He poked among the embers to stir the flames and added another log to the fire before sitting down with Prudence.

"Do you remember, Prudence, sitting here by this fire the first day we met? Marcy brought us tea, and I was so nervous I was afraid I'd drop my cup."

Prudence laughed. "You were nervous? I thought I was the only anxious one. Everything I said came out wrong, and I was worried you would not find the school up to your standards."

He took her hand in his. "I was so taken with the schoolmistress, I scarcely thought about the school. I had already made up my mind about the quality of the school, but I was most interested in getting to know the teacher."

Before Prudence could reply a great commotion was heard at the back of the house and she bounced to her feet.

"What on earth? It was a scream. It came from the kitchen." She raced to the doorway with Calvin behind her. Flinging the door open, they collided with Marcy.

"Oh, Miss Prudence. Lookit *this*." She was so out of breath she could barely speak. "Charles jist brought it by, and I reckon you ought'ta see it right away."

Chapter Eight

"Calm down, Marcy. You're getting yourself into a dither. Whatever is wrong?" Prudence put her hands on the young woman's arms to hold them still.

"You're flapping like a chicken," Calvin put in. "All I see is that paper you're waving in the air. What is it?"

Marcy took a huge gulp of air and blurted out, "Why, can't you see? It's the *Liberator*. The new copy. I said Charles jist brought it by."

"Why is that something to scream about?"

"Because, it's all there in black and white -- Miss Prudence's own words. And now the whole county... the whole state of Connecticut is a-goin' to know about the school. Ain't that wonderful?"

Advancing into the room, she spread the small paper out on the desk, jabbed a slim black finger at the words, and read breathlessly:

"Prudence Crandall, Principal of the Canterbury, (Conn.) Female Boarding School, returns her most sincere thanks to those who have patronized her school, and would give information that on the first Monday of April next, her School will be opened for the reception of young Ladies and little Misses of color. The branches taught are as follows -- Reading, Writing, Arithmetic, English Grammar, Geography, History, Natural and Moral Philosophy, Chemistry, Astronomy, Drawing and Painting, Music on the Piano together with the French language.

"The terms, including board, washing, and tuition, are $25 per quarter, one half paid in advance.

"Books and Stationery will be furnished on the most reasonable terms.

"Then it goes on with a hull list of names o' important gen'lemen people can call on if they need to know more about it.

"Ain't this splendid?" she panted. "I declare I'se 'most out of breath it's so exciting." She did find the breath to snatch Prudence's hands and go dancing around the room.

Calvin bent over the table and examined every word as if each one had a life of its own. His jaw was set. "So, the news is out. You lost no time, did you Prudence? I had hoped you would take at least a few weeks for a much-needed rest. There's so much at stake in this matter."

"All the more reason to act promptly." Prudence freed herself from

71

Marcy's clutches and came back smiling to Calvin's side. "So what do you think? Mr. Garrison printed it word for word, just as I gave it to him. Look how many names are there -- people who have supported me and promised to stand by me."

"Rev. S. J. May, Rev. S.S. Joycelyn, Arthur Tappan, Rev. Samuel Cornish, William Lloyd Garrison, George Benson." Calvin scanned the names of men he knew personally or by reputation. "All good men," he said, stroking his chin, "all influential, and all outspoken abolitionists."

Prudence's smile faded. "Is it a problem, Calvin? It sounds as if you don't quite approve."

"I do approve," he answered without hesitation. "I more than approve of doing away with discrimination, and I have nothing but admiration for your establishment of a school for 'little misses of color.' I am wholly in agreement with you from a philosophical point of view. It's just a personal matter that is a cause for my concern."

"Oh, Calvin. Do not be worried about me. This is a small affair in a small town, and I have been on good terms with everyone in Canterbury since I have come here. With the backing of Garrison and the others, I will have all the protection I need."

"I will say no more then," he answered. "After all, it is not my place to object, and I have great confidence in your ability to handle your own affairs. You may add me to your list of references, and I, too, promise to stand by you." He laid the paper down and grinned at Marcy. "Now, Miss Davis, is it my turn for a whirl around the parlor?"

Laughing, Marcy waved him away and left the room in high spirits.

Despite the excitement of her announcement in the *Liberator* and the promised adventure of the next day, Prudence slept well that night. The others were already gathered around the table the next morning when she came downstairs dressed in her warmest outfit. After a hearty breakfast, Prudence, Almira, Elizabeth, and Calvin donned their boots and coats and met Mr. Olney in the yard with the horse and wagon.

"Now, Papa, you must tell us where we are going," insisted Elizabeth as the wagon turned toward Packerville. The sun shone in a pale blue sky and the icicles festooning the bare tree branches dripped down upon the travelers as they rumbled along.

"I believe we are going to visit the Kneelands," guessed Almira. "They live out this way."

"You are almost right," Calvin said. "I'll give you a hint. You know, those hotcakes Marcy made for breakfast were good, but think how delicious they would have been with maple syrup instead of molasses."

"Sugaring!" squealed Elizabeth. "We're going sugaring!"

"*How wonderful,*" Prudence exclaimed. "I do remember now that Levi Kneeland has a grove of sugar maples, and it is certainly perfect weather for the sap to run. Do they know we are coming?"

"Oh, yes. Levi is expecting our help. We'll gather the sap buckets and bring them to the sugar shack, and I may even swing an axe a time or two to split logs for the fire. It takes a lot of sap and a long time boiling it to make a gallon of wonderful syrup."

"And maple candy," Elizabeth added. "That's my favorite thing."

Calvin looked thoughtful. "It is almost a mystery to me, even though I've seen it done year after year. The weather must be just so -- sunny in the daytime and cold at night -- for the sap to run. It looks almost like clear water when it fills the buckets, but after hours of boiling, it thickens and turns into gold. It's the sweetest taste on earth, I think. Another example of the refining process of fire."

"Also of there being a right time for every purpose under heaven," Prudence added. "It always seems you can find a sermon right under your nose, Calvin."

"Yes. I do believe nature gives the best sermons," he agreed, "if only we are paying attention."

"I have never heard you preach," she commented. "I hope someday I can come to Suffield and listen to one of your sermons."

"I say amen to that. I hope that day will be soon."

The horses were drawing near the Kneeland property. As the wagon clattered by a creek splashing over its stony bed, they could just make out a small shack on the hillside. The steam issuing from the place marked it as the sugar shack, where the sap was being transformed into sweet amber syrup. Before long, they were jumping out of the wagon and shaking hands with their host. Levi Kneeland, despite being a preacher by vocation, was a farmer by necessity and owned a fine pair of dapple-grey Percherons. They were attached to a wagon by complicated means of leather straps and ropes, and stood proudly ready to begin their day's work. Almira and Elizabeth, charmed by their beauty and friendliness, at once began rubbing their silky noses. Meanwhile, Mr. Kneeland explained to Calvin and Mr. Olney the layout of the sugar bush and the most efficient route for collecting the buckets and bringing them in. With two wagons at their disposal, they should be able to make quick work of the gathering process.

Into the sugar shack they went, inhaling the bouquet of odors from the crackling fire and the bubbling sap. Stacked upside down along the walls of the building were large, shiny pails. They helped themselves to as many as they could load onto the wagons, and after refreshing themselves with a drink of cider, they were ready to go. Elizabeth and Almira elected to ride with Mr. Olney, driving the team of Percherons, and Prudence and Calvin took their places in the conveyance which had brought them to the farm.

Soon they reached the sugar bush. The grove of maples which had flamed scarlet in the autumn now stood stark and austere against the winter sky. The drivers parted at the bend in the narrow roadway to begin making their rounds. Prudence and Calvin took turns holding the reins while the other hopped from the wagon, lifted the sap bucket from the shoulder-high spigot and replaced it with a fresh pail. Dipping her finger into the sap, Prudence tasted the clear liquid. "Why it's just like water. It has almost no smell and no flavor at all. Hard to believe it's going to become syrup."

The corners of Calvin's eyes wrinkled as he smiled to see her pleasure. The problems and cares of life whiffed themselves away in the bracing air, and the remainder of the morning in the sylvan grove was spent in joyful activity, more play than work.

"It's nearly dinnertime," Calvin said, glancing up at the sun. "Let's head back to the sugar house. I heard a rumor Mrs. Kneeland is fixing us a prime dinner, and I can always appreciate some good, woman-cooked victuals."

Mr. Olney and the girls were already at the sugar shack. While Mr. Olney emptied pail after pail of sap into the long metal pans, Elizabeth and Almira skimmed off whirls of foam from the hot liquid. The sap rippled over the long-handled spoons, becoming thicker and darker as the fire beneath hissed and crackled.

"Mmm. It smells so good." Almira leaned over and sniffed appreciatively.

"Do we dare leave it long enough to have dinner?" Prudence wondered aloud. "What if it gets scorched? Maybe I should stay here."

"Oh, no, that won't be necessary. It's not far to the house, and it won't take long to have a meal and come back." Calvin was already following Mr. Olney's lead and emptying the rest of the sap, and soon they were finished and headed to the Kneeland home.

At the long dinner table, spread with smoked ham, potatoes, squash, and piping hot bread, the conversation turned to the new school.

"Charles Harris brought me the latest copy of the *Liberator* yesterday," Levi said, "and I must say I was quite surprised to see your advertisement, Miss Crandall. In fact, I imagine it stunned quite a few of your good neighbors."

"I, for one, am very proud of you, Miss Crandall," spoke up Deborah Kneeland as she replenished Mr. Olney's cup with cider. "It shows women are as smart and progressive-thinking as men and not afraid to take a risk for a good cause. You're a heroine to be sure."

Prudence modestly acknowledged the compliment. "Thank you, Mrs. Kneeland. I am only responding to a need that has presented itself, and there are many others helping me fulfill the calling."

"May I ask," Levi continued, "what kind of reception do you think your new scholars will receive in Canterbury?"

"They are all good girls from good families. They will be kept in the school, and not allowed out and about town on their own. I hope once people see that all these young women desire is a chance to learn, they will put aside their unfounded fears and let us exist in peace."

74

"I assume, then, they are from Christian families?"

"Most definitely. Many of my supporters are well-known ministers of large churches in the adjoining states. The girls and I will attend the Congregational church across the Green. That should quiet any rumors about them being 'heathen.'"

"Reverend Hobbes is the minister there, correct? Isn't that where the Judsons and Frosts attend?"

Prudence nodded to both questions.

"Well, I hope your confidence is well-founded. I truly believe God can work on people's hearts, but if you should find their reception something less than warm, I assure you there will always be an open door and a welcoming handshake here in the Packerville Baptist Assembly. What do you say, Calvin? Would Prudence and her young ladies be welcomed by your parishioners in Suffield?"

Calvin had been silent during this exchange, concentrating on his ham and potatoes. He spoke slowly. "There are few people of color -- freed blacks -- in our area. It is hard to say for sure how people will respond to changes. I do think the Lord uses such things to show people their hearts. Of course, I, myself, would welcome Prudence any time."

Almira, reading a hidden meaning in Calvin's last words, gave her sister a poke under the table. Ignoring her, Prudence took another spoonful of squash.

Energized by the noonday meal, the sap brigade returned to their chore. "Les' hurry it up," Mr. Olney called. "Jack Frost be comin' back afore dark, I 'spect, and we be better off headin' home than lollygaggin' in th' woods ."

With a salute of agreement, Calvin headed back to the last stand of maples. The trees grew close together here, surrounding them with a chamber of peace and privacy as they continued their work. The afternoon sped by, and soon the old sun sent feeble rays to warn them it was time to make their final stop before returning to the sugar shack. Prudence jumped off the wagon to help Calvin with the pail, but she stopped his hand as it hovered above the full bucket of shimmering sap.

"Wait a minute, Calvin. Your daughter told me you could see your reflection in the sap, just like looking in a mirror. Let's see if it's true."

Smiling, they peeped into the container and glimpsed their faces side by side.

"You look happy, Prudence."

"I am happy. This was a wonderful idea, and I will always remember this day. I've so enjoyed being with thee Calvin... and Almira and Elizabeth, too," she hastened to add.

Calvin placed the pail back on its hook and turned to face her. "Do you know, Prudence, how very fond Elizabeth is of you? She even said to me yesterday she wished I was a pirate so I could kidnap you and take you home with us."

Prudence tossed her head and a peal of laughter echoed in the grove. "What an imagination she has. You'll have to watch out what she reads -- coming up with such an idea."

"Well, really, I considered it. It's not such a bad idea. Now don't look amazed. You know I would never take you anywhere against your will." His voice became husky with feeling as he cupped her rosy face with ungloved hands. Her pulse raced when his thumb brushed her lower lip. "Dear Prudence, how happy I would be if you would consent to come to Suffield with me as my wife. Share my life. Share my ministry. Be a mother to Elizabeth."

Taken by surprise, Prudence said nothing. He hurried on, almost afraid of losing his nerve.

"You could have a school there, if you want. The county is growing, and there will be a great need for schools.

"I have admired you from the first. I never expected to be in love again, but I am. You have won my heart. Oh, Prudence, I love you so. Will you marry me?" His arms encircled her, as his brown eyes searched her face, compelling a response.

Through her thick cloak, she felt the warmth from his hands radiate from the small of her back. It would be such a comfort to lay her head on his strong shoulder. A longing she had never before experienced surged through her, and her eyes closed. Ever so slightly, she leaned toward Calvin and lifted her face to his. His mouth was gentle upon hers -- almost shy -- but tasting her sweetness and feeling her tremble in his arms, he drew her closer and their kiss deepened.

Just as she was wishing the embrace would never end, a small, wrinkled black face pushed unbidden into her thoughts. In her head she heard the raspy, hopeful voice of Hattie Doud: *"We is allus' goin' t' be jus' workers... never had a chance t' learn... tha's why I wants t' help by givin' money fer Ann Eliza an' little Sarah."*

With a gasp, she pulled away from Calvin, and they stared at one another in confusion. "Oh, Calvin, no." Her voice shook, but her words were firm. "I am so sorry. I should never have kissed thee... never have let thee kiss me... for I cannot marry thee. I have made commitments, and people are depending on me. I dare not let my own happiness be an excuse for breaking my word."

"You do care for me, Prudy. I know you do, for you called me 'thee.' You call your sister and brother 'thee,' and you never call anyone 'thee' unless you love them.

"You told me you have not yet accepted any money -- you would accept nothing until they actually arrived, and you have yet a full month before then. People will understand. Marriage is a life-changing matter. You could likely sell your house to the town of Canterbury where they could set up another school to their liking, and after we are settled, you could start a school in Suffield. The same girls could come. It would only mean a delay..."

Prudence took another step away from him. "You have thought it all out without asking my opinion, it seems. Really, Calvin, I have put too much time and effort into this project to set it aside at this point. I place great value on the words 'there is a time to every purpose under heaven' and I know in my heart this is the right time and the right place for my school." She paused and took a deep breath. "If you are the right person, you have just come at the wrong time." She added in a sad voice, "I am not sure, Calvin, that I am the right person for thee, either. I am too independent, too plain-spoken, to be a Baptist minister's wife."

"You would be a wonderful wife," he began. Then seeing the stubborn set of her mouth, he stopped, hope fading from his eyes. For a minute, neither spoke. He put his arms around her once again. "Prudence, my Prudence. I already told you I would not kidnap you, and I'll not press you to abandon what your conscience tells you is right. At least let me continue to be your friend and hold to the possibility in some future day, a time will be right for us."

She returned his hug then stepped away, aware her words had stung him, but thankful he accepted her answer. "Yes, Calvin, I will always treasure your friendship."

The wind blew cold in the space between them, needling her face and arms. She shivered, ignoring the twinge in her own heart telling her she was closing a door that would never reopen.

"The days are so short now, aren't they?" She managed a brave smile. "Well, we'd better stoplollygagging here in the woods, as Mr. Olney said, and get these pails to the shack. The others will be waiting for us."

Chapter Nine

March 1833

The morning after the sugaring expedition, Calvin and Elizabeth left Canterbury. Prudence gave a fierce hug to Elizabeth, but only waved goodbye to Calvin. Everything had been said the day before as she and Calvin stood in the grove of maple trees, and now she must deal with her decision with dignity. At least she had the satisfaction of parting on amicable terms.

She launched into preparation for the new school, hoping to keep her thoughts of Calvin at bay. With characteristic purpose she forged ahead, making a whirlwind trip to New York, writing numerous letters, readying the house and larder with all sorts of provisions, and helping Marcy and Nerissa clean every corner of the house. She was on a small stepladder one afternoon with her hair under a mob cap and wearing a stained apron when Marcy poked her head around the door.

"Mercy me," she cried. "You have company, Miss Prudence. You best get that apron off and wash them smudges off your nose, 'cause you don't 'zactly look like a school teacher, and there's a passel of gen'lemen here to see you. They's in the front parlor."

"Do we have any refreshments you could serve them while I tidy myself up? On second thought, never mind. It won't hurt for them to see me at work, and I'm certainly not ashamed of getting my nose smudged in honest labor." So saying, she whipped off the apron, straightened her cap, and made her way to the parlor. She was not surprised to see the familiar faces of Dr. Harris, Mr. Frost, Captain Fenner, and Rufus Adams turn to greet her when she entered the room.

They wasted little time with pleasantries. "Good day, Miss Crandall." Mr. Frost took the role of spokesman for the group. "We have just come from meeting with a score of your neighbors here in Canterbury. We are shocked beyond words at your advertisement in Mr. Garrison's paper and have come to find out for ourselves if it is true. How can you possibly entertain the notion of bringing in foreigners -- colored girls, at that -- and setting up an institution for them here in our midst? What good could come from such madness?"

Looking at their stiff postures and disapproving frowns, Prudence forced herself to remain calm. "My purpose, sirs, is that of every teacher: to educate. I in no way desire to bring confusion to the town, but only to instruct the ignorant and prepare teachers for the people of color. Surely you must see the necessity for education if they are to elevate themselves as a people."

"I cannot agree with your ideas, Miss Crandall." Dr. Harris declared. "To educate people beyond their natural station is only to bring disorder. Their place in our society is clearly to be laborers, not philosophers or orators. Particularly the women."

Mr. Adams' high, thin voice expressed outrage. "Bringing young women into our town to mix with our sons and daughters is a shocking thing to do. It will encourage leveling principles. Who knows? It could even bring about racial intermarriage. And you call yourself a Christian woman."

Before she could stop herself, Prudence blurted. "You seem to have forgotten Moses had a black wife."

Choking on this impertinence, Adams was silenced.

"To plant such a concern right here in the middle of town," Frost continued, "would be an affront to the citizens of Canterbury. The village will be overrun with Negroes making themselves a public nuisance. You must abandon these plans at once."

"Must? Why is that? It is my right to teach whomever I please and who I think will benefit most from my teaching. I assure you, they will not cause any problems in the town. They are merely young women wanting to better themselves through learning, and as citizens, they have the right."

"What?" asked Rufus Adams. "What about our rights? They will surely become a burden on our town when they run out of resources and expect the town to support them. Besides, just their presence here in the middle of town will cause our property values to go down. How is this fair to your neighbors? Mr. Judson, especially."

"If that is the problem," Prudence reasoned, "I would be willing to sell this property and relocate elsewhere in the town. I assure you, you will never be expected to provide for their support. Not only are their families of moderate means, but Arthur Tappan and others of the Anti-Slavery Society will gladly post bonds for their support. The Society believes this is a crucial opportunity to demonstrate the abilities of the colored pupils and assert their rights to higher education."

Mr. Frost raised his voice. "You have not been listening. We do not want such an establishment anywhere in our environs. Not here. Not elsewhere in the town. Not in the state of Connecticut. Do not underestimate the strength of our numbers or of our principles. The Anti-Slavery Society be damned if they think they can whip us. We'll settle their hash in short order, and yours, too, madam. I advise you to take us seriously."

The others nodded their heads and murmured their agreement. Spurred by their support, Frost continued to deliver an ultimatum.

"We've appealed to you as neighbors and as friends, Miss Crandall, but you leave us no choice but to carry this to the next stage. This situation calls for a town meeting. You may expect to hear from us again in a less friendly manner." So saying, the men pompously marched out the door.

A less friendly manner? she mused. *That was hardly what I would call a friendly visit. I think I will keep this to myself. There is no use upsetting Almira and Marcy when we still have so much to do to get ready.* She put on her apron once more and resumed scrubbing the cupboards with vigor.

Hard work did not erase her sadness over her break with Calvin, but as she filled her days with organizing and setting up for the new school, her melancholy grew less intense. All the while, she kept in touch with Garrison, whose praise and support fueled her determination to make a success of the school.

Not a fortnight had passed since Mr. Frost's committee visited her when Almira returned from town one day with alarming news. She had scarcely removed her cloak before calling out, "Prudy, come quickly. We must talk." She pulled her by the elbow into the schoolroom.

"Sister, thee cannot believe what I have learned in town today. I overheard by accident some men talking in Mr. Coit's store. Mr. Judson, Mr. Frost, Dr. Harris, Captain Fenner, and the rest have called a town meeting. Thee can guess what it is about. They are planning to prevent us from having our school."

"I can believe it. They were very rude when they last called upon me. Truly, Almy, what can they do? The girls will be here in less than two weeks, and we will be ready to receive them. Besides, we are breaking no laws."

"That's just it. They intend to pass resolutions against thee to keep the school from opening. I doubt not they also will boycott our trade and refuse services to us. What can thee do in the face of such actions?"

"We shall see," Prudence answered. "Do not forget we have other resources they do not control. As a matter of fact, I will write a letter to Mr. Garrison, though I am not at all afraid of a town meeting. Who knows? It may turn out for the best and give me a chance to reassure our neighbors they have nothing to fear from a few colored girls who want to learn to be teachers. Enough talking, Almy. Please continue working on this stack of copy notebooks. I think the girls will like the colorful covers thee has started."

As a result of her letter to Garrison, Arnold Buffum, Reverend Samuel May, and George Benson arrived at the Crandall home two days later. May was a tall man of middle years who wore his dark hair parted on the side. He spoke in the well-modulated voice of an orator. At the supper table that evening, conversation soon turned to the business of the town meeting.

"Mr. Garrison regrets he is not able to be here," Reverend May told her, "but he has sent us to make sure you are represented at this town meeting tomorrow. He believes it is crucial your school not meet the fate of the one in New Haven."

"I heard something of that," Prudence replied, but the details did not reach us here in Canterbury. It was to be a mixed school -- without distinction of color, as I recall."

"A most infamous doing," George Benson said. "The founders appealed to the Declaration of Independence and planned to open an academy for twenty-eight white pupils and fourteen colored youths. They even took their plans before the town council, where the majority approved of their undertaking."

"Why then, what went wrong?" Prudence drew her brows together in perplexity.

"What usually happens," George stated. He helped himself to another serving of savory lamb stew before continuing. "Some ill-willed gossips started a rumor campaign, spreading slander and lies. Telling folks in the town that Negroes would be coming from the South and lining the streets with their huts. All sorts of rubbish you would expect a thinking person to laugh at. Instead, seventy men took it upon themselves to attack the academy."

"They did so," said Buffum in disgust, "apparently convincing themselves what was illegal for one person to do was justified because they had a mob."

"Terrible business, it was," George nodded, "and so they succeeded in bringing an end to a school that could have done much good for the town. Instead they brought disgrace upon themselves for their outlandish behavior."

"Oh, dear," Almira lamented. "How can people be so unfair?"

"All the more reason," Prudence said, "why we must calm their fears and share our hopes with them. I believe we may win them to our side after all."

Almira laid her napkin beside her plate. "Thee cannot possibly mean to go to the meeting, Prudence. Only the men of the town will be there, and it would be so unseemly for thee to go."

Prudence nodded. "I know, Almy."

Mr. Buffum patted Almira's hand. "My dear girl, this is why we have come. We will represent your sister at the meeting. Surely they will hear us out, and the rumors will stop before they get completely out of control. Have you ever heard our Mr. May speak?" He slapped his modest friend on the back. "I promise you, this man is eloquent.

"Besides, when we give them our personal assurance none of the pupils will be a burden upon the resources of the town, they will have to acknowledge they have nothing to be afraid of."

"I have prepared written statements for you, Mr. May, since you will be my representative. I have a letter of request for Mr. Bacon, who I understand will act as chairman."

Despite herself, Almira could not help but express another doubt. "What if he will not listen to Mr. May?"

"The laws of our country permit every man to speak, Miss Almira. It is our right as citizens."

Listening to the discussion as she bustled to and fro serving the meal, Marcy shook her head and sighed. "I don't know," she opined. "I'd like to b'leeve the best, but in my experience, I never seen a crowd o' white men meetin' to talk things over that turned out good for the coloreds. I b'leeve I'll take a walk across the Green tomorrow and have a look-see through the window to find out fer myself."

In spite of her confident words at the dinner table, Prudence spent a restless night. When she got up at first light to review the letters she had written for the men to read at the meeting, she was surprised to look out the window and see several horses and carriages were already outside the meeting house. She prayed the people would have open ears and listen to reason. After all, her purpose was only to improve the condition of a race of people who had for too long borne discrimination and misery.

At her desk, she began writing a postscript to the papers she would give Samuel May. Her handwriting sloped gracefully across the page with the words:

> *I have no wish to offend any of the citizens of Canterbury, and I authorize Mr. May and Mr. Buffum to enter into any reasonable agreement you see fit. I would be willing to sell my house and property back to the town for what I paid for it. I will gladly purchase another house in a less conspicuous location to continue my school, but I am determined to proceed with my venture.*

The atmosphere in the dining room was restrained as they partook of breakfast. They were unable to ignore the sounds of wagons and horses arriving on the Green in increasing numbers.

"Ain't there enough folks in Canterbury?" commented Marcy. "Looks like Mr. Judson's pack went all th' way to New London to bring in more."

Samuel May tried his best to reassure Prudence. He finished his last spoonful of oatmeal and dabbed his chin with the linen napkin. Looking up from under his strong eyebrows, he directed an encouraging smile at the sisters. "It is obvious to me Mr. Judson is the power behind this movement, Miss Crandall. I have had amiable dealings with him in the past and have a good relationship with him. I rely on that to gain his good will."

Prudence took a swallow of scalding tea and forced herself to smile at the good man. "I have confidence you will win the day. I assure you there are many prayers going with you to the meeting."

Shortly after the meal was finished, the three men crossed the Green and threaded their way through the throng of conveyances surrounding the meeting house. They waited until all were inside the building before making their entrance into the packed room. No one paid them any mind as they found seats near the raised dais where Mr. Asael Bacon, moderator for the meeting, shuffled some papers, preparing for his opening statement. Andrew Judson, seated beside him, nodded to a man by the door, who closed it with an ominous thud.

Back at the Crandall household, Prudence and Almira were drawn to the schoolroom windows where they had the best view of the meeting house. Almira counted the horses in the muddy yard and remarked, "My goodness, Prudy. Where have they all come from? I didn't know there were this many people in the county.

"Look." She pointed to an orange flash of fur outside the gate. "How did Whittington get out there? It looks like he has caught another vole. Suppose he dragged it into the meeting and dropped it at Mr. Judson's feet."

Prudence did not respond to Almira's attempt at humor. Her mind was too filled with anxiety imagining what was going on in that closed building. The hour dragged by, and at last she left the window, went into the parlor, and took up her sewing. Almira had lured Whittington inside, and finding his mistress at her stitching, he curled into a ball at her feet. He had brought no vole along, but his twitching tail bumped against her full skirt in a soothing rhythm.

Time for the noon meal came and went with no sign of the meeting being over. Marcy offered a light meal in the dining room, but the women ate very little.

"I did go 'cross the Green this morning," she admitted to Prudence, "but I couldn't see or hear much a'tall. The window was too high off the ground to look in, and 'bout all I heard was a bunch o' loud voices. I do think I heard our fine Mr. Judson's voice, but I couldn't make out what he was sayin'."

"Never mind," Almira said. "If it was Judson, we can guess what he said. I am surprised, Marcy, that you had the nerve to go over there at all. I wonder how much longer the meeting can last."

Just before tea time, Almira, who had been pacing the hallway, raced upstairs and burst into her sister's room. "It's over at last," she announced. "I can see men coming out of the building."

Prudence jumped to her feet. "Did thee see our friends?" she inquired, then hurried downstairs to the front door to look for them. Marcy joined them, staring out at the crowd dispersing on the Green.

"Some of those men don't look too happy," Almira observed. "I wonder what happened."

"We'll soon find out, I reckon. Ain't that George Benson?" Marcy pointed at the familiar figure emerging from the doorway. Behind him came Samuel May, who was engaged in conversation with Mr. Judson, and Arnold Buffum, following at a slower pace and frowning down at his boots. The four men paused before parting. Prudence noticed there was no handshaking at their farewell, and a hard lump rose in her throat.

"Marcy," she said, "have you put the kettle on? They will be wanting tea and a bite to eat, and then we will hear what they have to say."

Marcy scurried to the kitchen with Almira behind her, and Prudence stepped out on the porch. She waited in the open, breathing in the fresh, spring breeze. With her eyes focused on Mr. May and Judson, she did not notice a stocky fellow with a scarred face walking away from the meeting house in her direction. Pausing before the gate, the man stooped, picked up a heap of muddy slush, and packed it into a hard ball.

"Nigger lover!" he shouted. Before Prudence could step inside, he hurled his muddy missile straight at her. It missed her by only an inch and landed with a resounding splat on the door.

Open-mouthed in amazement, she withdrew into the house. She was still trembling when she heard George Benson's voice at the door. "What's this?" he demanded. "It looks like someone already delivered a most uncivilized message. I'll wipe it off before Miss Crandall sees it."

When Prudence threw open the door, he knew by the grim look on her face she was already aware of the insult.

"I know you have a report for me," she said, "but it can wait until you have had something to eat. You must be famished, and Marcy has food on the table for you."

The men nodded and moved to the dining room. While they ate, they made an effort to indulge in small talk, but at last they could put off their news no longer.

"We shall take tea in the parlor, Marcy, and you may join us, too. This news concerns us all." With a calm demeanor that belied her anxiety, Prudence led the way to the parlor.

When tea had been poured, George Benson took a position in the middle of the room and removed a thick black notebook from his pocket. "I have it all here, Miss Prudence, and you may be sure an account of the whole business will appear in the next issue of the *Liberator*. I only wish I had better news to report."

Prudence smoothed her skirt. Regarding Benson with solemn eyes, she nodded for him to begin.

"As you probably know, Asael Bacon was the moderator. He sat in the deacons' seat, along with Mr. Judson, who acted as clerk. The room was filled pretty nearly to capacity with even the galleries on all three sides packed, but we managed to procure a pew on the side aisle where we could hear and see everything.

"After Bacon read the usual warning, he proceeded to present the resolutions the committee had prepared. I'll spare you the exact wording of them, but the tenor of the whole was to emphasize the 'disgrace and damage' that would be suffered by the citizens of Canterbury should a school for the colored race be set up. They termed your school, Miss Crandall, 'an impending evil,' and appointed a committee of civil authorities and selectmen to wait upon you to persuade you to abandon your project."

"*Humph*. They already tried that. Much good did it do them."

"Ah," put in Arnold Buffum, "did they not convince you of the 'injurious effects and incalculable evils' resulting from such a school? I believe they referred to Miss Crandall as 'the person contemplating the establishment of said school,' did they not George?"

"Indeed," he chuckled. "As if she were a monster."

"I do not find this amusing," remarked Samuel May, rising to his feet and pacing the floor with his hands clasped behind him. "Especially considering what Rufus Adams said in his speech. I will not repeat the words, for they were reprehensible. Not only did he grossly misrepresent your character and motives, but he threw out several low insinuations against the Society and Mr. Garrison for encouraging your enterprise."

Marcy clicked her tongue and shook her head at this news, but Prudence sat expressionless, drinking her tea.

"Dear me," murmured Almira. "Did no one speak up for Prudence?"

"Not in the least," Benson answered. "In fact, the 'Honorable Andrew T. Judson' followed Adams with a tirade it would be hard to match. You might say he vented his spleen in the worst sort of hostility. He worked on every chord that could call forth all the baser passions of the crowd until they were fairly frothing at the horrible doom hovering over them and their precious families. He convinced them you were the heart of a conspiracy against them, and they must rise up against you and the wealthy outsiders who were aiding you."

Buffum interrupted the report. "Remember, George, there was one tall gentleman who attempted to speak in her favor. I believe I heard him referred to as Mr. White, a tanner in the village."

"Dear Jane's father," Almira said. "Bless him for speaking out. What did he say?"

"He said he did not at all believe the men were presenting a fair picture of Miss Crandall. He said his daughter had gained much good from being a pupil at the previous school, and while he was sorry Miss Crandall had closed the academy, he must implore them to hear her side of the story.

"'I know Miss Crandall to be a Christian woman,' he said, 'and I cannot think she is guilty of any malicious intent toward us.' He was soon shouted down by others in the crowd.

"One fellow shouted, 'I hear that woman justified intermarriage by saying Moses had a black wife. Next she'll be calling for polygamy because of the patriarchs. She must be stopped here and now,' and the rest of the crowd went wild."

"While the tanner was speaking," said Samuel May, "I handed Miss Crandall's letters over to Bacon. He glanced at them, then gave them to Judson. He shook his fist in our faces and demanded how we as outsiders could insult the citizens by interfering with local concerns. Overhearing what he said, some rough-looking farmers threatened us with violence if we opened our mouths."

"Even though Sam explained he was merely speaking on behalf of Miss Crandall, who had asked him to represent her, the moderator forbade them to speak in the meeting. He did say," George added, "Sam and Arnold could speak after the meeting."

"Which we attempted," continued Mr. May, "as soon as we heard the words 'this meeting is adjourned.' The men started pouring out of the building, so I leapt to my feet and shouted, 'Men of Canterbury, I have a word for you! Hear me!' About half of them had left, but those remaining turned to listen to my replies to the accusations made against Miss Crandall and her supporters. I called Arnold to my side, and he was only able to speak about five minutes when the trustee of the church came in and ordered us all out so he could lock up."

"I am sorry I could not do more," Arnold Buffum said, "but the oratory of Cicero himself would not have been able to control those people. In short, Miss Crandall, I fear we have failed in our mission."

"I thought I saw the three of you on the lawn speaking with Mr. Judson. I am nearly afraid to ask, but I must know what he said."

Samuel May reluctantly brought forth a parchment and turned to answer her question. "I am afraid I presumed too much on my acquaintance with that man. He was as cold as a codfish, and he gave me this copy of the resolutions passed at the meeting." In a flat voice, Mr. May read the words:

"Whereas it hath been publicly announced that a school is to be opened in this town first Monday of April next, using the Language of the advertisement, 'for young ladies and little misses of color,' the obvious tendency of which would be to collect within the town of Canterbury, large numbers of persons from other states, whose character and habits be various and unknown to us, thereby rendering insecure, the persons, properties and reputations of our citizens. Under such circumstances, our silence might be construed into an approbation of the project Thereupon resolved -- that the location of a school for the people of color at any place within the limits of this town for the admission of persons of foreign jurisdictions meets with our unqualified disapprobation and it is to be understood that the inhabitants of Canterbury protest against it in the most earnest manner. Resolved -- that a committee now be appointed to be composed of the Civil Authority and Selectmen, who

shall make known to the person contemplating the establishment of said school, the sentiments and objections entertained by this meeting in reference to said school, pointing out to her, the injurious effects and incalculable evils resulting from such an establishment within this town and to persuade her to abolish the project."

Silence gripped the small group in the parlor.

Prudence spoke in a small voice. "Then I suppose I will need to move the school... perhaps to Packerville or even New London."

May shook his head. "No, Miss Crandall. I regret to say it would make no difference." He leaned his spare frame against the mantel, frowning as he spoke. "Judson took care to inform me he means such a school shall not exist anywhere in the state of Connecticut. In his view, the colored people can never rise from what he calls 'their menial condition,' and makes no secret of his dedication to the cause of colonization."

"I am familiar with his fanatical ideas," Prudence said. "He thinks of them as inferior beings who can never be equals of whites and should be sent back to Africa to civilize the natives, if they can."

George Benson again referred to his notebook and his face grew redder. "I have his exact words here: 'The condition of the colored people can never be essentially improved on this continent. You are violating the Constitution of our republic which settled forever the status of the black man in this land. They belong to Africa. Let them be sent there or kept as they are here. The sooner you abolitionists abandon your project, the better for our country, the niggers, and yourselves.'"

As George snapped his notebook shut, Almira burst out, "What a *hateful* man. We ought to send him someplace... I won't say where..."

Prudence held up her hand in a calming gesture. "We ought not return evil for evil, sister. Now that we know the opposition we face, we can be prepared to meet it." She looked around the circle and smiled at her supporters. "You must not blame yourselves for this outcome, gentlemen. You have done your best, and that is all that is required of any of us. Now I must do my best to carry on in the work I have been called to do. Others will hear of what happens in Canterbury, and perhaps they will be strengthened in their own resolve to stand for what is right."

Chapter Ten

The morning of April 5, the Crandall household was bursting at the seams. Sarah Harris returned to the school along with her young cousin Mary, but they were the only local students. Ann Eliza Hammond and her younger sister Sarah had arrived before the end of March, and after settling themselves in the smallest room, they helped the other girls move in as they arrived.

Little Sarah Hammond acted as the unofficial welcoming committee. Prudence smiled to watch her making friends with the older girls. She had already made a great comrade of the long-suffering Whittington and carried the cat under her arm as she greeted the newcomers with her ingenuous questions.

Upon learning Eliza Glasko's name, she remarked, "Eliza -- that's my big sister's middle name. We have two Elizabeths as well. Elizabeth from Providence, where I come from, and Elizabeth all the way from Philadelphia. We'll have to call them Elizabeth One and Elizabeth Two. Oh, I near forgot there's an Ann Elizabeth coming from New York. What a mix-up."

Besides Sarah Harris and her cousin Mary, there were three other girls from towns in Connecticut. The rest came from the states of Massachusetts, Pennsylvania, Rhode Island, and New York. Rooms that had been shared by only two girls before now held three or four, but somehow each one claimed a spot for herself. Prudence and Almira gave up the luxury of their privacy and became roommates so Amy, Theodosia, and Jerusha could occupy Almira's room.

No one complained of the tight quarters because they were so happy to be in the school.

Marcy was in her glory as she rang the dinner bell and the pupils crowded around the table to partake of the first meal in their new home. Prudence explained the custom of pausing for each one to say a silent prayer, and a quiet mood settled upon the whole group as they ate. It was one o'clock before Prudence and Almira summoned the girls to the schoolroom to introduce them to their lessons.

They entered shyly, scarcely believing the tidy, colorful room was meant for them. When each found her assigned place, Prudence opened her book and began to read her rules for the school. The pupils listened with respect as their teacher admonished them to work diligently and accept the responsibility which accompanies the privilege of learning.

When Almira distributed the books she had prepared for them to use for their compositions, their eyes shone with pleasure. "The subject of our writing today will be virtue," Prudence explained. "Think of the

88

many virtues which grace a woman's character and choose one you believe to have the highest value. Describe this virtue, and tell me why you believe it to be the most important quality to cultivate."

They meekly took up their pens and began their first assignment. The scratching of quills was punctuated by occasional sighs and the sound of raindrops against the windows as the hour passed.

Prudence was in no hurry to present her students in public, so she was not sorry the April rains kept them indoors for the entire week. Nothing disturbed their tranquil days and harmonious evenings.

Friday afternoon, Marcy came to Prudence's room. "I thought we had food a-plenty in the pantry, Miss Prudence," she said. "But these gals has healthy appetites, and I'm gettin' low on flour. Is it all right if I make a quick trip to Mr. Coit's store? I'll be back in time for tea."

She started off alone, armed with a shopping bag and an umbrella, avoiding the puddles in the streets and humming to herself.

She had not been gone long when Prudence looked out and saw her returning. The shopping bag hung by her side like a deflated balloon, and the mud-caked hem of her gown trailed along behind.

"Oh, Miss Crandall," she wailed, meeting Prudence in the kitchen. "How many times has I been to that store? But today Mr. Coit wouldn't let me through the door. He was mean as a varmint and said he wouldn't sell me so much as a spool of thread, no matter how much money I planked down... And what in tarnation does 'boycott' mean?"

Prudence frowned in disapproval of Marcy's language but answered her question. "It means he has decided to refuse to do business with us because of the resolution passed at the town meeting. It's simply another way of expressing the community's censure of our school -- trying to force us to bend to their will."

Marcy's mouth dropped open in shock. "Well, I never in all my born days thought he could be so lowdown and orn'ry."

"I am not surprised, only sad. I expect we will find the other merchants joining the boycott. It is a good thing we are well-stocked with most goods."

"Whatever will we do, Miss Prudence? Soon or later we'll run out, and the girls'll have to go home. We can't starve them." Tears gathered on her dark lashes.

Prudence took her by the shoulders. "Marcy, you are not to tell any of the girls about this. We do not want to spoil their first week here with bad news. It will only worry them."

"Worry *them*? Aren't you worried? How long can we keep on--"

"As long as God wills, Marcy. Even if He must send manna from heaven or ravens to bring us food. Remember all the times He fed the children of Israel in the desert and provided for the prophets? Now stop those tears, my dear Marcy. I will help you get the tea ready."

Thus it was the young ladies ate a hearty meal that evening, never suspecting anything was amiss.

The next day was Saturday, and the girls kept busy preparing for their first Sunday in new surroundings. As they washed their linens and found places to hang indoor clotheslines, Mariah Robinson from Providence exclaimed in excitement, "I'm glad tomorrow is Sunday. It's my favorite day of the week. Ain't we lucky to be right close to the meeting house? I do hope there's lots of singing."

Almira glanced at Prudence in consternation.

"What is thee planning to do, Prudy?" she whispered to her later. "I fear we will not be welcome at the meeting with our new scholars. Shouldn't we just stay home and have a meeting for worship in the Quaker way?"

Prudence looked thoughtful. "I have given it much consideration, Almira. I think if we wait to go in until just before the meeting starts and sit in the back, we will not draw too much attention to ourselves. There have been coloreds at the meetings before, and no one objected. It seems the church should be the one place where people would let down the barriers and worship together.

"Let us be sure all our charges are suitably dressed and give no offense with fancy clothing. We need them to be models of virtue and keep their eyes down in modesty."

Almira had been holding her breath during this speech, and let it out shakily. "As always, thee has thought of everything. I pray thee is right."

In the morning, though clouds hung low in the sky, the rain had stopped. After a simple breakfast, the girls prepared for church. They wore their Sunday best. Every gown was clean, well-pressed, and perfectly fitted. The subdued colors did not call attention to the wearers, and every head was covered with a cap or simple bonnet. Prudence and Almira both wore grey gowns, and they escorted the young ladies across the Green with Prudence in front, Almira in back, and the pupils walking two by two between. Approaching the front door just as the bell ceased ringing, Prudence felt she had timed their arrival perfectly. She cast one last glance over her shoulder to inspect her charges before entering, and when she turned back toward the door, she was startled to find the tall figure of Captain Fenner looming over her.

"Miss Crandall," he intoned in the hollow tone of one standing sentinel at a house of death, "you must stop here. It is my duty to tell you the doors of this place are closed to you and those of your so-called school. We are here to worship our Lord, and we cannot have the sanctity of this place disrupted by bringing in foreigners. Go back home at once, and when you have sent these persons back to their own homes, you and your sister will be welcome with us again."

Prudence was stunned into silence. She had been prepared for a cool reception, for heads turned the other way and lack of civility, but she truly had not expected the doors barred against them. When she found her tongue at last, she said, "Goodbye then, Captain Fenner. Our prayers today will reach God's ears better from my parlor than from your meeting house."

The young ladies had heard the exchange, and in shame turned around to walk back the way they had come. Some hung their heads, and others had tears in their eyes, but Prudence marched with her head held high, even though Captain Fenner's words stung her soul. Most of all, she hurt for the girls who had such great hopes for this first Lord's Day in their new home. She racked her brain, trying to think how to soften this rejection and what to do when they reached the house.

"Miss Crandall, I have a suggestion." Julia Williams, oldest of the pupils, stepped forward from the group of students.

Julia was from Boston. Twenty years old, she had already had some music training. Her goal was to become a music teacher. A tall, handsome girl, she exuded leadership and confidence.

"I know many songs familiar to most all of the girls. If Miss Almira will play the piano, I'd be glad to lead us in singing. I b'leeve the singing's the part of the service we was lookin' forward to the most. I happen to know Harriet Lanson knows lots of the prayer book. She'd be a good choice to do some prayin'."

Prudence seized Julia's hands in gratitude. "Oh, thank you, Julia. You have given me strength for this trial. We will gather in the schoolroom and begin as you say. While you are singing, I will select some Scripture to read, and perhaps some word will come to me that I can share."

The cloud of dejection which hung over them did not lift upon entering the schoolroom. They took their accustomed seats and bowed their heads in humiliation until Julia came to the front and filled the room with a voice like a velvet summer night. When Almira joined in on the piano with the familiar chords of "Wade in the Water," their strong young voices rang out, lifting their hearts and spirits heavenward.

"Wade in the water, children,
Wade way out in the water, children.
My Lord's gonna trouble the water..."

Song after song followed, until all traces of shame were replaced with shining faces and clapping hands. When Harriet Lanson prayed, she thanked the Lord for "this haven of learnin'" and for the "dear Miss Crandalls", and concluded her prayer with the words, "and as for the pore folks back in the meetin' house, Father, forgive them, for they don't know what they do."

After the meeting dispersed, Almira spoke to Prudence. "Sister, today I am ashamed of being white. I am ashamed of the so-called

Christian people of this town, and I believe the whole country should hear about the dignity Julia Williams showed today. George Benson ought to write about what happened in the *Liberator*."

"I think thee is right about that, Almy. After our evening meal, thee and I should take the farm wagon and drive out to see the Kneelands. Remember, he told us our girls would be welcome to worship in Packerville."

Almira nodded. "I almost wish we had gone there today, except for the lesson the girls taught me." Her blue eyes shone with determination. "Prudy, I no longer feel afraid. I know more troubles will come from the likes of Mr. Judson and Captain Fenner, but somehow I have found courage to face it. We cannot let these young ladies down."

The sisters embraced and mingled their tears and confidences until the aroma of Marcy's cooking and the sound of voices drew them to the dining room.

That evening, Levi Kneeland and his wife received Prudence and her sister cordially when they arrived at their home. They were not surprised Prudence and her pupils had been blocked from the meeting house, and agreed with Almira that George should report the story for Garrison's paper. "As a matter of fact, George will be stopping by this week," Levi told them.

"I do hope he'll report the facts only, and not make it sound like an outrage." said Prudence.

The minister smiled. "Even though it was," he commented. "Next Sunday I'll send one of my deacons to Canterbury with a wagon. Between your wagon and mine, we should be able to get everyone here safely. I know it's only a few miles, but I don't like the idea of those young girls walking, the atmosphere around here being what it is. Have your Fred Olney drive for you. Perhaps that'll be a bit more protection."

The following week passed in relative quiet. When the girls ventured out for a walk, they were followed and taunted by groups of youngsters, but Prudence and Almira instructed their young ladies to walk with decorum and not allow the bullies any satisfaction of seeing them react in fear. When Sunday arrived, true to his word, Mr. Kneeland sent a gentleman to accompany them to the service. When the wagons came to a stop before the simple white building, the girls sat glued to their seats.

"Here we are, ladies," Prudence encouraged them.

Still, they did not move. They stared blankly at their Bibles on their laps and fidgeted with their bonnets.

Then the door to the church swung open. Levi and Deborah Kneeland descended the steps and crossed the lawn, followed by a group of worshipers. With smiles and outstretched hands, they soon welcomed the newcomers and led them through the doors of the Packerville Baptist Assembly.

*****

On Monday morning, Sarah and Mary Harris got an early start to school. George Fayerweather, as had become his custom, collected them in his buggy and dropped them off in front of the gate.

"I wonder if Miss Crandall has read the comp-a-ti-shun I wrote last week," said the younger girl as she pushed open the gate and started up the walk.

"Composition," Sarah corrected.

"Well, it's the hardest comp-a-zis-shun I ever wrote, and I'm 'fraid I made lots of mistakes-- What's that awful smell?" Mary stopped in her tracks.

Sarah let out a shriek as the stench reached her. "Don't go another step, Mary. I can't believe it! They've smeared barnyard manure all over the front steps!"

It was true. Piles of hog and cow manure covered the steps in a heavy slime which hordes of flies were feasting on.

"How wicked!" cried Mary. "They ought to be cowhided! How can anyone be so mean to Miss Crandall? An' her bein' white, too."

Sarah and Mary dashed to the back of the house and called for Marcy. When she saw the disgusting mess she wasted no time in finding shovels and brushes to remove the filth. Working quietly as possible, the three hiked up their full skirts and shoveled away until Mr. Olney and Nerissa happened along and pitched in.

"Ye get back in the house," Fred told the women. "I'll finish cleaning up afore Miz Crandall sees it. Them polecats whut done it oughta be cowhided."

"That's exac'ly what I said," put in Mary. "Miss Crandall, I s'pose, would tell us to forgive 'em."

Muttering less than forgiving words under his breath, Olney put his back into another shovelful of manure while Sarah and Mary went to Marcy's room to clean themselves up for school.

"How come yore so early today?" Marcy asked as she dug in her bureau for a clean cap for Sarah.

"Why, George wanted to get a jump on his work in the blacksmith shop, so he brought us early, and it's a good thing he did," she answered as they moved to the kitchen.

"Well, then, you might's well join us for breakfast. I'se ready to stick my biscuits in the oven, an' you can make the tea. Let's not tell Miss Prudence 'bout the steps, Sarah. She's got enough to worry 'bout. Mary, you fill this pitcher with water an' set it on the table."

The biscuits were done just in time for the Crandall sisters and their boarders to sit down to table. After the customary grace, Prudence reached for the tureen of porridge and Almira poured out a cup of water for Julia, who was sitting beside her.

With a wild whoop, Marcy dashed into the room, jostling Almira's elbow and knocking the water all over her lap.

"Don't nobody touch that water!" she hollered. "Oh, Miss Prudence, I'se so sorry! The water's been poisoned. Did anybody drink any? It's poisoned fer sure!"

"Poisoned? Whatever are you talking about, Marcy?" Prudence picked up the water pitcher and held it to her nose. Revulsion spread over her face when the rank odor of manure rose from black flecks of animal excrement floating in the water pitcher. She pushed back from the table and stood. Everyone else at the table followed suit. The meal was ruined.

"Call Mr. Olney," she commanded.

Almira and the others looked on from the yard as Prudence grimly followed Mr. Olney to the springhouse. Grunting and mopping his brow, he managed to shove aside the heavy stone protecting the well and drew up a bucket of water. The worst had come to pass.

"Looks like a boodle of devils come in the night, Miz Prudence, and dumped a load of manure in this here well. I dint wanna tell you this, but me an' the girls cleaned a pile of manure off'n the front steps already this mornin'. Reckon it's the same bunch."

Prudence sat down on the grass. Her composure crumbled. "What an awful thing to do. Anyone who drank any of that water on the table would have become seriously ill. We've always had the best water in our well," she cried in discouragement. "Will we ever be able to use it again, Mr. Olney?"

"It'll take some time," he said, shaking his head. "Some time an' some doin'. It hasta be cleaned, pumped out 'til it runs clear, an' if worst comes to worster, we'll git a new well dug. Now," he said, his practical side asserting itself, "whut's to be done meantime?"

Drying her eyes, she stood up and glanced toward the worried group in the yard. When her gaze rested on Sarah, her jaw set in determination. "Mr. Olney, how many empty casks do we have in the barn? Load them up in the wagon and drive out to the Harris farm. I'm sure William and Sally will let us have fresh water from their well to tide us over until the problem is solved. They are outside the town, and no one in Canterbury needs to know the Harris's have helped us. The cowards who did this will be expecting me to give up and come begging for mercy, but we are not beaten yet."

*****

The Crandall household cheered when Mr. Olney returned in the middle of the day with enough fresh water to last for some time. He had begun the task of unloading the water, when much to everyone's surprise, Pardon and Reuben Crandall drove into the yard.

Almira rushed to greet her brother and father. She threw herself into her big brother's arms and kissed her father's weathered face. "Oh, how I have missed thee. We have so much to tell about the past weeks. Prudy is in the back parlor. I cannot wait to see her face--" She did not have to wait, for Prudence, too, had heard the wagon and rushed out of the house with a huge smile of welcome.

"It appears we arrived just in time to help Mr. Olney with a heavy task," Pardon said. "We'll give him a hand now and visit later."

"We've heard some of the news already, Almy," Reuben sent his sister a smile of encouragement. "Look what's inside." He uncovered one corner of the wagon, revealing an astonishing assortment of goods from the farm.

Almira squealed in amazement. "How did thee know? Thee has brought the very things we need -- butter, cheese, ham, and cider. Here's a basket of fresh fish and a whole sack of flour. Marcy will bless thee. Marcy!" she called. "Come see!"

Hearing the commotion, Marcy scurried into the yard and peeked into the wagon. "Oh my, oh my." She grinned at Reuben and Pardon. "Miss Prudence, did you see all this? I b'leeve these are the ravens you was tellin' me about, bringin' provisions from the Lord."

Reuben and Pardon worked steadily with Mr. Olney, unloading the heavy water casks as well as the goods in their farm wagon. By the time they finished, the sun had set. The three men washed up in the yard, removed their boots, and came the back way into the kitchen. Marcy, of course, had heated some stew and served them liberal portions in gratitude for their generosity.

"How did thee know to come, Father?" Prudence asked. "Thy arrival could not have been better timed."

"Daughter, thee may think Canterbury is an isolated country town, but I tell thee the whole state has eyes on the doings here. Not just because of Garrison's paper, but the ordinary citizens are closely following developments, and news travels fast about the Canterbury affairs. We heard a few days ago about the general store boycotting your business, and we knew thee would need supplies."

Reuben wiped the inside of his bowl with a thick crust of bread and bit into it with relish. "Believe it or not, Mr. Judson himself accosted us on the road as we were on our way here."

"*Threatened* me, he did." Usually mild-mannered, Pardon pounded his fist on the table. "How dare he forbid me to bring my daughter supplies? He said I should be sorry if I came again, but I promised him as long as I had breath in my body, my daughters should not want for any necessity."

"I believe," added Reuben, "by the rumors we have heard he has every intention of running thee out of town. Has thee heard of the

Pauper and Vagrant Law?"

Prudence drew her chair closer to the table. "Isn't that an old law that persecutes the poor? I did not know it was still in the books."

Her brother nodded. "Any person who is not an inhabitant of a given town can be warned to leave. If he, or in this case, she, does not leave, she can be fined one dollar and sixty-seven cents a week for every week she stays in the town."

"Ridiculous," Prudence said in disgust. "Suppose they do not pay?"

"Ah, there is the bad part." Reuben lowered his voice and glanced sideways at Fred Olney, who sat quietly with his head in his hands. "According to this law, if the person fails to make payment to the town treasurer, the poor unfortunate shall be whipped."

"*Whipped?* How monstrous. How could such a thing be in a civilized country? Who would carry out such an atrocity here in Canterbury? I am astonished such a law still exists."

"Thee has not heard the worst," said Pardon in agitation. "I could not believe it myself, and I looked it up. Listen to this." He delved in his pocket and produced a paper. "'After a warning has been given to the vagrant as aforesaid, and such person hath no estate to satisfy the fine, such person shall be whipped on the naked back not exceeding ten stripes, unless he or she depart the town within ten days next after sentence is given.' There's more jargon there, but thee can see Judson is a desperate and determined man who will stop at nothing to bring this school to ruin."

"Even if it means whipping an innocent girl?" exclaimed Prudence. "Oh, Father. Does thee have any advice for me?"

"My dear daughter," Pardon said, "were pride not a sin, I would be nothing but proud of thee, and Almira, too. I cannot help but wonder how far thee should go in this matter. Mayhap this is not the time, nor the place, for thee to proceed with the school. I have wondered if thee should sell the property here, send the young ladies back to their homes, and wait for a better time. Judson is a powerful man. Not a fellow to trifle with."

Prudence buried her face in her hands and was silent, picturing one of her dear pupils with back bared to receive ten lashes on her body. Who, then, would be the scapegoat? Beautiful, gifted Julia? Precious Harriet, whose strong spirit was not matched with a robust body? Surely not Ann Eliza Hammond who had arrived at the school carrying Hattie Doud's money in a leather pouch around her neck. Yet she knew Andrew Judson could not win. No matter how many laws were on his side and how many people were cowed into following him, he was crusading on the wrong side. She rose from the table and went to her father.

"Father, how I love thee. Thee and Reuben have made me glad today by coming to see us. Not only have thee provided our needs, but strengthened our hearts. I cannot believe the Providence that watches over us all will abandon us in any trial. Sell this home? Give up the cause of human rights? I cannot, and I will not. Do not ask me to ever believe it is better to live in comfort with an evil conscience than to suffer for what is right."

Her father's strong arms encircled her. "I knew thee would not give in, my Prudence. I had to give thee a choice. Know we will support thee in every way we can, and whatever comes of this battle, thee is a chosen vessel of the Almighty One."

Chapter Eleven

It was Saturday afternoon, and Prudence was having a hard time concentrating on the columns of figures in her ledger. Sounds of scurrying feet, clapping hands, and laughter from outside the room kept interrupting her efforts. Before long, the puckish face of nine-year-old Sarah Hammond peered through a slowly opening doorway.

"Miss Crandall? C'n I... may we come in?"

The "we" included Sarah, Amy, Polly, and Emilia, four of the younger set of students. Prudence motioned for them to come in, and the quartet shyly approached. Sarah, of course, was nudged to the front, and it was she who said, "Miss Crandall, did you notice what a beautiful day it is? Just right, don't you think, for goin' outside to play?"

Prudence found it hard to resist Sarah's dancing eyes and lopsided grin. "Play." she teased. "This is a school for serious studies, young lady, not a dame school for children's games. Besides, it sounded to me as if you were having plenty of fun just now."

"Wal," Sarah continued, "we got tired of playing knick-knack, and besides, Marcy's scoldin' us for using her spoons. We'd ruther go outside, cuz it's like summer today. Don't you hear the birds, Miss Crandall? If we could jist go over past the Green to the woods beyond, we'd have ever so much fun playin' hide an' go seek. We might even find some wildflowers to pick for a bouquet for you," she finished her request with shameless wheedling.

Prudence had a momentary vision of the girls running pell-mell across the Green, frolicking in the woods, and being seen by Mr. Hobbes or his wife. "No, girls, I cannot allow you to run free in the neighborhood." Seeing their crestfallen expressions, she relented.

"There are plenty of places for hide and go seek in our own yard. If you do not go beyond the fence, you may go out until tea time. I trust your chores and studies are all done, of course."

"Oh yes'm," they chorused.

"Thank you ever so, and truly we'll be good 's gold." Sarah grinned.

Wasting no time, they disappeared from her presence. Soon she could hear a merry commotion outside, and glancing out the window, she noticed some of the older girls had joined in the fun. Smiling, she returned to her ledger.

The hide and go seek game was a great success as the little misses slipped through the shrubbery, hid behind the stable, and concealed themselves among the trees. Ann Eliza had come into the yard to keep an eye on her young sister, and it was her turn to be the seeker. She buried her face against a large tree and counted to one hundred, then shouted out, "Ready or not, here I come!" Just as she ran to look behind the hedge paralleling the front drive, she saw an imposing-looking gentlemen approach the gate.

"Hey, there!" he hailed her. "You there! Come here at once." he stopped on the slate path, tapping his boot in impatience. "I have some papers here to be delivered to Miss Crandall. They're very important. Can you be trusted to take them in?" He narrowed his eyes and studied her. "What's your name, girl?" he demanded.

Gazing at her feet, she answered. "I'm Ann. Ann Eliza Hammond."

"Well, then, Ann Eliza Hammond," he sneered, "these papers will be of interest to you as well. Get going now, and take them to the lady of the house."

The girls who had been in hiding shrank back into the shadows until the man was gone, then followed Ann Eliza into the house.

Prudence looked up from the ledger in surprise when Ann Eliza burst into the room without knocking.

"Miss Prudence, a man met me in the yard and told me to bring you this. He said it was important. He said it was about me."

With a reluctant hand, Prudence accepted the documents. "Please close the door, Ann Eliza. Tell the girls in the hallway to go to their rooms." She opened the seal and skimmed to the snaky signature at the end, "Rufus Adams, Justice of the Peace."

"What is it?" Ann Eliza's fear grew as she watched her teacher read the paper and saw the color drain from her face.

"Sit down, dear. Listen carefully, but do not be afraid. I had hoped to shield you from this atrocity, but I see now I must tell you what has been happening. You have done nothing to deserve this and are only being singled out because you have been here the longest of all the out-of-state students.

"You see, there is a wicked law that should surely be obsolete, but some of my persecutors have unearthed it and are trying to use it as a ploy to close the school. This old law says any person who is not an inhabitant of this state can be warned to leave town, and if they ignore the warning, can be fined for every day they remain, up to ten days. Remember the day we found the manure in the well?"

Ann Eliza nodded. "I can never forget."

"It was the same week I received an official warning you were being required by this so-called vagrant law to depart the town. Perhaps I was wrong not to tell you about it then, but I gave a bond for $10,000 to Mr. Judson right away. It was signed by the Reverend Mr. Samuel May and other abolitionists of Brooklyn, and I believed that would put an end to the matter."

"Who is he?" asked the bewildered girl.

"He is a minister who lives nearby -- in Brooklyn. He is a particular friend of the man who prints the *Liberator*, and when he heard about this school, he came to see me and said he would do all in his power to help me. He even came here to the town meeting, and when he found out some people were planning to expel my students from town by bringing out an old vagrant and pauper law, he and the others gave a bond to the town."

"I don't understand. What is a bond?"

"It simply means the men of Brooklyn are giving money to the town of Canterbury so if any of my pupils were to cause a financial burden to the town or incur a fine, the money would already be there to cover the cost. The men of Canterbury have interpreted this old law to say you, the so-called vagrant, must pay the fine yourself, or bear the penalty."

Unable to sit still a moment longer, the stricken girl jumped to her feet. "How much money do I have to pay? Maybe Hattie and my mother can get the money--"

"I fear it has gone beyond that at this point. The fine is just an excuse. Since more than ten days have passed, they are now demanding you appear Monday morning at one o'clock at Asael Bacon's house."

"What will they do to me?" Something about the unspeakable horror on Miss Crandall's face called to mind tales she had heard from Hattie Doud.

"They will beat me?"

Prudence's silence told her the truth.

"Then that is my lot -- my part in the struggle. Hattie told me she had been beaten, and many of the massuhs in the South beat their slaves. I will be proud to be beaten for the cause of freedom, Miss Crandall, if only God will give me the strength to endure it." Her words were a whisper, and a hot tear trickled down her smooth, brown cheek.

Prudence wrapped her arms around the trembling girl. "Oh, Ann Eliza. I cannot believe they will go through with this. They are trying to frighten us, to be sure. I am going to send Mr. Olney to Brooklyn immediately to find Samuel May. Surely he will be able to stop this crime... it is too awful..." They clung together, crying.

*****

The next day, the group attended Sunday services in Packerville, but they did not linger for any visiting. Prudence sat beside Mr. Olney on the wagon ride home, questioning him about his errand to Brooklyn.

"You did go straight to Mr. May's house, did you not? You did give him the letter I wrote him?"

"Yes, Miz Crandall. I shorely did go straightaway like you tole me to, an' put the letter into his hand my own self."

"He sent no reply? Did he read it?"

"The man open it right up and look at it, then he say thank ye an' tell Miz Crandall not to worry. He say he take care of it. Tha's all. An' I" come straight home."

"It's easy to tell someone not to worry, isn't it?" Prudence said to her sister later that afternoon. "If only I knew what he meant by taking care of it. Oh, if only he would come."

The day and evening passed with still no word from Samuel May, and Prudence spent yet another restless night.

On Monday morning, she was far too distracted to stay in the schoolroom, so turning the day's lessons over to Almira, she waited in the parlor with Ann Eliza. She made an effort to be calm and assuring for Ann Eliza's sake, still, she paced back and forth from the parlor to the front door, looking out again and again, hoping to see Samuel May's familiar form trudging up to her door. Dinner time drew near, and still the man had not appeared.

"Oh, Miss Crandall, I know I can't eat a bite of dinner," Ann Eliza said. "Let's go now. I only want to get it over with."

Only Marcy came to the door to see them off. She hugged Ann Eliza wordlessly, her heart too full to speak. Prudence was dressed in gray, and Ann Eliza's dark brown cotton dress fell straight from the shoulder. Although the day was warm, she wrapped her slim body in a dark shawl, hugging it around her shoulders for protection. The solemn procession of two headed straight to the main street of the town and arrived just before one o'clock at the large house of Mr. Asael Bacon. They were led to a high-ceilinged room which served as his office. Long bookshelves lined one wall of the room opposite an ornate fireplace. Mr. Bacon and half a dozen more sour-faced men sat upon hard benches in the center, and Mr. George Middleton, Justice of the Peace of Windham County, sat behind an oak desk which dominated the room. A household servant offered Prudence a straight-backed wooden chair, but Ann Eliza was made to stand facing the desk. Middleton cleared his throat. The noise echoed in the room.

"Are you known as Ann Eliza Hammond?" he demanded.

"I am, sir," her voice was a hoarse whisper.

"Speak up, girl. Are you aware of the wording of the writ signed by Rufus Adams and delivered to you on the last day of April?"

"I am, sir."

"I quote, in part, from that writ: 'The Select Men of said Canterbury-_'"

Prudence burst out, "Where are these brave Select Men of Canterbury today, sir. Do they lack the courage to appear and speak for themselves?"

"*You will be silent, miss.* You will have a writ served upon you in short order for receiving this Hammond girl as your pupil. Now, where was I? 'The Select Men of said Canterbury did warn the said Ann Eliza Hammond, to depart the town of Canterbury aforesaid, and Notwithstanding said warning, she, the said Ann Eliza, against the provision of said statute, and against the peace, did continue in said town of Canterbury the full period of ten days by means whereof the said Ann Eliza Hammond hath forfeited and become liable to pay the Treasury of Canterbury aforesaid for the use of the town of Canterbury aforesaid the sum of one dollar and sixty seven cents per day, and a right of action hath accrued to recover the same, and the defendant hath never paid the same, and now to recover the said sum of $167 and cost of suit, this action is brought--'" He broke off abruptly, seeing the girl before him trembling like a reed in the wind.

"Here now, these facts are already established, and there is no need to read the whole document since you admit you are that person. I take it you do not have with you the aforesaid sum of payment?"

Prudence sprang forward to stop Ann Eliza from collapsing. "This is *wrong*," she protested. "She has done nothing against the peace -- nothing at all to the town of Canterbury -- and a bond of one thousand dollars has been posted as security for my pupils--"

With a wave of his perfumed hanky, Mr. Middleton cut off her words. "The point is, Miss Crandall, I have no alternative but to carry out the provisions of the law, to wit, 'to satisfy the fine, such person shall be whipped on the naked body not exceeding ten stripes.' In view of the young age of this offender, leniency is called for, and the whipping shall be reduced to merely five stripes."

"I am ready." Ann Eliza's voice shook. "Since this is the part I have been called to do..." She untied the shawl around her shoulders and let it slip to the floor."

All at once they heard a great uproar outside the office, and four men came crashing through the door.

"Stop this unspeakable outrage at once!" A red-faced Samuel May, accompanied by George Benson and two unknown gentlemen descended upon the astonished Justice of the Peace.

Prudence caught Ann Eliza in her arms and led her to a chair.

Without waiting to be addressed, Samuel May leaned across the desk, filling the space with his imposing presence. "I presume you are that man from Plainfield, George Middleton, called here like Pilate of old to do the dirty business of the self-righteous yellow-bellies of this town. Where are they? Hey?

"They had best be advised I am here. I have brought with me the power of the pen, which is mightier than the sword. This is George Benson, reporter for the *Liberator* who has the ear of the whole nation. What infamy will the men of this county be branded with when it is known they have resorted to a public whipping of an innocent schoolgirl. None but knaves and fools would presume to enforce such atrocity.

"And here is the power of the law at my side. Meet Charles C. Burleigh. You have heard of him, yes? A lawyer of great renown, he is well-informed of the facts of this travesty, and witness, besides, to the ten thousand dollar bond given to and accepted by the town of Canterbury."

"*Shame* to Miss Crandall's persecutors." George Benson could hold his peace no longer. He brought down a hard fist upon the oak desk. "Burning shame to the gallant and noble inflictors of stripes upon innocent and studious females.Shame to you, too, sir. Remember the old adage, 'A whip for the horse, a bridle for the ass, and a rod for a fool's back.' Oh, I intend that a generous public will know to whom these words should be applied."

Mr. Middleton suddenly had much to do, wiping his perspiring brow with his perfumed handkerchief, causing the writ against Miss Hammond to mysteriously vanish, and backing out of reach of his irate visitors. "I had *no* idea, gentlemen. I see I was not apprised of all the particulars. Uh, Miss Hammond, Miss Crandall, you are released -- I mean, you are free to go..." Mumbling and weaving, he slithered out of sight, and Mr. Bacon's desk sat in the middle of the room, emptied of its menace.

Beaming, the Reverend Mr. Samuel May shook Prudence's hand, hugged the tearful Ann Eliza, and ushered them into the fresh air. "I regret the anxiety I caused you by my late arrival, Miss Crandall. I fully intended to be here hours ago, but I had to gather my forces, you see." He nodded toward George and proceeded to make known to her the brothers Charles and William Burleigh, the lawyers he had brought.

"To put a fine point on it," he said, "William is not yet an official lawyer, but a student of the law. However, what he lacks in credentials, he exceeds in image management." He slapped the younger Burleigh on the shoulder. There could be no doubt his meaty fists, wild red whiskers, and rumpled attire had been of great value in intimidating the pitiful Mr. Middleton.

Everyone welcomed the heaven-sent gentlemen to the Crandall house that afternoon, and all rejoiced over Ann Eliza's release. Sarah (who had been up to this point unaware of the threat hanging over her sister's head) clung like a burdock to Ann Eliza and wept. Marcy (who had kept silent during the entire ordeal) could be heard shouting, "Praise Jee-SUS!" all over the house.

Though much relieved by Ann Eliza's rescue from the dreadful punishment, Prudence spoke little throughout the evening. When at last Samuel May and the others took their leave at the front door, she voiced her concerns.

"Even though a battle was won today, I do not underestimate the extent of Mr. Judson's bigotry. Do you think for a moment he will let go of his schemes against this school?"

"Not at all." Samuel May cocked his head. "Beware of that chap. It would be interesting to know why he harbors such passionate prejudice against the colored race. I heard a rumor once about a colored housemaid his wife sent away -- but never mind. He is an intelligent man, and ought to know, even if his ridiculous idea of colonization should succeed, the colored population will continue to grow. The only question is will we recognize the rights God gave them as men and assist them to become all they are capable of, or will we deny them the privileges we enjoy and bring God's judgment upon ourselves. It appears this quiet little village of Canterbury is the place where that question will be answered."

"The legislature is now in session," the lawyer Burleigh said quietly. "I would not be surprised if Judson introduced some bill forbidding the establishment of a school such as yours anywhere in the state."

"Every citizen has a right to education. Would a law like that be constitutional?" Prudence was shocked.

"*I think not.*" Mr. May exploded. "Who knows how Judson might press and how the legislature might be wrought upon? I assure you, Miss Crandall, if such a law is passed, I will contend against it to the very last -- even to the highest court in the land."

"Then I am content to do what I must, and to wait for the cause of freedom to be vindicated." She shook the hand of each of her visitors. "Your arrival today saved a young girl from a heinous punishment, and I cannot say enough how I value your counsel and your defense. God bless you all."

Closing the door quietly, Prudence retired to her room and fell to her knees. She whispered an earnest supplication to the Almighty One for protection and strength.

Why do I feel so alone? She crawled into her bed and pulled the quilt over her shoulders. *Almira is always by my side. Garrison and the others are with me every step of the way. Father has assured me of his support. And yet... if only...*" She turned over on her side and closed her eyes, not allowing herself to finish the sentence. Nevertheless, she fell asleep thinking of Calvin.

In the days that followed, she did her best to cheer her students. All of the girls worked hard, and most of them showed strong aptitude for learning. She remarked to Almira that they were the most motivated group of students she had ever taught. As the lessons proceeded, she listened constantly for a sinister knock on the door that would bring her school to an end; however, no such interruption came.

The May days continued, sunny and temperate, and scores of birds gathered in the trees along the drive to serenade Miss Crandall's young ladies. One Friday afternoon, she closed her geography book and smiled at her students.

"Girls, we have had a wonderful week. All assignments have been done on time, and you have been diligent in your work. Would you like to go outside, perhaps for a walk across the Green, and look for wildflowers? There are sure to be violets and bloodroot in bloom, and perhaps some oxeye daisies along the way."

"Oh, let's do." Julia said. "We can bring back specimens to sketch for our plant studies."

Before they could put away their books and pens, the loud clanging of church bells invaded the schoolroom. The girls ran to the windows.

"What's that?" Sarah Hammond's piercing voice cried out. "They never ring the bells on Friday. Do you s'pose someone died?"

"Look at all the people. They're runnin' across the Green and in the streets. Let's go find out what's happenin.'" Julia headed for the door, and the others followed close behind. Without warning, a thunderous boom shook the house. Shrieking, the girls dove under tables and chairs and shrank into the corners.

Mr. Olney burst through the front door, shouting, "Git back, li'l ladies. Doan go out thet door. They's firin' a cannon in the street, an' it ain't safe a'tall." His eyes were wide with fear.

Prudence peered out through a crack in the door. It was true! A group of laughing townspeople had just fired a cannon in front of her house and were now moving down the street, hauling the cannon on the back of a wagon. They were singing and dancing and jeering as they made their way along.

"What are they saying?" she asked Mr. Olney. "I can't understand a thing. It just sounds like a lot of noise. What are they celebrating?"

"Oh, Miz Crandall, you doan wants t' know. They's up to sum'pn evil fershure."

"I must know." She waited a moment to make sure there was no immediate danger of being fired at, and then stepped outside.

Most of the people were at a distance, but a few stragglers saw her and whirled around to taunt her.

"Howdy, miss. Gonna join the celebration parade?"

"What are you celebrating?"

"We're gettin' rid of the nigger gals. Sendin' 'em back where they come from. No more little colored tarts settin' themselves up to be ladies in Connecticut. Thanks to Mr. Judson, there's a law now!"

Prudence's heart sank. So, Judson had succeeded after all. There was no point in following the revelers or seeking more details. She was sure to find out the whole of the law soon enough. Back she turned to face her quailing pupils and tell them of this new challenge.

Before the evening had passed, Samuel May and Charles Burleigh were at her door. Both were visibly distraught.

"Any civilized state should be ashamed of such a law," Mr. May said. "Judson had his way with the Legislature after all. Listen to this:

"Be it enacted by the Senate and House of Representatives, in General Assembly convened, that no person shall set up or establish

in this State any school, academy, or literary institution for the instruction or education of colored persons who are not inhabitants of this State; nor instruct or teach in any school in this State; nor harbor nor board for the purpose of being taught or instructed in any such school, any person who is not an inhabitant of any town in this State, without the consent in writing, first obtained, of a majority of the civil authority, and also of the Selectmen of the town, in which such school, academy, or literary institution is situated.

"I shall not read any more of this villainous act, Miss Crandall, but it is my duty to warn you the penalties for violation are severe, and your persecutors are determined to visit them upon you." He folded the document and lowered his eyes.

Prudence squared her shoulders. With head erect and eyes aglow she spoke. "Then I shall be prepared."

"So shall we," May's voice held sober determination. "The fight has only begun."

Chapter Twelve

"So, Reuben, what does thee think?" Prudence and her brother were enjoying a private conversation as they picked peas from the garden in back of the house. He had arrived earlier in the day with a welcome load of supplies from the farm. Since the town merchants still refused to do business with Prudence, she was dependent upon the generosity of her father and brother. She also relied upon the Harrises, who continued to bring water for the needs of the school.

"I think fresh peas and new potatoes swimming in hot milk are a delicacy fit for a king." He split open a pod with his thumb and popped the emerald gems into his mouth. "Mmm. Sweet."

"Thee knows that's not what I'm talking about. What does thee think about thy sister being a lawbreaker?"

Since the passage of the Black Law, Prudence had continued to do the very things forbidden in it -- harboring and teaching colored pupils. Indeed, several more girls from New York had arrived last week, bringing the school population to a total of twenty-four. Her primary concerns were the instruction of these young ladies and provision for their basic needs. Though economy was practiced in every way possible, Prudence felt the daily struggle to keep food in the mouths of twenty-nine dependents. Nor was there a shortage of visitors to share their bread and tea, for many abolitionists and readers of the *Liberator* were stirred by news of the school and came to see Prudence's brave experiment for themselves. Busy as she was, she had little time to contemplate what might happen to her should her enemies take action to enforce the penalties of breaking the law.

"I seem to remember thee quoting Garrison's views to me, Pru. Something about right and wrong not being dependent upon popular opinion. So how can an unjust law based upon popular opinion require our obedience? I would think less of thee for obeying such a law."

"Exactly," Prudence said. "Garrison also said 'That which is not just is not law,' so I can scarcely consider myself a lawbreaker, but rather a citizen standing for the rights of all human beings."

"Thee does not need to worry what I think of thee, sister, but thee should have a caution what thy enemies think. Does thee know the penalty of continuing in violation?"

"Imprisonment."

"Just the same as for a common horse thief or murderer?"

She nodded.

"Then truly this is a black law. Thee would face this indignity for the sake of a cause?"

"Not for just any cause. For the cause of abolition and freedom, I would go to jail if I must. Surely if I were imprisoned, it would draw attention to the evil nature of the Black Law."

The pea-picking continued in silence, as the brother and sister moved up the row, filling their baskets with the first of the harvest. When they came to the end of the row and started back toward the house, Reuben introduced a new topic.

"How is Calvin Philleo these days, Pru? What does he have to say about the doings in Canterbury?"

Prudence looked away in annoyance. "I have no idea. I have not heard from him since he took Elizabeth home. I have had no time to write to him nor to wonder about his business. I know he is in sympathy with my work, as he is with all endeavors for equality."

"He has no special interest in Miss Crandall, of course."

"Why ever should he?"

"Why, I have no idea," Reuben answered innocently. "I suppose he gives gifts to many females and comes to spend holidays with them. Just what has thee done with thy Kashmir shawl?"

"I suppose enduring this teasing is the price I must pay for help in the pea patch." Exasperated, Prudence plopped onto the step and began shelling the peas for supper.

"What teasing? I was just curious about the fancy shawl." Reuben ducked inside the house to dodge the pea pod she threw at him and called over his shoulder, "Be sure to add a pat of butter to my peas and potatoes."

Reuben spent the night at his sister's home and was preparing to leave early the next morning when he saw an official-looking pair approaching the house. He stepped into their path.

"Good morning, Friends. May I help you?"

The men looked startled, "No, sir, I believe not." They produced papers identifying themselves. "We are officers of the law and are here for Miss Crandall. Where is she?"

Reuben frowned. "There are two Miss Crandalls living here. What is your business?"

"Oh, we have come for the older one, Miss Prudence. The one who sneaked all those colored girls into town and brought calamity upon us. For the past month she has continued to break the new law of the land, and we have come to arrest her."

Knowing nothing he could do would dissuade them, Reuben took them into the house. "Wait here in the hall and make no noise," he warned. "Classes are in session, and Miss Crandall is busy teaching. I will bring her to you."

The girls looked up from their studies in surprise when Reuben entered the schoolroom. Taking Prudence's arm, he led her out a side door.

"They have come for thee, Prudy. The sheriff and the constable are waiting to arrest thee. I fear they mean to take thee to prison this very day."

"I think they would rather not do that," she answered wryly. "They will expect my friends in the Anti-Slavery Society to post bonds to keep me out of jail. We have a surprise in store for them. I must go to my room and collect some personal items.

"Reuben, do not wait for me. Go straight to Brooklyn to the house of Samuel May, and tell him what has happened. He will know what to do."

In much distress, Reuben left the house and turned his wagon toward Brooklyn.

The sheriff and the constable soon escorted Prudence across the Green to the meeting house where Asael Bacon and Rufus Adams awaited her. The trial did not last long, since the outcome had already been determined.

Adams pronounced the judgment against her. "You are ordered to appear at the next session of Superior Court, which begins in August. Until then, you are in the hands of the sheriff. Do you understand?"

"I understand perfectly well."

The two justices exchanged glances. "I fear you do not understand," Bacon sneered. "We cannot take a chance on your leaving town. Unless you can give bonds in the sum of five hundred dollars, you shall be taken this day to the jail in Brooklyn."

"I understand perfectly," she repeated, "and I am prepared to go at once." She picked up the small satchel she had brought from the house and put it over her arm.

The men were nonplussed. Surely this woman could not intend to go to jail. "Do you not mean to give the bond money? Have you no friends or supporters to aid you?"

"I have many friends and supporters, none of whom have it in mind to give bonds."

"This is an outrage," squeaked Adams. "You would put yourself in jail?"

"I agree. It is an outrage, sirs, but I do not put myself in jail. It is you who are sending me to prison through the passage of this appalling law, and it is in your power to cancel it and set me free to do my work. Summon Mr. Judson. I'm sure he has the power to free me if he does not want his name linked with this scandal. "

"We cannot do that," said Bacon, "but we can send word to Samuel May." He scribbled something on a paper and motioned to a young man standing by. "Make haste to find Mr. May and deliver this message.

"If he will procure the five hundred dollars and meet us in Brooklyn, you can save yourself the embarrassment and disgrace of being put in jail."

Prudence was unmoved. "Embarrassment? Disgrace? It is not I who shall be disgraced, but you and Judson and all your kind who would make teaching colored girls a crime and thrust me in prison like a common felon."

The justices threw up their hands in exasperation. "Take her away," Adams directed the sheriff and constable. "Perhaps a glimpse of the prison cell will change her mind."

"Well, I have never had an official escort before," Prudence commented blithely as her captors seated her on the seat between them, "nor traveled in such a fine spring wagon."

The men were shamed by her cheerful conversation on the way to Brooklyn and answered only in gruff monosyllables. The six-mile journey passed quickly, and soon the jail came into view. "There's the Reverend May," said the sheriff. "Now we may have some sensible answers."

"Who's with him?" asked the constable.

"My brother Reuben," answered Prudence, "and my good friend George Benson from the *Liberator*, of course."

They hung their heads as they helped Prudence from the wagon. Benson was the last person they desired to see. Who knew what the reporter would say about their part in locking up a harmless female teacher. Certainly nothing very flattering.

Reuben quickly came to her side, casting a glance at the dismal building looming before them. "Oh, Prudy, is thee certain this is the way thee must go? I doubt not we could raise the money for the bonds from the Friends and others in sympathy with the cause."

Prudence also gazed at the prison walls. The edifice was an indeterminate mix of brown and gray. Superficial cracks, smudges of oil and mud crept to the sills of the heavily barred windows. She hesitated only a moment before giving her brother a tremulous smile. "It will be all right, Reuben. I know it would be easier to call for help, and I am sure many would spare me the ordeal of going to jail, but I believe this is the best way. When we say 'way will open,' it does not always mean the way will be an easy one."

"Then why...?"

"Nothing but my imprisonment will so quickly show the public the wickedness of this Black Law, and they will clamor for it to be repealed."

Samuel May had been speaking with the constable and the sheriff, and now appeared ready to accompany them inside the jail. "I have spoken to the sheriff," May told her, "and he has agreed to put you in the best cell they have. It is not much; in fact, the last prisoner held in it was a murderer who was hanged last year for killing his wife. George and I brought a bedstead and clean bedding from my home, and we will make you as comfortable as possible."

Inside, a few men were standing about in a room bare of all

furnishings but a few hard benches, and a desk with a chair. The sheriff seated himself at the desk and began writing orders for the jailer. One of the fellows approached Samuel May.

"What kind of people are you stinking abolitionists, who would allow one of your own people -- a woman at that -- to be thrown in jail and not lift a finger to help her? Too confounded stingy to pay the bonds?"

Ignoring the man's question, May answered, "What kind of people would pass a law in the state of Connecticut that a woman could be fined and imprisoned for teaching a few dozen colored girls? Are her persecutors mad? Have they taken leave of their senses?"

The sheriff at last rose from his desk and led Prudence and her friends down a narrow passageway. A smirking man joined them in the hallway. It was Andrew Judson himself. They continued down the murky corridor until the jailer met them with a bunch of keys dangling from his belt. The sheriff halted, and with a glance at Judson, he released Prudence's elbow. "Good night then, Miss Crandall," Judson spoke with a voice full of venom. "Since you refuse any help, this is where I shall leave you. You will remain here until your trial in August." He turned on his heel and left.

The jailer was taken aback at having a female prisoner, but he showed her to her cell with the best manners he possessed. "It's the best we got, ma'am. 'Tis true, our last guest was a murderer, but that was more'n a year ago, and I 'spect the wind has blowed away any pestilence left from him."

Prudence was not the least soothed by this intelligence, but she tried not to cringe as she peered through the doorway of the narrow room with its sparse furnishings and single high window. At least the bedstead and clean linens from Mr. May's home had been installed and the cell appeared to have been cleaned, with no refuse in the corners nor cobwebs hanging about.

"Take heart, Miss Prudence." Samuel May grasped her arm. "I do not intend you shall be here for long. Only until your sacrifice has served the purpose of arousing the public against your disgraceful treatment and the base nature of this law."

"I will stay as long as I must, but I would rather be doing my work."

"The work you are doing here," Samuel responded, "is equally important."

Reuben hugged her tightly, and she clung to him until the rotund jailer cleared his throat. "Sorry, gents, I have to ask you to leave now. Don't worry none. She'll be safe, I'll look after her me own self."

I'll not be able to sleep a wink. When Prudy lay down that night, cast iron blackness made it impossible to see the hand she held up before her face. Intermittent clanging of metal and short, sharp cries jabbed the silence. The faces of Rufus Adams, Asael Bacon, Mr. Judson, and her other foes crowded around her, and the events which had brought her to this bleak cell replayed themselves in her weary mind. She turned over on her left side, her favorite sleeping position, and with the shift in her body came a change in her thoughts. She thought of the sweet dark faces of her schoolgirls with sheets pulled up to their chins as they bade her good night. She thought of Marcy's smile as she lifted the blue willow teapot and poured out the steaming amber liquid into a delicate cup. She thought of her dear father, ignoring the threats from Judson and faithfully piloting his wagonload of provisions to her back door. She thought of Reuben's affectionate hug, and the good Samuel May's promise to her. She slept.

"Ye have a visitor, ma'am," the jailer announced outside her door next morning.

"Come in," Prudence answered from the other side, for she was as presentable as she could be with the minimal comforts afforded by her cell.

"Helen," she exclaimed. "How good of you to come." The comely young lady who entered her room was none other than George Benson's younger sister who happened to be betrothed to William Lloyd Garrison.

Pretty, dark-haired Helen carried a hamper under her arm and was dressed in a green and yellow sprigged muslin gown. She looked as welcome as the sunshine. "I would have come yesterday, but I did not find out you were here until this morning. Look. I have brought you such a feast you shall forget you are in jail." As her visitor began unpacking delicacies from the hamper, Prudence's mouth watered. She had scarcely eaten the day before, and the fragrances wafting from the dishes Helen placed on the small wooden table reminded her how hungry she was.

"I can't say how hot the tea is, though," Helen apologized. "I wrapped it well, so perhaps it will do."

To the prisoner in the musty cell, the aroma from the teapot rose like incense from an altar. "It is more than I deserve. Certainly more than I expected," She leaned forward in expectation as her ministering angel filled a mug.

"Nonsense. You deserve every bit and more. I can't tell you how I admire your courage, Prudence. George and William are praising you to the skies."

"That is also more than I deserve." Prudence helped herself to a slice of ham. "I am merely doing my duty."

"How long, do you think you will be here? How will you pass the time?" Helen looked about her at the crumbling plastered walls. "I should have thought to bring flowers."

"It is possible I may be here until my case goes to trial in August. I hope it will not be that long, but I must be prepared for the worst. As for how I will pass the time, I hope friends will visit, and bring me more books. I have only my Bible with me.

"I don't suppose they would allow me to have my sewing for fear I should stab my jailer with a needle and escape from here." She winked at her friend. "I did bring paper and pen. They say great literature has been produced in a prison cell, and many people in my situation have recorded profound revelations. Even if I don't have any great insights, I can at least keep a record of what happens each day and a journal of my thoughts."

"Perhaps your sister will come."

"Marcy, perhaps, but I doubt Almira will be able to. You see, she is in charge of the school now and must keep the young ladies at their studies. A huge responsibility for one so young as she. Oh, I am afraid I shall do nothing but fret if I am confined here long."

Helen poured out more tea and gripped Prudence's hand. Her fair skin flushed with feeling. "Don't worry. George was furiously scribbling an article for the *Liberator* first thing this morning, and I am sure William will write an editorial which will scorch the ears of all who read it. As soon as people hear how shamefully you have been treated, everyone living in the state of Connecticut will rise in indignation and demand the law be changed."

Prudence pondered Helen's words throughout the day as she paced the room. She finally sat at the small table and began to write.

June 28, 1833

Never did I expect to be writing from a jail cell. Yesterday I was arrested for breaking the recently passed Black Law, and at the advice of Mr. May and my other patrons from the Anti-Slavery Society, I have allowed myself to be put in jail rather than give Judson and the others the satisfaction of posting bond ($500.) They were shocked and angry, realizing how their actions will make them look before the public eye, and indeed they care for nothing so much as the good opinion of men. Had Andrew Judson simply let Sarah Harris attend my school, none of this would have happened, but perhaps it is for the best these things come to light and the fundamental right to education be granted to all.

All day I have been waiting. Waiting and wondering what is happening outside these walls. I have seen no one except my jailer -- a fat fellow who seems greatly embarrassed by my presence here -- and dear Helen Benson who brought me food -- nay! More than food! She brought comfort and hope.

June 29, 1833

I did not sleep so well last night. The bed is not uncomfortable, considering I am in jail, but I miss my home. I wonder how Almira is coping with all the girls, and if Marcy is letting Whittington into the kitchen. I miss the view from my window, and the wonderful music of the wind sweeping across the green. This is only my second day, and already I am consumed with homesickness. I have still heard nothing from Samuel May nor anyone else. Helen did not come today, but then, I am sure she has more to do than tend my needs.

June 30, 1833

Another day of waiting. I spent the morning writing out instructions and lesson plans for Almy, and I hope I can find a way to get them to her. No one from home has been to see me, but I did at least get a letter from Almy, delivered by my friendly jailer. (I am so lonesome, I am even glad for his occasional rounds.) Almira says the girls are all praying for me morning and evening. Some are writing poetry for me. How sweet they are. She also says she is having a little trouble teaching the moral philosophy lessons. The pupils keep raising questions which have no easy answers. I am sending word for her to focus on other things until I return, whenever that will be.

July 1, 1833

I am still in jail, but today I was gladdened by a visit from Marcy. She brought (much needed) clean clothing and enough food to last a week. I dearly hope I will be home long before! She was full of news of Almira and the girls, plus all the doings around town. You would expect people would be hanging their heads in shame for the way they have acted, but apparently they are not. Almira is afraid to take the girls out walking now. The first time they ventured out after my imprisonment, ruffians followed them up and down the street, even daring to fling stones at them.

July 3, 1833

Two more weary days have passed. I have been feeling poorly, and hope I am not catching a cold. It is awful to be kept in this dismal cell when the sun is shining outside. Last night I thought I heard mice gnawing in the walls. It made me shudder. If only Whittington were here, he would make short shrift of the creatures! I had to force myself to think of something to be grateful for. I decided to be grateful for the longer days of summer because it means less time in the dark. Prisoners are not allowed candles or lamps, so as soon as the sun goes down, all is inky darkness.

July 4, 1833

Irony of ironies. Today is the birthday of our nation, the celebration of freedom, and here I am in a jail cell for daring to offer an education to young ladies of color. I sit here blowing my nose, my head aching. Mary brought me honey and lemon to put in my tea, and it did soothe my throat. She also brought flowers to cheer me. I have now changed my mind about the blessings of summer. Bugs have invaded my cell, and that, combined with the heat, have made this place unbearable. Bear it I must.

July 6, 1833

At last my cold is better. Except for a sore, red nose and a bad temper, I am all right.

July 7, 1833

Finally it seems things are beginning to happen! When Helen came today (Oh, she brought the fluffiest, most delicious cake.) I told her if all prisoners were fed like this, they would be clamoring to be arrested. Mr. May came also. It was later in the day, and he brought a copy of the paper. The headline said, "SAVAGE BARBARITY! MISS CRANDALL IMPRISONED!!!" It went on to say "the authors of this infamous proceeding are friends of the American Colonization Society," listing names of the prominent members (including Judson), exposing their prejudice and condemning their actions. Mr. May is very hopeful the article will open the eyes of the public. I hope I may now be released!

Prudence's hopes were at last realized. The next day Samuel May returned. "Your waiting is over, dear lady." The smile on his plain face was nearly as wide as the Quinebaug River. "You have finished the course and kept the faith. Already the news of your trial has spread abroad and our cause has gained much good support. I have with me the money required for the bond, and I shall pay it now and return to take you home. Are you ready to go?" He looked around the small cell and the stalwart woman sitting on the bed. Her always neat appearance had been altered. Her face was drained of color, and there were dark circles under her eyes. His joy faded.

"Were we wrong to require this of you, Prudence? I think perhaps this was too great a price to ask you to pay. I am deeply sorry."

"Don't think of that," came her answer. "What is done is done. I am only glad to be going home and getting back to my school. I have paid dearly for the right to teach these girls, and I intend to do it with all my might."

He left her to gather her few belongings and tidy her appearance as best she could while he went to pay the bond money. She was pinning up her tangled hair when the jailer thumped on her door.

"A gentleman to see you, ma'am."

"Come in, Mr. May. I am ready."

The last person she expected to see entered her cell. His tall frame filled the doorway even as his smile filled her soul. "*Calvin.*"

Impulsively, he took her hands and pulled her to him, but she backed away in uncertainty. "I am a mess." She covered her hair with a cap and put her hand self-consciously over her nose. "I haven't been well."

"Dear Prudence, you are a beautiful sight to me. What other woman would have the courage to do what you have done. When I found out you were in jail, I came as quickly as I could. I met Samuel May in the passage and heard the latest news. He is paying your bond even now, and I will take you home directly. I have Jackson outside with the chaise." He put one arm around her waist and picked up the satchel.

Without another glance at the rude cell, she leaned gratefully into his strength. "Oh, Calvin, take me home."

Chapter Thirteen

A heartfelt homecoming awaited Prudence when Calvin ushered her into the house. "Here she be! Praise Jee-SUS!" shrieked Marcy in delight. Almira fell upon her sister's neck with such tears and expressions of sympathy Prudence protested she was being drowned. The girls descended upon her like a family of bobbing quail, clucking and cooing in anxious concert.

"It wasn't so horrible," she said in answer to all their questions. "I had a reasonably clean room and enough food to eat. The worst part of jail was having so little to do."

Despite her declaration that she was "perfectly fine" and ready to go to work, Calvin and Almira saw the signs of fatigue.

"You'll be 'finer' after a few days of rest," Calvin insisted. "You've been through an awful ordeal."

"You needn't fuss over me. I am itching to get back to the schoolroom. I don't doubt, Almy, thee can use some relief."

Her sister waved her away. "Nonsense. I have managed all week on my own, and can certainly do it for one more day. Come, young ladies, back to the schoolroom, and let Miss Prudence rest."

Without further protest, Prudence allowed herself to be led away by Marcy for a hot bath, "a cuppa tea," a decent meal, and a nap. Opening the door to her bedroom, she chuckled to see Whittington curled up in the middle of her bed. He lifted his head and gave her a reproving gaze as if to say, "Where have you been all this time?" He rolled over and unfurled himself in a glorious stretch, displaying his pearly claws and elegant tail. She scooped the animal into her arms and tucked his head beneath her chin. "Oh, I did miss thee, Whittington, and I tell thee I am glad to be home." So saying, she lay down on the bed and fell fast asleep. By mid-afternoon she was feeling much rested and ventured down to the parlor where Calvin sat deeply engrossed in a theology book. He looked up eagerly when she entered the room.

"You're up." he remarked. "You look refreshed. Even your nose looks better," he teased.

She shook her head in mock reproach. "You will not curry favor with me by pointing out my flaws. Even though as a clergyman, I'm sure you excel at finding faults."

He laughed heartily at her quick retort and came to her side. "Prudence," he said, "it's a lovely day. Too beautiful to waste indoors. Let's go for a walk, shall we?"

"Oh, I'd love that. I'm sick of confinement."

Birdsong and breezes accompanied them as they wandered down

the walk and past a field dotted with fragrant piles of freshly-cut hay. A farm hand on top of a hay wagon swiped his face with his sleeve and waved to them. By the time they reached the creek flowing through the grove of trees beyond the Green, the summer heat had taken its toll. Calvin tossed his hat on the ground, spread his topcoat in the shade, and loosened his shirt collar. "Come, Prudence," he beckoned. "Dare you to put your feet in the creek."

She laughed and sank gratefully to the mossy ground. "Oh, there was a day I would have taken the dare. Almy and I loved splashing in the creek when we were girls. I guess it wouldn't do for a spinster schoolteacher -- especially one whose respectability is already in doubt. I am now a felon, you know." She untied the blue ribbons on her straw hat and laid it beside his coat. A zephyr ruffled her honey-colored hair. "Ah. It's so quiet here. It soothes my soul and makes me forget all the turmoil in the world."

Calvin stretched his long frame alongside the creek and trailed his fingers in the cool water. He did not look at her as he said, "You have had more than your share of turmoil these past months, Prudence. I am so sorry you were put in jail. Though I understand why Samuel May and the others wanted you to go through with it, I think they asked too much of you."

"Oh, they did not force me to do it at all," she insisted. "They were willing to pay the bond at any moment if I had but asked them to. It was a chance for the world to know not only the monstrous use of the Black Law, but the cruel character of those who framed it. Much good will come of my imprisonment. I am sure of it."

"Your zeal does you credit, my dear." He turned on his back and looked up at her. "You give much thought to what is good for the cause and what is good for others, but scarcely any thought to what might be good for you. You are supposed to love others in the same measure as you love yourself, and I sometimes think if you practiced this, your care for others would be very small."

Her mouth dropped open in surprise. "Whatever do you mean?"

"You *see*. Even the idea of thinking of your own good is strange to you. I think I must take on that job for you and help you see it is not only the colored girls who have rights. You, Prudence, have a right to live your life and to choose happiness."

"I am happy..."

"Are you?" he challenged. He pushed himself up on his knees and took her face between his hands. "Or have you convinced yourself self-sacrifice less of a risk than love?"

It was not only the July heat which caused her cheeks to flame. She turned away from his gaze and swallowed hard. "It is love that motivates my sacrifice, Calvin." Her voice was so low he could barely hear her. "A god-given love of all mankind."

He sat cross-legged on the ground and stared at the sky. No cloud marred the royal expanse. No sounds could be heard save the soft voice of the creek and the chirping of hidden choristers.

"I may be leaving Suffield, Prudence. There is a church in Ithaca, New York, in need of a minister, and they want me to come there."

Shock left her practically speechless. "*Ithaca.* So far away. Do you mean to go?"

"Does it matter to you, then? Oh, Prudence, that is what I need to know. I have been thinking of nothing but the distance it would put between us, and if there is the least chance you care for me, I would not go. More than anything, I hoped this latest persecution would end your resolve to stay in Canterbury. Not that I want your school to fail. I do not. Neither do I want to see you harassed by cruel bigots or used by idealists to promote their cause. You are not a pawn in a game, Prudence. You are a woman. A strong woman, yes, but not invulnerable. You are the woman I love. When I heard you were in jail, I was wildly imagining all sorts of things and knowing there was nothing at all I could do. I want you by my side -- with me in Suffield -- where I can love and protect you."

She reached out to touch his cheek. "It's not always possible to protect someone from the mills of the gods, even when you love them."

He caught her hand and gently kissed her palm, then held it to his heart. "My little jailbird, say you love me," he whispered.

"Calvin, dear Calvin. I am not free to give my love. I am caught in the eye of a storm and I cannot escape it. I did not ask to be here, but I am. This is the thing I was born to do, here in Canterbury at this day in history. Maybe it is only a small piece in the struggle for freedom, but it is my part -- the part I must do." She rose to her feet, brushed off her skirt, and picked up her hat. At once he rose to join her.

"You speak of my right to happiness, but I could not be happy if I had to live knowing I had been untrue to my conscience.

"Besides," she gave a shaky laugh as she fixed her hat in place, "I can't leave town. I am out on bail, and I have to go to trial on August twenty-third."

His arms encircled her waist. There was longing in his eyes. "I know you too well, Prudence. There is no use pleading my cause, but I refuse to give up all hope. You say it is love that motivates the sacrifice... remember that when you think of me." They stood cheek to cheek in a moment of silence until he at last released her.

"I wish I could be with you at the trial in August," said Calvin as they walked back to the house, "but I shall be in Ithaca by then, and my work there will occupy me at least a year. The congregation has some financial problems I must work out, and they are also expecting me to build them a new bell tower."

"I will write," promised Prudence. "I hope all will be settled by the trial, and I can continue my work in peace."

"I've not been to that part of New York before, but I have heard it is a pretty place. Beautiful farmlands, gorges, waterfalls, and lakes."

"I would love to see it, then," she commented, "and to hear you preach. Do you realize I still have not had the honor?"

They continued on with polite banter the rest of the way home, using words as armor to shield their tender feelings. He did not stay for tea, and his abrupt departure surprised both Marcy and Almira.

"What happened?" Almira asked as they prepared for bed. "Why did Mr. Philleo leave so suddenly? Don't say it's 'nothing,' and don't thee pretend not to know what I'm talking about."

"I never pretend," Prudence answered brusquely. "What happened is exactly that. Nothing. He is in a hurry to get home, because he is getting ready to move. He is taking a church in Ithaca, New York."

Almira's hairbrush stopped in mid air. "Oh, no, Prudy. Did thee not hope... well, I had hoped that he... and thee..."

"Really," Prudence turned her head away so her sister could not see the tears. "I am past the age for that sort of thing, Almira. I shall never marry. Thee should be thinking of thy own prospects, and not worry about mine. Thee is still young."

"Twenty-nine is not old," Almira insisted, "especially if the man is older."

"I must introduce thee to the young Mr. Burleigh, Almira. There is a man in need of a wife."

Almira laughed. "William Burleigh? I did meet him. He does need a wife, judging from his wild appearance. But I am not the one to tame him."

So Prudence succeeded in diverting her sister's attention, but as she lay in bed watching the moon walk in silver slippers through the clouds, she could not deny the emptiness she felt inside. *He said he would be there at least a year, so I must not hope to see him. Maybe in a year, I can turn the school over to someone else, and then... No. There is no use considering impossibilities. It is better this way. He has his work to do, and I have mine.*

No one would have guessed from Prudence's outward demeanor that her time in jail had any effect upon her. Resolved to see the school succeed, she blazed ahead with plans for recruiting more students, and even hired Mr. William Burleigh as a teacher. She foresaw the trial coming in August would require her attention for an indefinite time and did not want to burden Almira with the additional responsibility for teaching all the classes. Despite his great size and rough exterior, the younger Mr. Burleigh had a gentle spirit and a keen mind. Fortunately, he had also studied French. He was an effective teacher, and, as Samuel May pointed out, having a strong male presence about the place gave added protection to the young ladies.

There was, however, no protection from the malicious lies spread abroad about Miss Crandall's school and her pupils. Newspapers printed false statements about the "promiscuous young colored women overrunning the town of Canterbury, luring the innocent youth into miscegenetic relationships." It was even reported that "colored men were seen walking arm in arm with those who ought to be respectable white females."

The members of the Colonization Society repeatedly printed articles opposing the school, saying it was under the patronage of the radical Arnold Buffum, and he not only intended to use the school as a platform calling for immediate abolition but as an open door for blacks from slave states, who would turn Connecticut into "the Liberia of America."

"I can't understand," Almira said, laying aside a copy of the *Windham County Advertiser.* "Why doesn't Samuel May write something in the *Christian Monitor* refuting these insults and telling people the truth?"

"I am sure he would," Prudence answered, "but even though he is the editor, the paper has some long-standing policy of not printing anything relating to neighborhood or personal quarrels. Since the majority of people in the state are in favor of the Black Law, editors of other papers have also refused to print Samuel's columns."

"Then we can do nothing about these lies? Listen to this: 'Miss Crandall herself has been seen consorting with black men in a most familiar manner.'"

"I suppose Mr. Olney was helping me out of the wagon. People see what suits them. Take heart. Mr. May told me yesterday he has written to Arthur Tappan for help."

In response to Samuel May's plea, Arthur Tappan himself came to visit the school. Seeing firsthand the excellent work being done at the Canterbury school, he commissioned Mr. May to issue a paper and send it all over the country so people would know the truth.

"The cause of the whole colored race will be much affected by what is happening here at Canterbury." Tappan shook Prudence's hand after his visit. "You have endured more persecution than I had even imagined, and yet you and your pupils are stalwart as soldiers. You have my whole-hearted approval and support. This may be a long and expensive struggle. You may consider me your banker, for I will underwrite whatever it costs." He turned to May. "See to it she has the best lawyers available for the trial. Try to engage Ellsworth. He's one of the finest."

Two days later, Samuel May sent word to Prudence he had found a printing office in the village and had leased it for a year. Although the press and types came with the office, he needed some help in getting it set up for operation. "Could you spare Mr. Burleigh for a day or so?" was the request.

"After all, since Mr. May is doing this for us," Prudence explained to the girls, "I can hardly refuse him. We will manage for a day or two without Mr. Burleigh. Now, let us get ready for our walk. Take your parasols. The sun is fierce today."

Their occasional walks had become happier times since Mr. Burleigh's arrival. Few of the village hooligans were willing to risk their necks around his muscular six-foot frame. The girls joked that "burly" was a good name for him. Even though he was not with them today, several weeks without incident had given them a sense of security.

"C'n I... I mean may I... walk with you today, Miss Crandall?"

Prudence did not need to look around to know it was her little shadow, Sarah Lloyd Hammond, skipping up behind her. Her brown dress under a white smock came just above her ankles, showing the new shoes her mother had sent last week.

"Yes, you may, Sarah, but please do walk instead of skipping. We will save the skipping for later." The sun blazed down upon them as they made their way down the street. They were the only people to be seen outdoors today. No doubt most were fanning themselves in their parlors or finding shade behind the houses. "Did you remember to get a good drink of water before we started?" Prudence asked her.

"Yes'm, I did." Sarah was ever eager for her teacher's approval, and if she ever broke a rule it was purely unintentional. Her worst fault was talkativeness, and even Prudence had a hard time being stern with her.

"Where is Harriet today, Miss Crandall? Why isn't she walking with us?

"She's not feeling well this afternoon, dear."

"What's the matter? Is she still coughing?"

"Her cough does seem to hang on, but I am more worried that she is running a fever."

"I think I might have a fever, too," Sarah said. "I feel very hot today."

Prudence smiled. "I think we are all feeling rather hot today, but it is not the same as having a fever. A fever is a sign of illness. Perhaps I should call for Doctor Harris," Prudence mused, more to herself than to Sarah.

"I think we should pray for her. Harriet prays about everything."

"Does she, now? Harriet is a very faithful Christian."

"Oh, yes'm, she is. I think she is the most forgivingest body I ever did see. She never says anything mean about anybody." Her eyes grew round in wonderment. "I even heard her pray for the slave owners. I pray for them to be hurt like they hurt their slaves, but not Harriet." The child closed her eyes, lifted her chin, and intoned in the most pious tone she could manage. "She says, 'O, Jesus, lay not this sin to their charge, but bring them to repentance and to light.' Wherever did she learn such fancy prayers?"

Prudence suppressed a smile. "Why she is the ward of a very religious man, the Reverend Simeon Jocelyn. He is the minister of a large church in New Haven. Temple Street Congregational."

"Then he must be a white man. That's why he teached -- taught Harriet to pray for the white slave owners."

"No, Sarah. He is not in sympathy with slavery. He is an abolitionist, just like Mr. Garrison and Mr. May and Mr. Benson. He has both black and white people in his congregation. Whether a person is white or black does not matter at all. We all need to be forgiven for our faults, and we all need to forgive those who wrong us."

This nugget of wisdom apparently gave young Sarah something to think about, for she was quiet for a change. Reaching the end of the avenue, Prudence led the company around the corner and crossed to the shady side of the street. All the girls were looking somewhat damp and flushed, and she began to question the wisdom of sticking to habit when nature was in a contrary mood. However, it was pleasant to be able to stroll down the street without being plagued by horn-blowing and mockery, so she continued on the regular course.

Canterbury is such a lovely town, she reflected, looking at the stately, well-kept homes. Vegetable gardens wore their abundance proudly, tall hollyhocks stood sentry beside drowsing flower beds, and an occasional dog meandered across their path. Cows grazed in the meadows beyond. *It looks like a perfect Eden. If only we could all live in harmony here.*

"Prudence, wait!" she heard Almira's voice calling from the back of the line.

"What is it? Is there a problem?"

"Not exactly," Almira replied, "but I think we should cut our walk short. Two young ladies are in a hurry to reach the necessary, and all of us are very thirsty. Let's just take the shortcut and not go 'round the Green today."

Almira so seldom offered a suggestion to change the routine that Prudence made up her mind to listen. The girls did look worn out. Their faces were shiny with perspiration, and they held their pretty parasols limply over their shoulders.

"All right, then, Almy. Please take the lead from here, and Sarah and I will bring up the rear."

"So now," commented Sarah, "we are in last place instead of first. I don't mind. It just means we get to stay outside longer."

Soon the house came into view and Almira stepped up the pace. They were within yards of the property when a disheveled figure plunged toward them, crying out, "Oh, stop! Don't come this way, ladies! You must go 'round the back way -- *please!*"

The creature held out her arms like a possessed scarecrow, rushing wildly toward them.

"Is that Marcy?" asked Almira in wonderment.

The girls pressed forward, and then stopped in their tracks, screaming and crying as if six demons had crawled from the earth to devour them.

"What on earth..." Prudence was too far away to see the source of their terror, and Marcy was doing all in her power to prevent her from moving forward.

"Don't go there, Miss Prudence. You mustn't. You mustn't. There's more manure, and a broken window, and they threw rotten eggs at the house and the fence--"

As Prudence pushed Marcy aside, the stench of rotten eggs overpowered her. Then she saw what Marcy had tried to shield her from.

Whittington! The cat's lifeless orange body dangled from the fence. The striped head she had so often stroked hung at a bizarre angle. His gaping mouth appeared frozen in a final yowl of pain. The innocent creature had been impaled on the cruel tines of a pitchfork, and his soft white belly was purpled with gouts of blood. All that was left of Whittington's lordly tail was a gruesome, bloodied stump.

Horror wrapped icy fingers around her neck, squeezing a moan from her parched throat. "Nooooo..."

"Prudence!" screamed Almira.

A collective cry of alarm rose from the young ladies and little misses of color. Miss Prudence had fainted.

Chapter Fourteen

Prudence was carried to her bedroom and there she stayed until the next day. Meanwhile, when word of the atrocity spread through the neighborhood, Deborah Kneeland brought a group of housewives from Packerville, armed with scrub brushes and buckets, to attack the revolting mess in the yard. Sarah Harris hurried home and enlisted her mother and father to join in the cleanup, and Marcy acted as supervisor of the whole project. As darkness fell, Mr. Olney buried Whittington's remains behind the stable. Long after the stink of rotten eggs and manure had been purged away, the bitter smell of hatred lingered in the sultry heat.

No lighthearted chatter was heard in the house that night. No girlish games enlivened the parlor. When Marcy grimly summoned them to dinner, the girls sat wordlessly at the supper table and nibbled the lukewarm food. Almira tiptoed through the halls after the girls were in bed and heard sobs coming from behind the closed doors.

It was late when Almira crept to her own bed. Prudence's face was toward the wall, and a terrible silence forbade any speech.

In the morning, Almira gathered the heartbroken girls in the schoolroom.

"I don't understand it," Ann Eliza blurted. "How could they be so cruel to Miss Crandall? She didn't do anything to hurt anyone, and besides, she is white."

"How could they torture poor Whittington?" wailed Jerusha. "He was only an innocent cat."

"I just *hate* them all." Eliza Glasko's dark eyes glowed with rage.

Sarah Hammond's tears spilled down her face. Between sobs, she said, "Me, too. Me and Miss Crandall were talking... while we were walking... just before we found Whittington... about forgiving. I don't know as I can forgive. Miss Almira, how can you forgive those who are so awful?"

Almira was saved from answering by the opening of the door, and the calm appearance of Miss Prudence herself. Her face was pale, her jaw clenched, and her eyes empty of expression. She carried a large rock in her hand. Without comment, she walked to the front of the room and placed the stone in the center of the desk.

Julia Williams was first to speak. "Miss Crandall, are you all right?"

Prudence nodded briefly. "Good morning, girls. Forgive me for being late today. I was collecting evidence of the damage done by our visitors yesterday. This is the rock someone with a very good aim threw into my parlor, smashing the window."

125

The rock was white granite with streaks of black jetting through. It was larger than her small hand, but just the right size to fit a man's open palm. All eyes were riveted on the stone.

"I do not know who threw this rock, but I can imagine many faces behind the deed. Mr. Judson? Mr. Adams? Captain Fenner? The boys who have thrown stones at you girls? Merchants in the town? It could be anyone.

"I know the right thing to do... forgive. When I want to get revenge... I must forgive. When I want to cry out in anger... forgive... because there is power in forgiveness. Unless I can look at this stone without hatred and passion in my breast, the man who threw it is my master. He has won. I cannot truly say I have reached that place of peace, so until I do, the stone will stay here on my desk as a reminder..." Her voice trailed away in a whisper. "A reminder that I need to forgive."

She bowed her head and said, "Let us begin our morning meeting with a time of silent reflection."

Prudence never again spoke of the stone, nor did she talk about Whittington. Even though she continued fervently as ever in her tasks, some of her joy was gone.

*****

Many worries filled her thoughts. The upcoming trial was foremost, but other troubles pressed upon her as well. Poor Harriet Lanson was getting worse day by day, and Prudence could not dismiss the likelihood she was suffering from advanced consumption. Marcy confirmed her suspicion when she reported Harriet's laundry contained many blood-stained handkerchiefs.

Prudence had just settled into bed one night when she heard a rapid pounding on her door.

"Miss Prudence." Julia Williams' low voice held a note of alarm. "It's Harriet. She's coughing up blood something awful. You'd better come."

Prudence and Almira donned their robes in a flash and ran to Harriet's side. A sheen of sweat covered her waxen face as she labored to breathe between attacks of coughing.

"I must go for Doctor Harris," Prudence whispered to Almira. "Stay here and try to keep her comfortable as you can. Julia, can you please get some water and cloths. We must try to get her fever down."

She sped away in the darkness, running as fast as she could to Dr. Harris's house on the main street of town. The wind whistled a fearful dirge through the night air, warning her there was no time to waste. There was no light in the house. She pounded the knocker for some minutes before the door opened a crack and the wavering lamplight revealed the gray hair and lined face of the doctor's wife.

"I'm so sorry to come at this hour," Prudence gasped, "but one of my girls is very sick. Coughing blood, and an awful fever. Please ask Dr. Harris to come at once. I will pay whatever he asks..."

To Prudence's shock, the doctor's wife shook her head. "No, miss, I'm sorry, but the doctor can't come. He's been forbidden by the selectmen to tend to anybody at your house. Besides, he's sound asleep."

"*Please*. She is desperately ill. He is a *doctor*. He cannot refuse to help her. She may die. I beg you to try to persuade him. Just go and tell him how serious this is..."

"I'll see." Pressing her lips in a thin line, the woman turned and disappeared into the house. In a minute, she returned. "I'm sorry, Miss Crandall, but he won't see you. He says it's most likely consumption, and he couldn't help her anyway. Burn all her bedding and such when she goes just in case it's catching. He wants you to know he can't come for any reason to your house, so don't ask again." The door closed with a click of finality.

All night the three women nursed Harriet as well as they could. Every remedy they knew was applied to no avail, and toward morning it became evident the patient was slipping away. She knew it, too.

"Don't cry, dear Julia." Between bouts of coughing, she comforted her weeping roommate. "You have been... the best friend to me... God has given... you... strength... to be... a leader. He has... a future... and a hope for you... here... but He... is calling me... home. Home to see my mother."

Early in the morning, fifteen-year-old Harriet Cassie Lanson died. Never to know her earthly father, she was received into the loving arms of her Heavenly Father. The next day Reverend Jocelyn came to preach her funeral sermon, and she was then buried in the colored cemetery outside of town, even in death deemed unworthy of a place among the whites.

Prudence and Almira told no one about Dr. Harris' refusal to come to Harriet's bedside, but they doubled their efforts to see to it everyone in the household ate well, drank pure water, and got plenty of exercise. All were cautioned not to venture out into the dank, night air. Prudence also visited Sally Harris and obtained a number of herbal remedies and poultices. "We just need to be prepared," she told Sally. "You never can tell when someone might get sick or have an accident."

Her spirits sank lower and lower. When her lawyers came to discuss the upcoming trial, she gave vague, noncommittal replies to their questions. The faith she had clung to since childhood had failed her. Where was the spark of the divine within every man and woman? Was it in Dr. Harris as he turned her away in the middle of the night? Was it in Mr. Judson's pomposity, or in the Canterbury villagers who drank in his poisonous rhetoric like mother's milk? Even the children of the town had become bestial, torturing a harmless cat. Forgiveness was as impossible as climbing to the moon.

It was Sunday morning. Low-hanging clouds sucked in the humid air and pressed close to the earth as the Crandall household made their way to the Sunday meeting at Packerville. In vain Prudence wished for a breeze as she got out of the wagon. The inside of the church was slightly cooler, and Prudence and the others sat gratefully in the shadows of the high-ceilinged sanctuary.

She found her mind wandering as one of the deacons read the announcements. A baptismal service at the river next Saturday... a quilting bee at Mrs. Smythe's house... prayer needed for a sick mother... None of those things concerned her. She was longing to remove her bonnet; the stiff black ribbon was making her neck itch. They were all in deep mourning for Harriet, and thus she must wear black, no matter the season.

Levi Kneeland came to the pulpit. He had been looking unwell lately, too. Perhaps the summer's heat was affecting everyone. He announced his text and began reading from the third chapter of the Gospel of John. Familiar words. "'Verily, verily, I say unto thee, except a man be born again, he cannot see the kingdom of God.'" The old story of Nicodemus, the ruler who came to Jesus by night, looking for answers to his questions about life. Her thoughts drifted.

Levi is a good man, she mused, *and a sincere preacher, but his manner is unimpressive. Now Calvin, on the other hand, has the voice and the manner of an angel. If only I were in Ithaca hearing him preach this morning.* She shifted to a more comfortable position and sighed. *I wish I had gone with him after all. Nothing is turning out as I thought it would. I knew the way would be hard, but I never imagined how hard. How can people be so evil? How can these things be?*

"'How can these things be?'" Levi Kneeland's voice broke in upon her like an echo of her own thoughts. "'Jesus answered and said to him, "Art thou a teacher of Israel and knowest not these things?"'" Levi placed the New Testament on the pulpit and gazed out over his slumberous congregation.

Prudence sat up straight, feeling he was looking directly at her. *Yes,* her heart responded. *I am a "teacher in Israel," yet I do not understand how such things can be.*

Patiently, Levi continued to expound the Scripture. He quoted the familiar sixteenth verse: "'For God so loved the world, that he gave His only begotten Son, that whosoever believeth in Him should not perish but have everlasting life.' Because we have heard this often, my friends, we think we know what it means. In these familiar words lies the secret of the Kingdom. This is what Jesus means when he tells Nicodemus he must be born again. There is no flesh that can be saved without a new birth though faith in Christ Jesus and His sacrifice on the cross.

"We may believe God exists and we may even strive to be good people, but if we believe not on the name of the Son of God, we are condemned already." Once again he lifted his New Testament. "Listen to the words of Jesus: 'He that believeth not is condemned already, because he hath not believed in the name of the only begotten Son of God. This is the condemnation, that light is come into the world, and men loved darkness rather than light because their deeds were evil. For every one that doeth evil hateth the light, neither cometh to the light, lest his deeds should be reproved. He that doeth truth cometh to the light.'"

Stunned, Prudence turned these words over in her mind. It was not only the men of Canterbury who were of the darkness. She herself was condemned because she had thought believing in God and living a good, moral life was enough.

And the light? Did it not come from within?

"We must come to the light!"

Oh, now I see. Jesus is the light that has come into the world. When we come to Him, we become part of Him and we are in that light and that light is in us!

When the final prayer was said and the people filed out of the building, Prudence turned to her sister.

"Almy, I should like you to take the girls home and leave me here for awhile. I feel a great need to talk with Mr. Kneeland, and I will find my way home later."

Almira opened her mouth to protest, but Prudence took her arm and said, "This truly is important to me, Almy. Please do as I ask."

The girls were full of questions when Miss Prudence was left behind, but Almira avoided answering them, and by the time they were seated at the dinner table, they had turned their minds to more practical matters. Almira spent an impatient afternoon, and was relieved to hear a buggy in the driveway just before twilight. There was peace in Prudence's eyes when she came into the room.

"How was your visit with the Kneelands?"

"It was wonderfully refreshing, Almy. Levi and I had a long conversation, and he explained many things to me from the Word of God. I know, now, what is meant by 'being born again.'"

"Oh, yes, what he preached about this morning."

"It is so easy to think we understand something because we are familiar with the words. I have always believed in the Truth, but never known what it was-- I mean, Who it is."

"I am not in a mood for riddles, Prudy. What is thee saying?"

"First of all, I am inviting thee to come to my baptism at the Quinebaug River next Saturday."

Almira was astounded. "*Baptism.* Does thee no longer mean to be a Quaker? What will Father say?"

Prudence hugged her sister impulsively. "I am a Quaker in every fiber of my being. That will never change, Almy. Now, I will be more than a Quaker. I will be a *new* Quaker in Christ Jesus."

Bewildered, Almira stared at Prudence.

"Ever since the day Whittington was killed, Almy, I felt bitterness growing inside me like a hard stone in my heart. I could not forgive those who had done such an awful thing, though I knew it was the right thing to do. I was nearly ready to abandon the school. I knew my hatred would eventually destroy everything we have worked for."

"I remember what thee said to the girls that day, Prudy. As long as thee has hatred and passion in thy heart, the one who has wronged thee is thy master." Understanding began to dawn on Almira, even as tears welled in her eyes. "Has thee now been able to forgive?"

"No, sister, not I. I had to come to the foot of the cross and admit my own failure and sin. It is Christ who has freed me from my bitterness and given me power to forgive. Oh, Almy, such a burden has gone from my heart."

The sisters had a long talk after that, and Almira was the first to notice in the morning that the white and black stone was no longer sitting on Prudence's desk in the schoolroom. Her students happily observed that day Miss Crandall was humming as she went about her duties.

*****

On August twenty-third, Pardon Crandall's chaise arrived at Prudence's house early in the morning. He wore a dark gray broad-brimmed hat with his best trousers. A dark cravat, or Quaker band as it was called, contrasted with his white shirt. He might have been courting, for all his fine appearance, but in fact he was driving his daughter to court. The day had arrived for her long-awaited trial, and he intended to stand beside her through the whole proceeding. She came immediately from the house and climbed onto the seat beside her father, giving him a dutiful embrace.

"Is thee ready, daughter? I would that I could have shielded thee from this testing, but now it has come, I only wish for the truth to be heard and justice done."

"I am prepared for whatever may come, Father. My lawyers, Mr. Ellsworth and Mr. Strong, are the finest available, thanks to Arthur Tappan's generosity, and they intend to prove my innocence by challenging the Black Law. They believe, as I do, that it is unconstitutional. I fear it is going to be a long day, but since I will not have to speak at all, my part is trifling. All I need do is sit calmly and behave modestly throughout the proceedings."

She certainly looked the part of modesty, wearing her best black silk dress and Quaker bonnet.

"I'm told the case is being heard by Judge Eaton. His prejudice is well known, Prudence. He is one of the legislators who not only passed the law, but actually wrote it. Thee will not have a sympathetic ear from him. I consider him little more than a henchman for Judson." Pardon endeavored to remain calm, but it was hard for him to stifle his worries. Judson was prosecuting the case, and besides being an able lawyer, the man had a vindictive streak Pardon himself had been a victim of. More than once Judson had threatened bodily harm to him when he dared to bring food and water to his daughter.

They had arrived in Brooklyn, the seat for Windham County. As the carriage rolled past the house where General Israel Putnam had lived and died, Pardon remarked, "I wonder what General Putnam would make of this so-called Law. I doubt when he and his men were risking their lives for freedom in 1776, they had it in mind that in scarce sixty years it would be a crime to teach young colored girls."

The courtroom was packed. Judson's friends and supporters were out in full force. They were easy to identify by their hostile expressions. There were many curiosity seekers as well, looking for a day's entertainment and an opportunity to raise their status by carrying the news to their own neighborhoods. Prudence scanned the mass of faces, grateful to see many Friends present. Her own counselors came quickly to her side and brought her and her father to their places before the bench.

"Take heart, Miss Crandall." Henry Strong kindly placed a tumbler of water on the table before her. "Our defense is ready, and I am confident the jury will be fair. By George, it's hot in here. Let me know if you need a break."

Judge Eaton set forth the indictment against Prudence, two counts which actually amounted to the same thing, namely "with force and arms she received into her school and with force and arms she instructed colored girls who were not inhabitants of this State without having first obtained in writing, permission to do so from the majority of the civil authority and selectmen of the town of Canterbury, as required by the law."

Andrew Judson had rehearsed his opening statement well. He took care to explain that the Black Law passed by the General Assembly in May existed for the purpose of keeping out of the state "an injurious kind of population" and was necessary for keeping the peace.

"This law is not, as the defense will lead you to believe, discriminatory. It does not deprive any inhabitants of this state, whatever their race, from receiving an ample and generous education. All children in Connecticut may enjoy the advantages of public education provided by the common schools, which are under the supervision of the proper officials in every town.

"It is not fair nor is it safe to allow any person, without the permission of those officials, to come into the state and open a school for any class of people she might care to invite from other states." He paused dramatically and cleared his throat. "Especially when the class of people is regarded by all states, North and South, as being persons respecting which there should be some special legislation. If not for such laws, what would prevent any state from freeing all their slaves and sending them to Connecticut?"

Pardon Crandall was barely able to suppress a snort at the last comment. "Ridiculous," he muttered under his breath. Ellsworth gave him a sideways glance, as if to say, *Just wait. Our turn is coming.*

William Ellsworth's opening statement was clear and to the point. "The question in this case is not whether thirty or forty girls should be educated in Canterbury, but whether all blacks enjoy the rights of American citizens. Even the common law of England boasts equal principles regardless of color. In America, we have built our freedom and our nation on the belief there are certain inalienable rights not restricted to color. The right to an education is one of those basic civil liberties. Miss Crandall cannot be held guilty of violating a law which is unconstitutional in its very essence."

Her lawyer's arguments sounded so obviously correct to Prudence, she could not imagine how they could be refuted. Surely the trial would end quickly, and she could get out of this stuffy, uncomfortable courtroom. She looked around the room, trying to read the expressions of the crowd and particularly the members of the jury as Mr. Judson droned on.

"You may say," Judson went on, "This is a small matter, concerning only a few dozen persons, but do not be mistaken. On this point at least, I am in agreement with the Honorable Mr. Ellsworth. The implications of this trial are far reaching. You are called here to decide more than the fate of an individual, but on a principle of law. Did Miss Crandall board and instruct even one colored pupil from outside of this State? If so, she is guilty of violating the Law, and so we intend to prove."

That shouldn't be hard to prove, since I have never attempted to deny it. Nevertheless, she was somewhat bothered when Levi Kneeland was called to the stand as a witness. She looked at Mr. Strong and frowned.

He leaned toward her and whispered. "Don't worry, Miss Prudence. He'll say nothing to harm you. He didn't want to testify, and is only doing so under the threat of being put in jail."

A worried look was on Kneeland's face when he took the stand.

"Just what is your relationship to Miss Crandall?" the oily voice of Judson inquired.

"She has recently begun attending my church."

"Meaning, of course, you are the minister. The Packerville Baptist Assembly, is that correct?"

"Yes."

"Does Miss Crandall come alone to the meetings?

"No."

"Well, whom does she bring with her?"

"Her sister. A man who works for her. Students from her school."

"I see. Are these people colored?"

"Yes, some are."

"Do you have any knowledge of where these students come from?"

"I do not know their addresses. All I know is they come with Miss Crandall."

"Do you mean to say you know nothing about them? Have you never spoken with them outside of the church?"

Levi asked for a drink of water while he considered his answer. He reluctantly told the court he had prayed with the girls at the school several times, had eaten with them, and had heard them recite lessons.

"Yet you know nothing of their backgrounds? Where they lived before they appeared in Canterbury?" Judson challenged him.

"I can't say exactly. I am under the impression some of them come from New York and Rhode Island, but some are local. From Connecticut."

"No further questions, Your Honor." Judson smirked.

When Mr. Ellsworth declined to cross-examine the witness, Levi stepped down from the witness stand with an apologetic glance at Prudence. She nodded, accepting the situation with grace.

Her father nudged her and nodded in the direction of a man who was waiting to testify. "Who is that? Does thee know him?"

Prudence recognized Philip Pearl, the father of her former pupil, Hannah Pearl. The man nervously avoided looking at her. Soon he was called to the witness stand.

"Now, Mr. Pearl," began the prosecutor, "what is your expertise regarding the law?"

The witness replied he had headed the legislative committee in the state which wrote the school law. He confirmed the Constitution of the State of Connecticut gave Negroes all rights and privileges of white citizens except the right to vote.

"How would you describe the condition of the colored population of our fair state?" Judson asked.

"Very favorable," he spoke without hesitation. "They have equal rights in education, persons, and property. Not only that, they have freedom to choose any occupation they choose."

"Then you would say Negroes are, as a class of people, very well-treated in our state?"

"Objection," Ellsworth broke in. "Calls for an opinion from the witness."

"I'll withdraw the question." Judson said. "So far as education is concerned, what is the legal duty of our state to educate those from other states or countries?"

"We have no such duty," Pearl said with emphasis. "Whatever their race may be. Obviously, if we were to set up schools for them, many of them and their families would take up residence here."

"Why would that create a problem?"

Again Ellsworth objected. "Calls for a conclusion with no basis in facts."

"Overruled," Judge Eaton said. "I'd like to hear his answer. Mr. Pearl, answer the question."

"It is a fact confirmed by long experience that colored persons are an appalling source of crime and pauperism. Why you have only to look at the numbers. Criminal courts, prisons, asylums for the poor -- all are largely populated with people of color. Clearly we have reason to legislate against the education of blacks from out of state."

"Thank you, Mr. Pearl. That will be all."

"Mr. Ellsworth, you may cross."

"Mr. Pearl, if what you say is true regarding the colored population, do we not have a duty to raise their moral consciousness through education?"

"Well, yes, to an extent. We ought to help Negroes, but we as lawmakers have a greater duty. We must first protect our own citizens. We can't have a lot of colored emigrants rushing in from here and there filling our schools."

"Should we never, then, provide for their higher education?"

"Perhaps. There could be circumstances which would warrant such a decision, but the decision ought to be left up to the civil authorities of the particular town, certainly not to any individual."

Prudence saw with dismay the sympathetic nods from the jury. She hoped Mr. Ellsworth would be able to turn their opinions when he explained the unconstitutional nature of the law. Judson, of course, had said nothing about the most disagreeable features of the Black Law, and done his best to present it as merely a sensible protection for the citizens. She found that her part, to sit calmly and behave modestly, was not so trifling after all, but a great difficulty.

The proceedings wore on for hours with Ellsworth insisting the law was unconstitutional. "Under Article 4, section 2 of the United States Constitution, the citizens of each state shall be entitled to all privileges and immunities of citizens in the several states. The law against the school is clearly unconstitutional. Blacks are citizens, and the State of Connecticut cannot deprive those from other states from one of the privileges of citizenship, education."

Judson, as expected, contended first of all that blacks were not citizens, because they did not have the right to vote. He emphasized the "states rights" and argued that according to the Constitution, the federal government has no control over education. "The State of Connecticut has held this power since before the Revolution," he practically shouted. "Shall we nullify a right held by our states since 1717?"

Long before the lawyers made their final arguments to the jury, Prudence was wearied of listening. It was a relief when Judge Eaton at last sent the jury to their chambers with their instructions.

"Prudence Crandall is charged with a violation of a certain statute of law in this state, forbidding the setting up of a school for the instruction of colored persons, not inhabitants of this state, boarding or harboring them for the purpose of instruction. The State Legislature thinks this law is constitutional. The defense holds it to be unconstitutional."

He laid aside his spectacles and looked directly at the jurors.

"It is my opinion the law is constitutional and obligatory on the people of the State. If you believe the law to be constitutional and think the prosecution has proved that Prudence Crandall has violated the law, you must find her guilty. If you believe the law to be unconstitutional, a higher court will decide her guilt or innocence."

With a great scraping of chairs, shifting of weight, and abundance of sighs, the jury arose from their seats and shambled from the room.

Chapter Fifteen

"What do you mean, they couldn't decide?" Almira's voice rose in near hysteria. The entire household plus Sarah Harris, George Fayerweather, and Charles Harris had gathered to wait for the outcome of the trial, and Almira's nerves were on edge when Prudence and her father arrived home.

"Just that. The jury could not agree on a verdict. Seven voted for conviction and five voted for acquittal, and they said it was unlikely they would ever come to an agreement. Judge Eaton sent them out three times, and each time they came back with the same vote." Prudence slumped into a chair in the parlor and took off her bonnet. She was exhausted beyond belief.

"All that talk and no action." Marcy snapped.

Her fiancé, Charles, soberly shook his head. "So I s'pose this means you'll have to face a new trial with a different judge and jury. Did they give you any idea when it will take place?"

Prudence sighed. "Probably not until December. I hate having it hanging over my head, but at the same time it does give my lawyers more time to prepare their arguments, and leaves me free meanwhile to carry on with my work."

"Well, I'm sure Mr. Garrison will put everything that's happened in the *Liberator*. Miss Prudence, do you know how much mail the paper has received since this whole thing started? There's a bushel of letters from people who are wholly on your side," Charles said.

"Miss Prudence gets lots of mail here, too." Marcy's voice held a note of pride. "She's even heard from some far-off place called Scotland. A bunch o' ladies sent her a Bible with a real nice inscription inside the front cover. Too bad some o' them wasn't on that jury. They'd make up their minds right quick which was the true side."

"In the end," Pardon assured them, "the right will triumph. It always does, but it may take a long, weary time. It may not even be in my lifetime."

Prudence and Almira looked at their father with concern. He had aged greatly in recent months. Though his eyes were still bright and his mouth firm, his clothes hung a trifle loosely on his once-erect frame. His daughter's trouble was taking its toll. For his sake alone, they longed for the question of the school's existence to be decided and their lives to return to a normal pattern.

When they went to their room that night, Prudence confided to her sister. "Almy, I am just worn out. I am tired of being a symbol for a cause. I am worried about Father."

"Thee would not quit now." It was not a question. Almira knew her sister's nature too well for that.

She crossed the room and took a letter from the highboy. "I have been saving this. It was delivered this morning, and I believe this is the right time for thee to read it. It's a letter from our dear Elizabeth."

"Elizabeth? Calvin's Elizabeth?" Prudence seized the paper and scanning the familiar penmanship, she smiled in delight. "Oh, she describes the country there, and tells about her Papa..."

"Go ahead," Almira encouraged her, "read it aloud. Of course I've read it, but I like hearing it again."

So Prudence read:

"Dear Miss Prudence and Miss Almira,

"Papa and I are all settled in Ithaca now. It is a beautiful place, so green it almost hurts my eyes to look out across the fields. There are many rolling hills, and I am sure in a few months they will be bright with autumn colors. We have a housekeeper and a manservant, and a lot of people about the place (we live next door to the church), but I miss you and the school very much. Papa is very busy with his pastorly duties, and though he takes me with him when he can, I am alone much of the time. That is when I think of you the most.

"My education is not so exact anymore. I have hardly done any mathematics. I do drawing on my own, for there are many beautiful places to sketch when we go out. I am sending you a small sketch of a place known as Taughannock Falls that we drove past last week. I am sorry I cannot put the sound of the waterfall on paper, for it is bodacious. (That is a new word I learned.)"

Here, they both laughed, and then passed the sketch back and forth to admire the young artist's work.

"My Papa has encouraged me to read, but the books in his library are quite boring. For example, he gave me a long-sufferish book called **Institutes of the Christian Religion** *by an odd person named John Calvin. I say he is odd, for in the picture he wears a hat that looks like an upside down pie, and he has a long pointed beard, longer than a pirate's, that almost makes him look like a wizard. Papa says that is the very last thing he is. Papa says Mr. Calvin is a famous theologian who has influenced millions of believers, including him. Anyway, I have not made much progress in reading it, but I will keep trying, because it pleases Papa. I would rather read* **Ivanhoe,** *but it is not in our library. It is quite a new book, and very popular in England. Have you read it?*

"Everyone I meet is impressed when they find out I was a pupil at the Canterbury Female Boarding School because, of course, everyone has heard of Miss Prudence. They all want to know what you are like. I tell them you are pretty and kind, and a very good teacher. Then they tell me you are a heroine. Think of that, Miss Prudence. A heroine just like in a book. But to me, you are not a person in a book, but a real lady who has courage and love in her heart. If there is anyone I would want to be like, it is you. I think you are very brave to start a school for girls like Sarah Harris, for they do need to learn, and you and Miss Almira are the best teachers in the world. I am only sorry I had to leave and we could not all be in the same school together. I really liked Sarah, and next to Hannah Pearl, she was my favorite.

"Today my father is over at the church with a passel of workmen who are climbing up and down ladders and putting up scaffolding to fix the bell tower. Papa is trying to tell them it would be better to tear down what is left of the old and use all new materials in building a new one. He told them trying to salvage the old lumber was false economy. At dinner he was talking about it, and he said 'I think I must preach this Sunday about sewing a new patch on old cloth.' I don't know what sewing on patches has to do with it, but sometimes he has funny ideas, even if he is a 'learned man.' (That's what one of the deacons called him.)

"I am glad you were able to get out of jail, Miss Prudence, and I hope you never ever have to go back. It was very wrong of the men who put you there. My father was awfully upset about it. I cried so much when I heard Whittington had died. He was the best cat ever. Papa did not tell me why he died, but I hope he did not suffer, and I pray you can get another cat. We remember you every night when we say prayers, and Miss Almira, too, because we love you very much. Please write to me soon.

"Your devoted pupil,
Elizabeth Madeline Philleo

"P.S. I hope I have spelt everything right. I checked most words in Webster's Blueback Speller."

"Oh, what a darling she is." Prudence wiped tears from her eyes and touched the paper gently. "This is just what I needed, Almy. Isn't she a caution?"

"I know," Almira laughed. "Did not thee love her description of John Calvin?"

"That word 'long-sufferish.' I have never heard it before, but I know exactly what she means."

"If it is not in the dictionary, it should be."

Prudence's face grew sober again. "Truly, Almy, there is nothing in this world that means more to me than knowing she thinks of me as a real lady with courage and love in my heart."

"The thing that touched me the most was her wish we could all be in the same school together. If only Judson and others like him could have the purity of a child and see the light..."

"Because their deeds are evil..."

"What?"

"Oh, I was remembering the scripture John three... something, 'men loved darkness rather than light because their deeds were evil.' Levi Kneeland preached on that. Remember?"

"I don't like to think of people loving darkness, even Mr. Judson." Almira frowned.

"Then pray for him, sister, for he, too, may choose to come to the light." Prudence carefully folded the thin sheets of paper and pressed them to her lips. "I feel blessed tonight by the words of this dear girl. I am no longer tired, Almira. I am renewed."

Almira hugged her fondly. "I am glad, then. Until December -- the next trial -- let us keep her words before us to draw strength for our labors."

When Almira laid her head upon her pillow, she heard a giggle in the darkness.

"What?" she said.

"Almira, do send the poor child a copy of *Ivanhoe*. Imagine Calvin giving a girl her age John Calvin's treatise to read. Elizabeth is right. Her Papa does have funny ideas for being such a learned man."

They stifled their laughter in their pillows before drifting off to sleep.

At breakfast the next morning, Marcy was unusually sober. After the girls left the dining room, Prudence folded her napkin and placed it beside her plate.

"All right, Marcy. What is bothering you? I can tell you have something on your mind."

"I do fer sure," Marcy answered. "Sarah and I need to talk with you. When school is over today, could we set down in the back parlor and have a chat?"

"Of course, we can sit down and talk."

Marcy nodded absently and left the room.

Throughout the day, she wondered what could cause Marcy to be so serious. Sarah Harris was also very quiet, and Prudence noticed her usually diligent student was decidedly daydreaming.

It was not long before Prudence learned the subject of Sarah's daydreams. When they were settled in the back parlor, Marcy poured out the inevitable cups of tea and began the conversation.

"Miss Prudence, Charles wants to marry me."

"Yes, I know. The first time I met him, he told me you were betrothed, and it is very evident you and he have strong feelings for each other."

"Well, they's gettin' stronger all the time. He wants to be married by Christmastime this year, and I do, too, but I know you need me here, and I can't see my way clear to up and leave you holdin' the bag."

Prudence was startled. It was true, she depended on Marcy's efficiency and loyalty in running the household. She could not imagine how she would manage without her. Before she could think of a reply, Sarah added her news.

"George and I want to marry, too. My father helped us buy a few acres of land outside of town, and George saved enough money from his blacksmithing to build us a little house. He's already started cutting the trees and has the plans all in his head."

"What about your schooling?" she could not help asking. Sarah's desire for an education was the catalyst that had changed everything in Prudence's own life.

"I'm almost finished with the training course, Miss Prudence. I will finish the classes, I promise, even after I am married. I don't want to keep George waiting. He is going to be the most wonderful husband, and I want to be his wife more than anything else." Her eyes shone with love.

"We want to have a double weddin'," Marcy said. "If we could have the weddin' here, it would be awful nice. If it's too much trouble," she hurried on, "Sarah's mother is willin' to have the doin's at her place."

Prudence set her teacup on the tray, folded her hands in her lap, and closed her eyes. She needed a moment to adjust to this sudden news.

Marcy and Sarah held their breath and looked at each other hopefully.

"Well," she said, after a moment's consideration. "November might just be a good time for a wedding. It will give us something to focus on while I am waiting for the new trial. Of course, thee must have the wedding here. Almira will be delighted to help with the plans. There is just one thing I must ask of thee, Marcy."

Gratefulness was written all over Marcy's face. "Anything, Miss Prudence. You know I'd do anything for you."

"You must not leave me. You and Charles may live here. We'll get a larger bed for your sleeping room -- Charles would never fit on that cot you have -- and we will refurnish this parlor for the two of you. You'll have your own home right here."

"I could cry, I'se so happy. Charles can keep on with his work for the *Liberator* and still work the farm with his pa. Livin' here, it'll be splendid. I can't wait to tell him."

"As for you, young lady," Prudence turned to Sarah in mock sternness, "no more daydreaming in class. You will marry your handsome George Fayerweather, but you must still finish your schoolwork. I am determined he shall have an educated wife.

"Now, let us tell Almira the news."

The anticipation of the double wedding kept all the young ladies in a state of animation. Even the ongoing drama of Miss Crandall's legal troubles could not dampen their enthusiasm. Both brides were to have new dresses, even though Sarah shyly suggested she had a brown dress which would do just fine.

"Oh, no," Ann Eliza insisted, "an old gown just won't do for marrying George. Especially brown." Her wrinkled nose showed her opinion of that dreary color. "You always liked yellow, Sarah. Why not a light yellow silk with an ivory veil? *I* know -- we could embroider tiny flowers all over the puffed sleeves and around the hem. I'll help make the dress. I'm quite good with a needle. We have lots of time."

"I don't need no furbelows," Marcy declared, "but I do love the color blue. If I could have a blue dress with a full skirt and fitted bodice, I'd be glad enough. 'specially if it was silk." She glided across the room, tossing her head and swishing the imaginary full skirt.

Poor Mr. Burleigh was at a loss in dealing with the "giddy females, who would as soon be sketching dresses and 'bo-kays' as attending to their mathematics." In the middle of a lesson one day, Sarah Hammond asked him, out of the blue, if he had ever thought of marrying. He turned red as the stripes on the American flag, and sent her from the room.

Finally, Prudence found it necessary to address her young ladies. She talked with them about the seriousness of the step Sarah and Marcy and their young men were about to take, and impressed upon them marriage involved commitment. "Married people go through many hardships in life, and godly character is far more important than fancy dresses and wedding parties. In the words of the traditional ceremony, 'marriage is not to be entered into unadvisedly, but reverently and discreetly and in the fear of God.'"

Her words had the desired effect, at least on their behavior in the schoolroom. Mr. Burleigh thanked her, pleased to be able to teach once again.

The month of September brought a long and glorious Indian summer. The bountiful apple harvest provided the school with a good supply of cider for the coming winter, and best of all, a new well was dug on the other side of property, so once again the household enjoyed the blessing of clean water. The young ladies in Miss Crandall's school continued their learning, and despite continuous resentment from the Canterbury residents, there were no major outbreaks of hostility.

Prudence was surprised the last week of the month to receive word her case had been reopened, and she was being called to appear in court October third.

"I thought it would be in December," she said to Almira. "I wonder why they changed it."

She tried to contact Samuel May for advice, but found he had gone to Boston for an extended visit. George Benson, however, came to call on her.

"It's all the doing of that capital blackguard Andrew Judson," he said, wrinkling his nose in distaste. "He couldn't wait for the regular session to begin in December, so he moved the case to Superior Court. He knows David Daggett's prejudice matches his own, and he'll try to use that to his advantage."

Prudence's heart sank. "Is there any hope of a fair trial, then?"

"It depends on the jury. Ellsworth is well prepared, and you may count on him to present the best possible case."

As it turned out, Judge Daggett's influence outweighed both the eloquence and the evidence presented by Ellsworth.

It was not hard for Judson to prove the facts of his case, that Prudence had harbored and instructed colored students who were not inhabitants of the state without gaining permission from the civil authorities in Canterbury. The question laid before the jury was whether or not the colored persons were to be regarded as citizens of the states where they were born, and if so, was the law Prudence broke unconstitutional?

As Daggett said to the jury, "This case is not about the evils of slavery nor is it about the blessings of education, but whether this law does clearly violate the Constitution of the United States."

Ellsworth did his best. Colored persons, he insisted, are citizens by right of birth in this country. Moreover, they are human beings, and there is nothing in the state or federal constitutions which deprives them of fundamental rights on the grounds of color. As for the claim that because colored persons cannot vote in the state of Connecticut and therefore, are not citizens, he pointed out that in several of the states where Miss Crandall's pupils were born, blacks had been granted suffrage. It would be illogical to say they are citizens in one state and not another. "Besides," he said, "citizenship cannot be tied to suffrage. Women and minors cannot vote, yet we recognize their rights as citizens."

In contrast to Ellsworth's well-reasoned arguments, Judson's manner was highly emotional. "If we accept the principles urged by the defense," he declared, "it would *destroy* the government itself and this American nation, blotting out this nation of white men and substituting one from the African race.

"The state does possess the power to regulate its own schools in its own chosen way, independent of the question of citizenship, and furthermore, it was never the intention of the framers of the Constitution to place persons of color on equal footing with themselves and make them citizens. It matters little what may be the opinion of a few madmen now, but what was the intention of the people of the United States at the time the Constitution was adopted? Slavery was the condition of the African at that time, and slaves were regarded as property. How could anyone think the founding fathers considered them voters or citizens?"

Prudence's eyes were on the jury as Judson spoke, and she saw the change in their faces as his passionate words stirred every latent fear and prejudice in their hearts. As Daggett gave his final charge to the jurors, she felt a cold wind blow through her soul.

"To my mind, it would be a perversion of terms to say slaves, free blacks, or Indians were citizens within the meaning of the term, as used in the Constitution. God forbid I should add to the degradation of this race of men, but I am bound, by my duty, to say they are not citizens. I have thus shown you this law is not contrary to the second section of the fourth article of the Constitution of the United States. Even if they were citizens, I am not sure this law would be unconstitutional, for it does not prohibit schools, but very suitably places them under the care of the civil authority and selectmen."

Andrew Judson's chest swelled visibly when these words were spoken. He was vindicated!

Daggett concluded his speech: "You will now take this case into your consideration, and notwithstanding my opinion of the law, you will return your verdict according to law and evidence. I have done my duty, and you will do yours."

In a very short time, the jury returned. No one, least of all Prudence herself, was surprised at their verdict. "Guilty, as charged."

The dull ache in her forehead intensified, and the mass of faces around her became an indistinct blur. She heard, from somewhere far away, the voice of her lawyer, Mr. Ellsworth.

"Miss Crandall. Prudence. *We are not beaten yet.* We shall file a bill of exception at once and take this case to the Supreme Court of Errors. I will take this to the highest court in the land before I am silenced."

Chapter Sixteen

January 1834

Dear Calvin,

It was Sunday afternoon. Prudence stared at the two words on the sheet of paper before her. She had received a letter from Calvin at the beginning of the year but had neglected to answer. Not exactly neglected. She had started several letters and destroyed them before writing much more than the two words staring back at her now.

What could she write about? The outcome of the trial last October had been published in many newspapers, including the *Liberator* and the *Unionist*, and the questions of citizenship for coloreds and the constitutionality of the Black Law thoroughly debated through the press. The everyday struggles and exploits of the school had not changed remarkably and would make dull reading. Writing about her own feelings was risky at best. At times, she longed to bare her heart to Calvin, but she felt she did not have the right since she had twice rejected his proposal.

Almost a year had passed since their adventure making maple syrup. The sweet syrup they brought back had long since been used up, but the memory of that day was a sweet treasure she would always keep. It had been at the center of her thoughts the day in November when Marcy and Sarah's double wedding took place. For some reason, it had come to mind yesterday when Sally Harris had dropped in to pay her niece Mary's tuition for the coming term.

Mrs. Harris laid the payment on the desk and waited for her receipt, and then, closing her reticule, she leaned forward with a gleam in her eye.

"I have a wonderful secret to share with you, Miss Prudence. I am going to be a grandmother. Sarah told me last week. She is so happy."

It was welcome news, and of course, she was pleased for Sarah and George, but in the midst of her joy a feeling of loneliness engulfed her. There was no husband in her future. No children. She had chosen to walk the pathway her conscience laid before her, and she was not sorry; yet there were days when the sacrifices she had made felt great indeed. Today especially, the memory of Calvin was bittersweet. She felt in great need of a confidant, and though she had forfeited his love, she decided she might at least write to him as a friend.

She dipped her pen in the inkwell and wrote.

Your letter reached me some weeks past, and at last I am finding time to reply. It sounds as though you are accomplishing all you had hoped to do there in Ithaca. What energy you have! The people must be so happy to have the new bell tower. There is something sweet and comforting about the sound of church bells, ringing out the daily rhythm of life.

Her pen paused. *Well, I used to find the church bells soothing. When I first arrived in Canterbury, I welcomed the nearness of their golden tones. Now the ringing reminds me of Captain Fenner turning us away that first Sunday. The bells are not a welcoming call but an echo of the church's hypocrisy.*

She shook the thought from her mind and continued writing.

I am glad to know you have found a good school there for Elizabeth. She will benefit much from the discipline of a formal education. You did not mention art classes. Perhaps if there are none in the school, you could find an instructor for her outside of school. She not only has talent, but a passion for drawing.

Now what am I doing, giving him advice about Elizabeth? I have no right to do so, although I wish I did. She is so very dear. I see much of Calvin in her, and I can't help loving her.

She considered a moment and finished the paragraph.

I am sure you know what a talented young lady she is, and will do what is best for her.

The school here is growing nicely. I am filled almost to capacity. Maybe I could fit in two more girls, but that would be all. It is a good thing I hired Mr. Burleigh. The girls not only respect him, but are very fond of him. He is kind and good-humored and knows how to challenge them. Anyone who thinks "colored" people have inferior minds ought to observe these scholars. They are not only quick learners, but they have a thirst for learning and a seriousness about their education that is gratifying to see. I do not regret the risks I have taken for their sakes, and I pray this school can become a model in years to come.

I am hopeful it will. Because of the conflict over its existence, thousands of people have heard of the Canterbury school. I have received letters of support, gifts, and many other kindnesses from people in America and also in the British Isles! I never thought my small enterprise would attract such wide attention.

145

I hope that doesn't sound prideful, but I am amazed at the outpouring of kindness and enthusiasm from so many people. Why, oh, why are my Canterbury neighbors so hostile to the presence of my pupils? Is it all due to Mr. Judson's antagonism?

Andrew Judson's political victories proved his power to sway the populace. A vision of his well-built frame flashed before her. His cold eye, his measured steps, and his satirical remarks in Judge Daggett's courtroom had filled her with dread. To think she had once considered him a good neighbor.

I only wish some of that kindness and understanding would extend to the people here in Canterbury. I still have doors closed in my face, and my pupils are subjected to constant harassment if they dare step out of doors. However, you might be interested to know I have found one person willing to do business with me. She is a widow who lives at the other end of town, and I have engaged her to do sewing for me. I have far too much sewing and mending to keep up with, and now that Marcy is married, she has less time than ever. (Charles seems to lose innumerable buttons and wear holes in his socks constantly.)

Prudence smiled as she wrote that sentence, knowing Calvin would understand her tongue-in-cheek remark. *I feel he has known me forever.*

This lady, Mrs. Farnsworth, is a singular person, not at all to be intimidated by the likes of Andrew Judson! It seems she lost both her son and her husband in the War of 1812, and she is very revered in the village for her patriotism. Therefore, she is not subject to the same rules as common people, and will do as she pleases. For example, she can (and often does) quote long passages of Scripture from memory, but she never goes to church and sometimes loudly criticizes the actions of its members. She is, by all reports, wealthy, but she makes no show of it, and lives very parsimoniously. I am sure she does not need to earn money sewing for me, but I rather think she is curious to know this old-maid schoolteacher who has brought such notoriety to Canterbury. Therefore, she welcomes my business. I, too, welcome my acquaintance with her, and we have had some interesting visits.

Again, she paused. *Should I tell him what happened last time I took my sewing to her? I was on my way home, carrying the dress she had altered for me since I lost so much weight last fall, and I ran into old Judson himself. What a coarse man! I can still hear him: "Dare you to go walking abroad by yourself, Miss Crandall? You've made more than a few enemies in town, you know. Perhaps you'd like me to find you an escort. I can think of a couple of darkies who'd be glad to help you home, if they can get sober enough to sashay down the street with a fine Quaker lady like yourself." His nasty cackle followed me all the way around the corner.*

Recalling the incident, she shuddered. *No, I won't tell Calvin that. He is always worried about my safety, and it will just prove him right. Does he still worry about me? He didn't need to worry, but still, it was pleasant to know he cared. He did ask about my health in his letter.*

> *You inquired about my health. I am tolerably well. I did have a bad cold last month -- no matter how careful I am, I seem to catch a cold a couple of times a year -- but I am thankful it did not go into my chest. I am fine now. My spiritual health causes me more concern. Since my baptism last year, I have a great sense of God's presence day by day. Still, at times I become discouraged, and especially since the hearing of my case is continually delayed. As anxious as Mr. Judson was to take me to court in front of Judge Daggett, there seems no such urgency to go to the Supreme Court of Errors. Perhaps this is a good sign, but still it weighs heavily on my mind. I am anxious for the question to be settled once and for all.*

> *I spend a good deal of time reading and meditating in the Psalms lately, and have committed several verses to memory. One which has given me much comfort is Psalm 43:5. "Why art thou cast down, O my soul? And why art thou disquieted within me? Hope in God: for I shall yet praise him, who is the health of my countenance, and my God."*

It's true -- my hope is only in God. Calvin will know what I mean. Oh, I am glad I wrote him. I can imagine the look in his eyes as he reads it and see myself sitting across from him. He will nod and smile in all the right places. Maybe he will read it more than once. If only he does not get the wrong idea and think I am in love with him. Well, that is a chance I will have to take. If I ever fell in love, it would probably be with him, but I am too sensible for that. Almira is the romantic one. It really doesn't matter anyhow, since he is so far away. There may be any number of spinsters and widows in Ithaca vying for his affections.

She added the customary closing and signature and popped the pages into an envelope before she changed her mind about sending it. She would mail it on Monday.

The long winter of 1834 gently bowed to an enchanting spring. The crocuses poked their hopeful faces through the melting snow, and birds fluttered about, building their nests among the golden leaves of the birch trees. The wind played tug of war with the girls' bonnets as they marched down the street, enjoying a break from their studies. The Crandall school was truly full now, for friends and supporters had provided resources for two more students to be added to the group.

Seemingly, the town bullies had tired of their entertainment and seldom followed the young women down the streets, but the girls were acutely aware of the hostile stares of any townspeople they happened to pass. Prudence avoided contact with her opponents as much as possible, but when a chance encounter forced a conversation, there was no doubt as to their antagonism.

One day they met Rufus Adams coming from his home. He looked up and down the row of young ladies and shook his fist at them. "You gals oughta be ashamed, parading yourselves out in front of the whole town. You don't belong here, no more'n a bunch of chattering monkeys. We'll soon see you all back where you belong -- Africa!"

He turned to Prudence with a sneer, his Adam's apple bobbing in his scrawny neck. "Just you wait until the next trial. You think the jury was quick to decide the matter last time? The Court of Errors will be ready and waiting to slap a fine on you and rid our state of these vagrants."

Prudence did not reply. She lifted her chin. "Ladies, let us move on."

She waited in vain to be notified of the date for her hearing. "I can't bear this suspense," she said to Almira and Mr. Burleigh one afternoon after school.

"I don't know whether to plan for the next term or not. We'll surely need more supplies -- the stationery is almost gone, and we'll need new copybooks soon. Marcy keeps peering into the larder and rolling her eyes as if she sees a famine on the way."

"We walk by faith, not by sight," William Burleigh reminded her. "My advice is to be optimistic about the outcome and not worry yourself about the trial. Who knows how long it will take those lawyers to come to the point? Seems to me procrastination is something they excel in." He ran his big hands through his unruly hair and smiled down at Prudence.

"I agree," Almira put in. "Think of all the times thee has told me 'take no thought for the morrow, for the morrow shall take thought for the things of itself. Sufficient unto the day is the evil thereof.' Let us just keep going, and hope for the best."

"I know thee is right," Prudence sighed. "We must endure and wait. That is the hardest part for me."

The waiting continued for months. The spring term ended, summer began, and yet there was no word of her case coming before the court. Sarah Harris Fayerweather had finished the course of study and retired to her cozy cottage to await the birth of her baby.

On her last day at school, she came to Prudence with joy in her eyes. "Thank you, Miss Crandall. The learning I have now will make me a better wife and mother, and I'll be able to teach my own children and others because of my studies here. George is very proud of me, too. If my baby is a girl, we are going to name her Prudence Crandall."

"You might change your mind about that," Prudence chuckled.

"Maybe you should find a name with less notoriety attached to it. She might not want to be associated with a rebel. I do thank you for the thought. I would consider it a great honor."

Prudence was teaching a geography lesson one sultry afternoon when Marcy opened the door to the schoolroom and cleared her throat. "Miss Prudence, you have a visitor. I showed him to the parlor."

The girls looked up from Morse's *Geography Made Easy* with curiosity. "Go ahead, Miss Prudence," Julia Williams said. "We can keep on with our reading."

It was not often Marcy thought a caller important enough to interrupt classes, so Prudence nodded to Julia to supervise the lesson and followed Marcy into the hall.

"Who is it?" she whispered, not knowing what to expect.

"It's a stranger. He called hisself Mr. Cleaveland," Marcy hissed. "I didn't know what t' do with him."

Prudence could see at once this was not a social call. He greeted her with an unsmiling nod and, without further preamble, presented her with a sealed document. "From the court," he said. "Your appeal will be heard by the Supreme Court of Errors on July 24 in the matter of Prudence Crandall, Plaintiff in Error, versus the State of Connecticut."

"*Hallelujah.* I have been awaiting this for many months. Thank you, sir, for you have brought good news."

He was startled by this reaction and stumbled out the door in a hurry.

For the next several weeks, Prudence's attorneys and supporters made frequent appearances at her home. Mr. Ellsworth, Mr. Strong, and another lawyer named Mr. Goddard reviewed the points of defense with her and added more historical proofs to their arguments. Mr. May and Mr. Benson came to offer once again their support and appreciation for all she was doing for the cause of abolition.

In the midst of all the activity, she found time to write a brief letter to Calvin Philleo.

It is here at last, the moment I have both anticipated and feared. At last the question will be decided, and the courts will rule on the constitutionality of the Black Law. It is well-named a "black" law, for it has caused a dark, oppressive cloud to hang over our state and blotted out the light of freedom for an entire race of people. The implications of the law have been widely aired, and I believe public opinion is shifting in favor of human rights.

This hearing not only has great personal significance for me, but for our country as a whole. The outcome will affect the Indians of our state, the free blacks, and even the slaves. I will soon know whether the cause I have embraced has been strengthened by our experiment here in Canterbury. If so, it will be worth it all."

The week before the case was to be heard, Prudence sent her students to their homes for a long holiday, then prepared to journey to the state capitol in Hartford. She traveled with her father, brother, and sister to lodgings William Lloyd Garrison had arranged for them near the courthouse.

Prudence came into the dining room the morning of July twenty-fourth wearing a cream-colored batiste gown trimmed in green. "I don't care if I do appear frivolous," she said to Almira, "I am not wearing black again. I nearly suffocated at the last trial, and if I am to be carried off to jail, I will at least be cooler."

"Oh, Prudy, how can thee be so imperturbable at a time like this? Everything is at stake."

"Then so small a matter as the color of my gown will hardly matter." Prudence popped a blackberry in her mouth and poured syrup on her hot cakes. Almira did not know she had spent hours in prayer last night, struggling with her doubts and fears, and had come at last to a place of peace. "It is in God's hands, Almira." She speared a bite of bacon.

After placing a tan bonnet on her tawny, blonde hair, she picked up her reticule and went outside. A contingent of supporters joined her in front of the house, including her father, Reuben, and George and Helen Benson.

Helen embraced her warmly. "You look fine, Prudence. Were you able to rest last night?"

"I feel very well, thank you, Helen. It is good of you to come along. I can assure you it won't be a picnic in there."

"I hardly expect it to be so," her friend replied. Since Prudence's time in jail, their relationship had grown. "I am praying we will have something to celebrate when it is over."

"Let's be going, Pru." Reuben, who was usually unperturbed, wore an air of anxiety. "The sooner we get there, the sooner it will be over."

Pardon chuckled. "That's not necessarily so, son. Thee wasn't there the last time. These court proceedings can't be rushed, or so it seems." Once again, he was dressed in his best clothes, looking dignified and noble.

Her brother took hold of her elbow and was just handing her into the carriage when a horse and chaise came dashing up the lane. Reining in his horse, a familiar figure leapt from the driver's seat.

Prudence's face lit up in surprise and delight. "Calvin! Calvin Philleo! What are you doing here?" she exclaimed. "I thought you were in Ithaca."

"I find my duties in Ithaca have come to an end," he announced, after shaking hands all around. "Although New York is a beautiful state, I find myself strangely drawn to Connecticut. It seems there is always something exciting going on here. It looks as though you are off for another adventure -- do I dare guess you are heading for the courthouse?"

He swept off his hat and bowed to Prudence.

"Miss Crandall, may I have the honor of driving you there?"

Reuben grinned at him. "A fine idea. I suspect our carriage will be rather crowded, and my sister will be more comfortable with you." He again took her elbow and helped her down.

Soon the caravan was underway, with Reuben in front, George Benson following, and Calvin last.

"I never expected to see you today," Prudence stated the obvious. With pleasure she studied his strong profile, noticing the widening of silver in his dark hair and the smile lines around his eyes. "Have you truly left your parish in Ithaca?"

"Yes, Prudence. When I received your most recent letter, I was just finishing up some details, and I found myself greatly motivated to be done with it so I could be here with you today."

"Oh, thee did not need to come--"

He silenced her protest with a shake of his head. "I am not here because I felt obligated, Prudence, but because I am vitally interested in the outcome. This case is the subject of discussion all over the country, and it means much to everyone who longs to see the end of intolerance. It's all very well to give lip service to equality, but this is a chance for putting it into practice. Besides, I have a very personal interest in the lady who started this school for 'young ladies and little misses of color.'"

He smiled down at her, the flecks of gold in his brown eyes holding her like honey snares a fly. Prudence felt her cheeks growing warm with an unbecoming blush and quickly changed the subject.

"Speaking of young ladies," Prudence said, "where is your dear Elizabeth?"

"She came with me to New Haven, and is staying with her aunt there. My wife's sister Emmaline is very fond of Elizabeth and begged to have her for a few weeks. She sends her love, and is eager to see you and Almira.

"By the bye, Miss Crandall, whom do I have to thank for the copy of *Ivanhoe* that mysteriously appeared in my house?"

The twinkle in his eye evoked a laugh from Prudence, but no confession. Riding beside Calvin, hearing the jingling of Jackson's harness, and feeling the caressing summer breeze lifted her spirits. It scarcely seemed possible she was on her way to a serious legal proceeding that would determine her future. She leaned back and took in the sights of the bustling town, and they soon arrived at the imposing capitol building.

Chapter Seventeen

The avenue around the State House was thronged by wagons and chaises, and clusters of people engaged in solemn conversation. Prudence immediately spied her lawyers, along with Samuel May, standing just outside the door of the stately building. As they pressed through the crowd to greet her, she heard a familiar voice in the background.

"It's Levi!" Calvin exclaimed, whirling to see his fellow minister approaching. "Levi Kneeland! How great to see you!" They clasped each other's hands and began an animated conversation.

Meanwhile, Prudence, surrounded by her counselors, was led into the packed courtroom. With each hearing, the crowds had increased in proportion to the controversy, and today the scent of battle was in the air.

"All rise. Hear ye, hear ye. The Supreme Court of Errors of the State of Connecticut is now in session this twenty-fourth day of July, in the year of our Lord eighteen hundred thirty-four." Chief Justice Thomas Williams took his place, followed by eight associate judges. They sat down, adjusted their spectacles, and soberly regarded the thick briefs stacked before them.

Prudence sighed as the proceedings began. William Ellsworth was clean-shaven and faultlessly dressed, his eyes gleaming like an avenging angel. Through heavy-lidded eyes, Andrew Judson took measure of the courtroom, calculating his odds and concluding Miss Crandall's school would not survive this day's onslaught.

The same arguments were repeated as in the previous trials, each man attempting to strengthen his position by citing historical and legal precedents. Judson then produced a heavy document he referred to as a memorial, decrying the increase in the colored population in the state and its negative effect upon the economy. The memorial was dignified (or in Judson's opinion, deified) by signatures of a long list of distinguished citizens.

"The black man," stated Judson, "has just emerged from a state of barbarism, and if native indolence should deter him from his toil, he has no qualms in applying to the public storehouse as a legal pauper, becoming a financial burden to the community.

"In the words of this memorial," Judson waved the document before the court, "whenever the black man comes into competition, the white man is deprived of employment, compelled to yield the market to the African, and is driven from the state to seek a better lot in Western wilds. Thus have thousands of our citizens been banished from home and kindred for the accommodation of the most debased race the civilized world has ever seen, and whom the false philosophy of enthusiasts is hourly inviting to deprive us of the benefits of civilized society."

Prudence's jaw dropped. The unfairness! The meanness! Indolence? She thought of the Harris farm, a model of industry. She remembered the hope in Hattie Doud's eyes, undimmed by her arms and back, scarred by years of hard labor. Dear Marcy, who had come into her life at a crucial time and taken on the task of running a bustling household. Barbarism? She thought of her small collection of scholars intent on mastering not only the practical aspects of learning, but the spiritual and moral as well. She wanted to jump from her seat and refute the string of lies issuing from Judson's mouth.

At this point, Judson placed the tome upon the table in front of him and laid his hand upon it as if it were holy writ. "These are the reasons, my fellow Americans, why I support the efforts of Colonization to Liberia. These are the reasons Miss Crandall's school is a peril to our society. These are the reasons, gentlemen, it is not only wise, but needful to abolish this school, for it is more than a nuisance and economic liability, but a seedbed of adulteration."

There was an agitation throughout the court, and Prudence wondered how Ellsworth would respond to Judson's dramatics.

He was equal to the task.

"I would urge the court," he began apologetically, "to pardon the Honorable Mr. Judson's use of the word *reasons*, for he has presented no facts at all, merely unproven and ungodly prejudices. And if I may further impose upon your indulgence, I would remind you that in his day Copernicus would have had no difficulty producing a long list of authorities endorsing the so-called 'Truth' that the earth was the center of the universe, but he and Galileo proved them wrong."

A wave of amusement stirred the rows of spectators.

"To return to the facts... the proper subject of a legal proceeding, there will never be fewer colored people in this country than there are now. Of the vast majority, this is their native land, as much as it is ours. It would be unjust and inhuman of us to drive them out, and even if they were willing to go, impractical to transport them across the Atlantic and settle them in Africa. As I said before, there will never be fewer colored people in our country than there are this day. Their population will grow with natural increase, and the only question is will we recognize their God-given rights and assist them to become all they are capable of becoming, or will we bring the wrath of heaven down upon ourselves by wickedly denying them the rights we enjoy.

"Education is one of the fundamental rights of man, and Connecticut is the last place this should be denied. Do not believe the invective my opponent has spouted. You are not children to be frightened by the bogeyman. The so-called memorial he has cited is no more than opinion. The academic achievements of Miss Crandall's pupils, mastering not only the fundamentals of reading and writing, but conquering advanced mathematics, French language, and moral philosophy -- these achievements, my friends, are the reality. Her colored scholars have proved themselves adequate -- no, more than adequate -- hungering and thirsting for knowledge." He paused, stretched to his full height, and ended his speech. "There is no reason to deny their right to an education. To do so, as we have repeatedly shown, violates the Constitution, the supreme law of our country."

"Talk about dividing the sheep from the goats," Mr. Strong whispered to Prudence. "Look at their faces. You can see which ones are on your side, Miss Crandall."

As she scanned the crowd, the face she searched for was Calvin's. He was in the second row, and his eyes were upon her, so full of hope and approval she had to blink away tears. The memory of the day she was released from jail came back to her. The busy scene in the courthouse faded, and her mind filled with the vision of Calvin stretched out beside her on the ground, his expressive hands dabbling in the creek. She recalled the earnest warmth in his eyes and the words he had spoken to her as they stood under the whispering trees. *"You say it is love which motivates the sacrifice. Remember that when you think of me."*

She had remembered it, and had wondered what he meant. Now, she understood. He did love her! Because he did, he was willing to sacrifice his own desires so she could be free to pursue her dreams. He had never tried to bend her will, but had patiently and faithfully stood by her in every test. He had come today. What would happen when the judges made their decision? His duties in Ithaca had ended, and no doubt he would be moving to a new location.

The voices of the lawyers droned on in the background, but Prudence was not listening. In this crucial moment when the future of her school was being decided, she was only thinking of Calvin Philleo. To tell the truth, he had never been out of her thoughts since the first day she met him. His keen mind and sincere faith had been a large part of his appeal, but that did not account for the happiness she felt when she was with him. The warmth of his touch, the light in his eyes, and the charm of his laughter had found a place in her heart, and that place would be forever empty if he disappeared from her life. Even if the school survived, knowing she had done her duty for the cause would be cold comfort without him in her life.

What was happening? Chief Justice Williams had risen and all the other judges prepared to leave the room.

"Where are they going?" she whispered to Mr. Strong.

He looked at her in surprise. "Why, to their chambers. The hearing is over, Miss Prudence, and they are now going into the deliberation process. We'll have a long wait, I expect, to find out their decision."

The spectators began to mill about the room, discussing the case in reserved tones.

"I believe the defense proved their case," one gentleman said to his friend. "How could anyone doubt the law is unconstitutional?"

"Judson was left with egg on his face," his companion laughed. "He's an adequate lawyer, but Ellsworth definitely got the better of him."

"Still," a third man offered, "it's a landmark case, and the outcome not to be taken for granted. I'm sure they'll take their time debating the merits. There's a lot of controversy over this one." He placed his hat over his thinning hair. "I don't intend to wait here, gentlemen. Will you join me at the tavern? I believe a pint of ale will cool our brains."

Helen Benson's thoughtfulness had provided them with a basket of food, and there was plenty to share while they awaited the court's decision. Calvin sat beside Prudence while they ate.

After a seeming eternity, the side door opened, and again the bailiff called for all to rise as the judges, looking as disgruntled as the spectators, returned to the room. No one was prepared for the Chief Justice's pronouncement.

"We have reserved our decision."

"What does that mean?" Prudence whispered.

Ellsworth turned to her, the creases in his forehead looking deeper than ever. "It means they are delaying their decision until some future time. There's nothing more for you to do, Miss Crandall. You may as well go home."

Her father's shoulders sagged with disappointment as he took her arm and walked toward the door of the courtroom. As they neared Andrew Judson, they heard him and his associates angrily cursing the court's delay. Spying Prudence, he whirled around, blocking her passage.

"So, we are still at bay, Miss Crandall. Do not think this is the last resort." He jerked his head at Pardon. "You, sir, had best keep that wagon of yours out of Canterbury. It's too wide for our roads."

"Step aside, Judson." Calvin's voice was low and tight. "You are too wide for this aisle."

"Why is everyone so upset?" Almira asked as they headed toward the carriages. "Doesn't this mean Prudy is free? Doesn't it mean the school can go on?"

"We don't know yet," Calvin replied. "We still have to wait for the judges to rule, and who knows how long it will be? It might take a week or more."

"What will you do, now, Calvin?" Prudence could not refrain from her anxious question. "Will you wait? Or do you have to go...?"

He put his arm around her waist and he held her lightly. "I will be here. I won't go, Prudence, until we know the outcome. The Kneelands have invited me to stay with them indefinitely, so you must get accustomed to my being in the neighborhood."

Relief flooded her. She would have plenty of time to talk to Calvin and think about their future.

Talking with Calvin did not prove to be as easy as she thought it would. For one thing, they had little privacy. For another, all week they were waiting for word from Justice Williams. Samuel May stopped by several times, shaking his leonine head in frustration. "I think the court is in a difficult position. Judson and his associates wield a great deal of influence, and even though the public opinion is leaning to our side, Williams doesn't want to cross them."

"Do talk about something else," Almira begged. "I feel like a sword is hanging over our heads. We may as well go to the schoolroom and prepare for the girls' return." So the week passed, as they did their best to distract themselves with everyday pursuits.

It was Ellsworth's associate, Mr. Strong, who at last brought word from the court. Prudence, Almira, Calvin, Mr. Burleigh, and Marcy gathered in the parlor to hear the news.

"Mr. Ellsworth sends his regrets, Miss Prudence. This is certainly not the outcome he had hoped for."

When Prudence scanned the document, the color drained from her face. Wordlessly, she handed it to Calvin.

"They are *evading* the issue. Listen to this: 'The defects in the information prepared by the State's Attorney were such that it ought to be quashed, thus rendering it unnecessary for the Court to come to any decision upon the question as to the constitutionality of the law.' This is the work of cowards!" he exclaimed in disgust. "They found a way out through a technicality." He rose to his feet and paced the length of the room.

"What course is open to me now?" Prudence's question echoed hollowly in the room.

Mr. Strong gave a lopsided grin. "Well, you could consider it a victory, of a sort. Your foes have failed to destroy your school through the legal process, leaving you free to carry on without fear of arrest."

"Indeed I shall." Her voice grew firm. "Though the court refused to acknowledge the truth, it has been proclaimed, and it is now up to us to prove by our actions we have a right to exist."

When Calvin bade her goodnight that evening, he stood hesitating with his hat in his hand.

"In another week, I will be going to get Elizabeth. I've been having some serious conversations with your father, Prudence."

Her heart jumped. *He's been talking to Father? About me?*

"He is such a fine man, Prudence. You know, this whole ordeal has been hard on him and Reuben, but particularly on him. He's disillusioned with the people here because of the way they have treated you. He has been talking about selling his farm and moving farther west.

Has he mentioned it to you?"

"Why, no. He was probably waiting to find out how the last trial turned out. Moving west? Closer to New Haven?"

Calvin shook his head and smiled. "Farther than that. He's heard great things about the farmland in Illinois."

"*Illinois.* It might as well be the end of the earth."

"A whole group of Quaker families from Plainfield and from Rhode Island are talking of heading to Illinois and starting a Quaker community there. I think he'd like to be part of it."

"What about Reuben?"

Again, Calvin smiled. "Well, Miss Prudy, you have been so involved in your struggles here you may have failed to notice Reuben has developed a deep interest in a pretty young Quaker girl in Rhode Island."

"Oh, Calvin, I am ashamed. You know more about my family than I do. I have been thinking of no one but myself." *Myself and thee.* If he had not been talking to her father about her, what did this have to do with them? Did she dare ask?

"As for me," he shifted his weight to his other foot and turned his hat around in his hands, "I find myself at loose ends. My work in Ithaca is concluded, I have no church appointment, and I find myself hankering to see some of that rich, black farmland in Illinois. What about you, Prudence? Are you tired of Canterbury yet?"

Thoughts raced through her brain. *Oh, yes, Calvin. I am tired of Canterbury. Tired of this burden. Tired of being alone. If you had asked me yesterday, I would have said yes. The court's decision -- rather their lack of a decision -- has changed everything for me.*

She dared not look into Calvin's eyes as she slowly gave him her answer. "Tired of Canterbury? You are asking me if I am ready to quit." She walked to her desk and gripped the back of the chair with both hands.

"How can I give up the school when Judson has lost? His attempts to manipulate the legal system have failed, and he cannot touch me now. In a few more months -- another year at most -- the courts will surely have to revoke the Black Law. I will not leave until the day I can see my pupils walk down the streets of Canterbury with their heads held high."

He gave his hat a final turn and placed it on his head. Crossing the room, he took her hand and drew it to his lips. His voice was sad as he released her hand. "Good night, Prudence." He pressed a light kiss on her forehead, and then he was gone.

Chapter Eighteen

"Wake up, Prudence." Almira bent over her sister's sprawling form. "Wake up."

Prudence opened her swollen eyes and stared. Almira drew back in surprise.

"Prudy, is thee ill?"

"No, no. I just did not sleep well last night. Is something wrong?"

"I think thee needs to get up. Something is very strange outside."

Rising, she threw a robe over her chemise and went to join Almira at the window.

"Look," Almira whispered. "What could it mean?"

It was yet early in the morning, but dozens of town residents had gathered around the perimeter of the property. Grim-faced, they stared at the house and spoke to each other in muted voices. Prudence opened the window and leaned out, attracting the attention of those closest to the fence. Seeing her, one man waved excitedly toward the window and called to his companions, "Look up! There they are!"

Startled by the sudden appearance of the Crandall sisters, the townspeople slunk away, but not without backward glances and surly expressions.

"What odd behavior." Prudence drew the curtains closed again. "I wonder what they are up to."

"Nothing good by their looks. Oh, Prudence, I feel frightened. Why ever would they be staring at our house?"

Prudence sat on the edge of her bed and rubbed her temples. She was longing to bathe her face and comb her tangled hair. After Calvin left last night, she had tossed restlessly for hours, filled with regret for the words she had spoken to him and even more for the things she had wanted to tell him and left unsaid. Now she had to begin this day faced with a new problem.

She drew in a deep breath, then spoke with sudden decision.

"Almira, I believe I need to make a trip to the seamstress today. I have some sewing that urgently needs attention."

"Sewing?" Almira was puzzled for a moment. "Oh, I see. Thee wants to find out if Mrs. Farnsworth knows any gossip--"

"Shh. Say no more. I never listen to gossip, but it so happens she is a fount of knowledge about the village of Canterbury, and if there is a cause for alarm, be certain she will tell me."

After breakfast, Prudence went to the linen closet, gathered some tablecloths that needed mending, and set off for the seamstress' house. Mrs. Farnsworth received her with open arms and invited her in for tea, even though it was only midmorning.

"I won't ask about the latest trial," she said, "for news travels fast. I already know the court was too lily-livered to give you any satisfaction."

"That's true," Prudence averred, "but at least I am no longer living under the bond. No one can say I am doing anything unlawful by conducting my school, and they have no reason to be against us now."

The widow pursed her lips. "Are you speaking of legal reason or human nature? Laws can't change the way people feel about things." She tipped the cream pitcher to her cup and then slowly stirred in a spot of honey. "I just happened to be in Mr. Coit's store yesterday when some of our neighbors were having a gab fest. You'll never guess whom they were discussing."

"Could it have been someone who is sitting in this room right now?"

"It most certainly could. One of them said, 'What if the case doesn't go the way Judson thinks it will? Is there anything else we can do to get rid of her?' Then they argued whether or not there was any other way to destroy the school."

"Well, there isn't," Prudence said flatly.

"Again, are you talking about legal recourse or human nature? If I were you, Miss Prudence, I would start packing my bags."

"You, Mrs. Farnsworth? I can scarcely believe you would run from trouble. You would stand up to anyone."

She shook her head. "You did not see the look on their faces. I do believe they mean to do you harm, and you have more to worry about than just yourself, my dear. Your sister is also in danger.

"I have done a bit of sewing for Rebecca Judson's father, Mr. Warner, and I tell you the man has deep pockets in his pants."

"Meaning what?" Prudence frowned.

"Meaning the man has money. He would not hesitate to use it to see things go the way his son-in-law wants."

"I pray you are wrong," Prudence said, "but I will be careful, and I thank you for warning me."

"I will keep my eyes and ears open and let you know if there is mischief afoot."

Prudence was reluctant to share Mrs. Farnsworth's suspicion with her sister. "She didn't hear anything definite," she said. "Just general grumbling.The usual comments."

Nothing out of the ordinary happened the following week, so she was glad she had not taken her friend's apprehension too seriously. Besides, she was preoccupied with all the changes happening to her family and dear friends.

Sarah and George Fayerweather were soon to become parents, and Marcy could talk of little else.

"Jist think of it," she gloated, "I'll be an auntie. Auntie Marcy. Don't that sound fine? Look at this blanket. I hope I get it done 'fore that baby is born. You never know about babies. They come when they's ready, whether you's ready or not. An' I do hope Charles is here when the baby comes, not gallivantin' around with Mr. Garrison's newspapers."

Reuben did bring his "pretty young Quaker girl" for a visit. Prudence was sure he had fallen in love with her, and it would be only a matter of time before they announced their betrothal. Her father owned land near Providence, and no doubt she and Reuben would settle there. As Calvin had forewarned Prudence, Pardon had acknowledged his plan to sell his land and move to Illinois, and just a few days ago, he stopped by with the news a gentleman from New London had made him a good offer for his property.

"I'm caught up in a tempest," she confided to Almira. "Everything I've come to depend on is being uprooted by the gale." Most of all, her heart was in turmoil over Calvin. He was staying with the Kneelands, and had come to see her only twice in the past week. Cordial and pleasant as always, he did not once bring up their last conversation, but asked if there was anything he could do to help her get ready for the return of her pupils.

"I won't be here much longer," he added. "Your father has convinced me Illinois is the new land of opportunity. I don't doubt there's room there for a Baptist minister. Who knows? I may go back to farming myself. I have wonderful memories of my early years working the land alongside my uncle."

Despite the heat of the day, Prudence felt herself grow cold. "I never thought of you as a farmer," she managed to answer. "What of Elizabeth? Will it not be hard for her to be so far from everything she has known?"

"As the saying goes, the young are resilient. Elizabeth is primed for adventure. Perhaps she will forget about pirates and become captivated with frontiersmen." He paused and became serious. "I do regret, though, she will not be able to say goodbye to you, Prudence. You mean a great deal to her."

"As she does to me." Prudence choked back the emotions threatening to undo her. "Everything is happening so fast, Calvin. My father moving. You leaving. Are you sure you need go quite so soon?"

His brown eyes regarded her gravely. "I have no reason to stay here, Prudence. I miss Elizabeth, and once I have reclaimed her from her aunt, I will continue heading west. You will be busy with your school again soon and have no time to think of me. You have accomplished your purpose here in Canterbury, and I am glad for you."

"No matter what I am doing, I shall always think of you, Calvin." She reached out to touch his arm, but he drew away and mounted his horse.

"I will come see you again before I leave," he promised. "When do your students return?"

"The new term starts September tenth."

"Then I will make it a point to come by the evening of the ninth to meet them all before I leave and to say goodbye to Almira and Marcy as well."

The days passed quickly, and despite her sorrow over Calvin, Prudence found herself caught up in preparing for the new term. It was marvelous to be free of the bond that had hung over her head for so long and to know now Mr. Judson and his ilk could say nothing about her legal rights to maintain her school. The girls returned one by one, rested from an extended break and eager to be in class again.

When Sarah Hammond opened the door in early September, Almira remarked, "You look as though you spent the whole of August growing. Why you are nearly as tall as your sister. She won't be able to call you her 'little' sister much longer."

Sarah smiled, showing a gleaming row of teeth, and her sister Ann Eliza laughed. "Taller doesn't mean smarter," she observed. "She'll always be my little sis."

All the girls were relieved Miss Crandall's trials were over, though disappointed the court's indecision had left their status open to further question.

"I don't mind so much what those old judges say," said Julia Williams. "I just want to finish my schooling so I can be a teacher. I met a young man this summer, Henry Garnett. He's thinking of becoming a missionary to Jamaica. Think how exciting it would be to go with him."

"I met someone in New York, too." Eliza Glasko flushed prettily. "He's also studying to be a teacher. He said I was the smartest girl he ever met, and he's very impressed by my learning, Miss Crandall."

Prudence was thrilled at her girls' progress and goals for their future, remembering what Hattie Doud had said months ago about opportunities opening to them when they got an education.

"It makes it all seem worthwhile, doesn't it?" Almira remarked.

"Yes, it has all been worthwhile," Prudence echoed, with only a small pang of misgiving in her heart. "I have an idea. Since the weather is so beautiful, let's have a gathering on the lawn tomorrow night. It will be a sort of celebration. We can have lemonade and cakes after supper, and sing songs... We'll have quilts on the grass to sit on and lanterns to keep the bugs away."

Her sister joined enthusiastically in the plan; but surprisingly, Marcy was hesitant. "I'll take care of the fixin's," she agreed, "but don't 'spect me to hang around. Sarah's baby may come any time now, and I promised I'd be there."

An almost full moon hung low in the eastern sky when Calvin Philleo arrived the evening of September ninth. He tethered his horse and carriage by the barn and tipped his hat to Mr. Olney.

"Wal, Reverend, looks like you's ready fer a journey. Headin' out West, I hear."

161

"I am, indeed, Olney. In the morning, I start for New Haven to get my daughter, and after that I'll be bound for Illinois. I want to get an early start, and I was hoping you could find a spot for me to stay tonight. I don't want to trouble Miss Crandall, seeing she has her hands full with all her students. How many are there, anyway? It looks like quite a group out there on the lawn."

Olney nodded. "More'n two dozen, I guess. They's an extry bed in our place, it so happens. That is, iffen yore willin' t' share a space." He began rubbing Jackson's glossy hide. "He remembers me. Wants more o' them oats, I reckon."

Turning his horse over to Mr. Olney's capable hands, Calvin wandered to the front lawn looking for Prudence. The same cream-colored gown she had worn for the last trial swirled around her trim figure as she came to him with outstretched hands. He caught his breath at her touch. Her sparkling eyes and animated smile filled him with wordless desire.

"Oh, I am glad to see you, Calvin. Come meet my girls and share some cake with me. Marcy made it especially for tonight. We're celebrating a new beginning."

The girls shyly greeted Calvin, and cast curious glances at their teacher, who stayed close beside the handsome man throughout the evening. Eventually, they settled down in groups on the quilts, chatting and laughing together as they enjoyed cake and lemonade. Julia Williams and Elizabeth Smith blended their voices in a melancholy tune, and soon the others joined in, the melody floating on the gentle air.

"Miss Almira," Calvin asked, "why aren't you singing along? My daughter tells me you have a fine voice."

"Sometimes I just like to listen. Their voices have a special quality that touches my heart. Even if they are not trained singers, their music is filled with emotion... with yearning."

She glanced across the lawn where Prudence was pouring lemonade for several girls. "You can see why my sister is so passionate about educating them. They are truly remarkable."

"In my mind, the students are no more remarkable than their teachers. You and Prudence are doing a wonderful work here. I hope you continue."

Almira looked down, tracing the squares on the quilt with her finger. "I don't know about me. I have been caught up in Prudy's mission, and I don't know if I have found mine yet. She is fond of quoting the saying, 'There is a time for everything under the sun.' I wonder how one knows when it is time for change."

Calvin's eyes followed Prudence as she moved among the girls. He shook his head ruefully. "I wonder that, too, Almira. I don't think I have figured that one out yet, and I am much older than you. Here I am on the verge of a total change in my life, and where I should be certain of my path, I find my heart unwilling to follow."

Prudence rejoined them. "What are you two talking about so seriously?" Gracefully, she sat down beside her sister.

"Mr. Philleo was just telling me that despite his great age, he has not figured out all the mysteries of life." Almira attempted to cast off the somber mood which had captured her.

"Well, I am quite old," he laughed. "I remember Elizabeth telling you I was nearly forty the first time we met, and now that I have passed that milestone, I am practically in my dotage compared to you, Prudence."

"I don't ever think of age." She knew that was not quite true. What she wanted to say, but did not have the courage, was that Calvin was the most appealing man she had ever known, and she never thought of the ten or more years between them as any kind of barrier. "That is, I try not to think of my own age," she corrected herself. "What is the mystery you have yet to solve?"

"Ask your sister to explain it," he said.

"I was only wondering," Almira murmured, "how one knows when it is time for a change. Thee knows, Prudy, how the Scripture goes, 'there is a time to be born, and a time to die, a time to laugh and a time to mourn,' and all the rest. Thee has always been so certain of the path. How is it so easy for thee to know the next step?"

"It is never easy," she contradicted. "I try hard to follow the leading of Providence and the teachings of the Word. That is why I spend much time reading my Bible. Then, once the decision is made, I don't look back."

"Ah," said Calvin, "then that accounts for your self-assurance. Do you never question your conscience? Are you never tempted to follow your heart?"

"I pray my heart will be one with my conscience," she answered, "and both submitted to the will of God."

"Miss Crandall, look!" One of the girls was pointing across the Green at the Judson home. "Did you see that? One minute all the lamps were burning, and then they all went out. All at once. Do you hear voices over there?"

Prudence strained to hear, but could not distinguish any sound coming from the darkened house.

"Perhaps it is a reminder," she said, "that it is getting late. We have classes in the morning, young ladies, and should pick up our things and get ready for bed now."

After a little good-natured grumbling that meant nothing at all, the girls moved toward the house. Some headed toward the quarters downstairs that had been converted to bedrooms since the number of pupils had increased, and the rest climbed the stately staircase to their rooms and were soon settled in for the night.

Prudence lingered on the front steps talking with Calvin, not wanting to say goodbye this one last time. "I would promise to write," she said, "but I have no idea if the mail is even carried so far west to where you will be."

"Illinois has been in the Union for more than a decade now, Prudence. It can't be that primitive. Maybe I'll settle near Springfield, where that Abraham Lincoln fellow lives. Be certain I will find a way to let you know where we are. Elizabeth would not want to lose touch with you. Nor would I." His voice was thick with feeling as he squeezed her hand. "I will save my goodbye for morning. I couldn't think of leaving without one of Marcy's famous breakfasts."

"Almira and I have a packet of things for Elizabeth. Books and so on. Goodness knows if there will be any schools out there."

"Perhaps you and Almira should come and start one. I hear there are Indian tribes out there who are just waiting for someone to come along and see to their higher learning."

"Now you are teasing me. As if I don't have enough of a cause to fight here, you suggest I start a school for the chief's daughters?"

"I think you would be capable, my Prudence, of doing anything you put your mind to. I was only half teasing you." He dropped her hand and stepped into the shadows.

She stood a moment on the porch, her eyes closed in wordless prayer as a jumble of images paraded through her brain. The cold eyes of Judge Daggett and the sneer on Judson's lips. The faces, both white and black, of her students. The echo of Elizabeth's words -- "I am only sorry I had to leave and we could not all be in the same school together." A vision of Calvin holding out his arms to her. She reached for him, and his face faded. It was replaced by the memory of Whittington's mangled body, and she bit her lip to repress a groan.

She pressed her throbbing head against the cool elegance of the porch columns. "How does one know when it is time for a change?" she whispered, remembering Almira's question. "Oh, I pray I am doing Thy will, Lord. I believe I am, for Thee has given me this work to do, but please show me if I am not. If it is time for a change, please show me quickly."

Tears welled up in her eyes, and a sob escaped from her full heart. The moon climbed higher in the sky and the air grew cold and still. At last she composed herself and tiptoed to her bedroom.

Chapter Nineteen

September 9, 1834

Prudence sat on the edge of her bed, weaving her blonde hair into a long braid. The only light in the room came from moonbeams filtering through the curtains. Almira's shape was a dark lump under the coverlet. Silence shrouded the house when at last she finished her braiding and slipped into bed. It had been a long day, and she soon fell into an exhausted slumber.

Trancelike, she moved into the kitchen where Marcy and Almira were fixing breakfast. The snap and crackle sounded reassuringly from the stove, but oddly, the women were wearing aprons over their nightgowns and moving around in silent slow motion. Just as Marcy opened the oven door, flames burst from the stove and Almira dropped the pan of biscuits on the floor with a loud bang.

Prudence awoke with a start. She had heard a noise in the room below!

The noise came again, louder than before. The blast of shattering windowpanes was followed by the thud of a heavy object striking against a wall. Hearing muffled shouts below her window, she bolted from her bed and peered down into the shadows. Almira stirred in her sleep.

"*Almira.*" Her voice was urgent. "*Get up at once.*"

"What's wrong?" Almira joined her at the window. She felt a sea of evil surrounded their home, full of dark creatures rushing upon it in murky waves. The sinister shapes, armed with iron bars and heavy beams, emitted grunts and curses as they circled the house. The gloom of night and smoking torches had transfigured the people of Canterbury into demons bent on destruction.

Paralyzed by terror, the women stared at the mob milling in the yard below. Prudence caught sight of a familiar face in the ghostly glow. Rufus Adams stood in the center of the group, his pale features twisted in contempt. "Pretending to be a school... nothing but a bawdy house for niggers... we'll show 'em..." Garbled words spewed from his mouth, and brandishing an axe he charged toward the house. At the sound of splintering wood, his companions rushed forward with a savage whoop.

Almira whimpered, and shaking in fright, collapsed in her sister's arms. Despite her own racing heartbeat, Prudence dragged Almira away from the window. "Hush, Almy. We must stay calm and think what to do."

She winced as another loud report of breaking glass reached their ears, followed by frightened screams within the house -- a crescendo in the darkness, even drowning out the horrible epithets being hurled at them by the assailants in the yard.

"The girls!" cried Prudence. "We must find them!"

Prudence raced down the stairs, driven by the cries of the terror-stricken pupils, while Almira rushed through the hallway to gather the girls shrieking outside their doors.

"Let's get downstairs with the others," Almira called, urging them toward the stairs. Just as they reached the landing, a heavy stone exploded through the Palladian window, sending missiles of glass in all directions. Stinging pain sliced Almira's cheek as she herded the girls through the rubble and down the staircase.

With heart pounding and legs shaking, Prudence stumbled to the downstairs bedrooms. "Into the hallway," she gasped. "Come with me. All of you."

Almira and her group met the others huddling against the walls of the hallway. The weeping girls clung to each other while pandemonium swelled around their home. "Jesus, protect us," wailed Ann Eliza, rocking young Sarah in her arms as a stone came sailing past them.

"They're coming in!" cried Mariah.

The front door shuddered under the heavy pounding, and raucous voices called out, "Yah, yah, ye fancy little darkies! Whut good's yore book learnin' now? Let us have a look at ye! C'mon out and sing us another song!"

Again the door groaned, and slurred obscenities whined through the darkness. "How 'bout a love song? Sing us a love song, will ya?"

"They're drunk." Julia's voice held both scorn and fear.

When the door held fast against their ramming, the men turned and attacked the stately fan windows with an iron bar until the hallway filled with a rain of glass.

"Over here!" someone roared. "Look it all this fancy glass! More'n enuff for a monkey cage!" The mob advanced to the schoolroom windows, methodically smashing every pane until nothing was left.

"Well, men, that's a good night's work, I say!" bellowed one. "There's no way now these darkies can stay."

"Let this be a warning to you, Miss Crandall!" another screamed. "There's no room in Canterbury for your kind of trash!"

"Go back to Africa, ya niggers!" shouted a hateful voice.

"Damn the abolitionists!" The crowd took up the chant until at last the clamor faded and the drunken mob stumbled out of sight.

Inside, sobs and moans filled the darkness of the house. On shaking legs, Prudence crept into the parlor and returned holding a small lamp. The flickering light revealed a nightmare of devastation. Stones and sticks littered the hallway. Blood smeared the floor where girls had stepped barefoot through the jagged glass. Almira's white muslin nightgown was splattered crimson with blood that still flowed from a deep cut by her right eye. The dank night air swirled through the broken windows like a miasma of death. Hastily, Prudence ripped a corner of her own gown and pressed the wadded cloth against her sister's wound.

"Marcy! Charles!" Her voice ricocheted down the murky hallway. "Where are you, Marcy?" *Dear Lord,* she prayed, *what has happened to her and Charles? What shall I do now with these girls? Where will they be safe?*

Her overwrought nerves lurched as Emilia screamed, "There's a man at the window! He's comin' in!" The hunched figure of a man stood on the porch, peering through a broken window pane. He held an eerily smoking torch aloft as he reached through the opening and groped for the latch of the door.

"Who's there?" Prudence demanded.

"It's all right," a faltering voice called out.

"It's Reverend Hobbes." Prudence recognized the pastor of the church on the Green as he held the light closer to his face.

"Don't be afraid. I've come to help."

Picking her way over the piles of glass and rubble, Prudence shoved the door open and let him in. His eyes filled with alarm as he surveyed the scene before him. "This is dreadful. Dreadful. This business has gone too far, and I am ashamed I let myself be intimidated by the wicked men who did this. God forgive me. I will be part of their hatred no longer. Miss Crandall, I have unlocked the meeting house. You and your students will find safe shelter there for the rest of this night."

With cries of relief, the girls followed Reverend Hobbes into the open. Prudence came through the door last, still carrying her lamp. The breeze shifted direction, and she raised her head in alarm. "Smoke! I smell smoke! It's the barn!" She rounded the corner of the house and saw Mr. Olney and his wife frantically battling blue and orange tongues of flame that licked the side of the barn. Mr. Hobbes thrust his torch in Julia's hand and sprinted toward the barn as quickly as his old legs would carry him. Nerissa's strong arms pumped like a machine, drawing bucket after bucket of water from the old well, as the men repeatedly doused the fire. In minutes, the crackling flames faded to angry hissing. The fire died. Choking on the smoke, Prudence dashed into the barn, freeing the terrified, screaming horses and leading them to fresh air.

"Praise be to Jesus," Mr. Olney panted, wiping the soot from his sweaty face, "my Nerissa's a light sleeper. We got that ole fire out afore it got a-goin'. Jist *wait* 'til we gets them varmints whut started it. An' Miz Prudence, ye saved them horses, shur."

She looked wildly around the hellish scene and saw Calvin's carriage in the same place he had left it, but there was no sign of him or of Jackson.

"Where is Calvin?" Her voice was a hoarse croak. "Have you seen him?"

Mr. Olney shook his head. "I'se been busy, Miz Prudence. I don't know where he's got to." He looked to his wife. "Rissy, did you see where Mr. Calvin done went?"

The woman spread her hands and shrugged. "I s'pose he's after them villains. I b'leeve I saw him ride off toward the woods. Or mebbe he jist plain run off."

Prudence whirled upon the Reverend. "Oh, Mr. Hobbes!" she cried, "Can you please see my girls safely to the meeting house? Almira will help, and Julia, too. I know Calvin. He would never run away from danger. More likely, he is heading straight into it. I must try to find him before something awful happens."

"I will do anything I can," Hobbes assured her, "to try to make up for my shameful treatment of you and your students. I should never have let Captain Fenner turn you away from the meeting that first Sunday, but I was a coward, you see. I don't know that there is anything you can do to help Reverend Philleo, but I understand your need to try. The girls will be safe with me and my wife. She is wonderful at nursing and comforting the injured."

Prudence scarcely heard the last part of this speech. She was calling for Mr. Olney to help her get a bridle on the mare she had just led from the barn. As she struggled onto the horse, Nerissa came running out of the house and tossed a coat to Prudence. "Put this on, honey, or you'll ketch yore death o' cold."

*****

Calvin Philleo tossed and turned on the lumpy cot in the Olney's humble house. He was glad for a place to stay the night, and reflected he had bedded down in less comfortable places, but he had too much on his mind to sleep. He hoped to get an early start to his sister-in-law's home in the morning, but at the same time, he was reluctant to leave. He had spoken truly to Almira earlier, although he had determined the new direction his life would take, his heart was loath to follow. It would be so different if Prudence were going with him to Illinois. How he would miss her friendship. She made him smile with her wit and good humor, she made him think with her sharp comments, and she made him proud with her high ideals. Most of all, she made him long for the intimacy of marriage and the feeling of her in his arms. The thought brought a groan from his throat, and he turned his face to the wall. It was hard to surrender one's dreams and desires to God's will, even if one was a minister. He tried in vain to dismiss visions of her sweet mouth and smooth skin as he finally fell into a sound sleep.

It was Mr. Olney's shouts which awakened him. "Fire! Fire! Oh, Lordy, Lordy..." The hired man dashed through the door as if pursued by the devil. "Git up an' he'p us, man..."

Quickly pulling on his pants and grabbing his boots, Calvin was out the door in seconds, filled with alarm at the sight of dozens of cloaked figures scurrying away from the yard. There was barely enough moonlight to see what had happened to the house, but it was clear the place had been vandalized. The Olneys were racing toward the barn, where a blaze had come alive in one corner. Rage hotter than flames sent blood racing to his brain. Would nothing put a stop to Judson's insane obsession?

At that moment, he saw a gray-clad form leap on a horse and head toward the woods. Resolve filled his heart. He would not let the miscreant go free! Those who had done this evil deed would be brought to justice and pay for their sins.

He ran into the barn, and within a few moments had Jackson saddled and was in fevered pursuit, but the figure on horseback had vanished. Following his instincts, he headed toward the wooded area beyond the Green and picked his way warily across the creek and toward the river.

Jackson moved under him, sure-footed and sensitive. He paused. With a soft whinny he lifted his head and changed direction, and before long came to a small clearing. There was a man on foot, running across the ground. Spurring Jackson forward, Calvin overtook the fellow. He sprang from his horse, hit the ground running, and brought the man down with a low tackle. A whoosh of air exploded from the vandal's lungs as his face smashed into the dirt.

The man reeked of rum and sweat, but he appeared to be unarmed. Blood spurted from a gash in his lip as he tried to spit out a broken tooth. Calvin pinned him to the ground. "Who are you, and how dare you attack innocent women in the middle of the night? Speak up! You live in Canterbury?"

The fellow rolled his pale eyes under a mop of greasy hair. "No, I ain't. I mean I don't. I live in... Plainfield. I was just passin' by. I didn't attack no women, neither." He plucked another tooth from his mouth and pressed his hand against the flow of blood.

Calvin felt an urge to smack the man. "A likely story. I saw you on the lawn there at the Crandall school." He saw the man was young and thin, but he did not look like anyone he had ever seen around Canterbury. "So, if you are from Plainfield, what are you doing here?"

"I heard all about that school. Everybody knows they've been tryin' to get them niggers to leave for a long time, and not even the law could make 'em go. They had another school like that somewhere a coupla years back, and the people there took it on theirselves to wreck the school, so they had to close it."

"So what?" Calvin grabbed his throat and shook him. "What does that have to do with you?"

The captive's eyes grew wider with fear. "I heard the people of

169

Canterbury was going to do the same thing here. They said they needed all the help they could get, and if anybody come along to help out, they'd give them money. So I thought I'd see for myself, and I come on over from Brooklyn-- I mean, Plainfield. I never attacked no one. All I done is throw a few rocks, and I ain't even that good of an aim." He tried to laugh, but the sound came out as a slurpy whimper as more red stained his shirt.

"You're a coward and a liar, whatever else you are. I'll see to it you're punished for your part." Without loosening his grip, Calvin said, "Maybe I'll take you back to the Crandall house, and if you'll tell us all you know about who's involved with this business -- especially who offered to pay you -- we'll show you some mercy. You ever see the jail in Brooklyn? It's not a nice place."

He dragged the young man to his feet and pulled his hands behind his back to tie them with a rope, when suddenly he heard the loud report of a rifle, and a slug whizzed by his head. Two men on horseback emerged from the trees.

"Stop right there," growled a low voice. "You're another nigger lover, hey? We've seen you hanging around that school with those Crandall women before. Are you after them or the tasty little black girls?" A squat, muscular man with a whip in his hand got off his mount and walked toward Calvin. A white scar across the man's cheek gleamed in the moonlight. The scoundrel looked familiar, but Calvin did not know his name.

"Let loose of that kid, old man." He flicked the whip in a menacing manner. Calvin let go of the young ruffian, who lost no time making his escape.

The other man, taller and wirier, grabbed Calvin from behind, holding him in a viselike grip. Calvin struggled to free himself, as the man laughed and breathed whisky in his face. "Let's show him just how we feel about white people who go up against their own kind, Ira. Give 'em a taste of that whip."

An ugly grin twisted the features of the man called Ira. "Nah, I'd ruther give him a taste of my knuckles." He came at Calvin with his fists, plowing first into his stomach and knocking the air from his lungs. The tall man snickered again, and jerked his arms tighter. "Go for it, Ira. I've got him."

By the feeble light in the clearing, Calvin Philleo saw the unholy power of hatred glitter in the man's eyes and knew he was about to get the beating of his life. "Dear Jesus, help me!" he cried aloud. A fist like a cannonball smashed into his jaw.

Chapter Twenty

Grateful for the moonlight, Prudence followed the road that led east from town, urging her mare forward as fast as she dared go. It was the dead of night, and Prudence shivered with cold despite the jacket Nerissa had given her. The events of the past hour were a blur in her mind. From the first crash of a stone coming through the parlor window to the appearance of Reverend Hobbes, the whole ordeal was a lurid dream. Now Calvin had disappeared. After the first shock wore off, she realized the futility of trying to find him on her own. What would she be able to do if she did find him? All she knew was he was in danger, and she had to rescue him. She was a few miles from George and Sarah Fayerweather's cottage, and it was there she turned for help.

As she neared the cottage, she was surprised to see lights in the windows. George's hound dog bounded off the porch, his mournful baying alerting the people in the house. George himself stepped out, followed by Charles Harris. Both were fully dressed and wide awake.

"Miss Prudence, whatever are you doing here in the middle of the night? Is something wrong?" Charles was the first to reach her side.

Gasping for breath, Prudence got off the horse. "I've come for help. We were attacked tonight. A mob of people set upon my house. They broke all the windows and smashed everything they could get their hands on. They even tried to burn down the barn *with the animals still inside.*"

"*Good Lord.* Was anyone hurt?" Charles was aghast. By this time, George and Marcy had joined them, and Sally Harris also came out of the house. As clearly and quickly as she could, Prudence described to her horrified listeners the violent actions of the mob and the condition of the girls she had left in the care of Reverend Hobbes.

"Cal-- Mr. Philleo is gone. He was spending the night, planning to be on his way to New Haven in the morning, and when he saw what happened, he must have given chase after some of the men who started the fire in the barn. They are all crazy drunk and capable of any violence. I fear what may happen to him if he falls into their hands."

Ever the man of action, Charles immediately took charge. "You saddle our horses, brother," he said to George, "and get your pistol, too. We'll take the dog along. Too bad we don't have something to give Bruno the scent."

"*We do.*" Marcy exclaimed. "That jacket, Miss Prudence, that's his, ain't it?"

In amazement, Prudence peeled off the jacket. Recognizing the blue worsted jacket Calvin had been wearing as he sat beside her on the grass that night, she stifled a sob. Nerissa must have grabbed the first coat she came to in the house and given it to her. It had to be Providence that guided her hands to Calvin's garment.

"I'm coming with you," Prudence declared, oblivious to the fact she was barefoot and in her nightgown. "I'm the reason Calvin is in trouble, and I have to help him."

Charles shook his head. "It won't help him for you to put yourself in harm's way, too, Miss Prudence. Besides, the mare is tuckered out and would slow us down considerable."

In a few minutes, George returned with the horses. "You wait here," Charles said to Prudence, "and pray. We'll find him and be back as soon as we can. We're wasting time now." He swung into the saddle and grabbed the reins. "Just pray we get to him before it's too late."

Prudence looked around in a moment of bewilderment. "What are you all doing here in the middle of the night, anyway? Why is Sally here?"

As the men galloped away, Marcy put her arm around Prudence's shoulders and drew her toward the house. "It's Sarah's time," she said quietly. "Her baby is comin' tonight."

Prudence's legs gave way beneath her, and she sank onto the porch steps. "Oh, my goodness. Is she in the house?"

Marcy chuckled. "Of course, she is. Where else would she be? An' things is goinjist fine. A little slow, but fine. Mother Harris knows all about bringin' babies. Now you go on inside, and soon's I see to this horse, I'll take care of you. Le's find you something to wear besides that nightgown."

*****

Still in a state of semi-shock, Almira and the schoolgirls followed Mr. Hobbes across the Green, many of them limping on bleeding feet. Mr. Olney went in the house with a lantern to survey the damage done while his wife cautiously entered the bedrooms, collecting blankets and other needful items for the girls' comfort.

Mrs. Hobbes met the group at the door of the meeting house, clucking like a mother hen gathering her chicks to safety. In shock, she noticed the bloody footprints on the steps of the meeting house. "Dear Lord in heaven!" she cried out. "May God punish the villains responsible for *every drop* of this blood. We need bandages, Mr. Hobbes. Run to the house and grab an old sheet from the upstairs linen closet."

Her first concern was caring for the injured, beginning with Almira. Once Almira's own wound was bathed and dressed, she helped Mrs. Hobbes remove the splinters of glass and bandage the cuts of the others. Mr. Hobbes moved among the girls, doling out warm blankets and words of comfort. Though the distressed girls gradually calmed down in the safety and warmth of the meeting house, there was no question of sleep for the rest of the night. In hushed voices, they prayed for Miss Crandall's safe return to them and agonized over the uncertainty of their future.

When Hobbes went to secure the door, he found his wife on her knees applying a scrub brush to the bloodstains on the steps. "What are you doing?" he asked.

"Why, I thought you'd want these steps cleaned off. They're a sorry sight."

He pulled her to her feet and took the brush from her grasp. "Let's leave them there. I want everyone who comes on Sunday to see what comes of bigotry..." His voice trailed away sadly as he pulled the door shut.

*****

Calvin lay facedown in the darkness. He hardly noticed the chill from the damp ground penetrating his thin, blood-soaked shirt. The night was silent save for the chirping of a few heedless insects. Groaning, he tried to push himself to a sitting position, but the pain in his chest mocked his efforts and he sank to the ground again.

His tormentors had tired of beating him and pushed him into a shallow depression. Barely conscious, he heard their threats and curses as they rode away.

He felt fortunate to be alive. He was sure he had a broken rib, and he could feel the lump on the side of his face and taste the blood coursing from his nose and lip. *What made them stop?* His desperate call to the Almighty must have shamed them into sparing his life.

What was he to do now? He spit a mouthful of blood on the ground and tried to whistle. Maybe Jackson would hear his call.

I don't dare lie here waiting to be rescued. Who knows what ruffians are still lurking around? Maybe Ira and his pal will decide to come back and finish me off. Wincing with every movement, he dragged himself a few feet forward. At least he was on level ground now, but still a far cry from being back to the house. The thought of the destruction he had left behind brought more torment to his soul.

Oh, Lord, don't let those innocent girls suffer any more. Protect my Prudence. Help her for once to be as sensible as she is brave. He felt himself drifting into unconsciousness again and fought to stay awake. *She's stubborn. I guess You made her that way. But I can be stubborn, too. If I ever get back, I'll make her see we belong together.* Tears flowed from his eyes, mingling with his blood in a salty river.

He whistled once more, this time with more effect. To his great joy, he heard Jackson's soft whinny and saw the horse coming toward him.

"Come here, old fella. That's it -- stand still. I've got to get back to the school." He managed to grasp a nearby sapling and painfully pulled himself to his feet. He got hold of the dangling reins in his left hand and stretched his right arm across the horse's back. Unsure of how to proceed, he clung to the saddle and gratefully leaned on Jackson's comforting bulk. With his strength ebbing away, he knew he could not hold on for long. *Lord, you have brought me this far. Now I need a miracle..."*

*****

George and Charles rode side by side toward the river. "It seems like Bruno wants to go this way, and we've got no better lead," George said. "I hate to say it, but I kinda feel glad to have something to do. I was getting mighty jumpy back at the house. I never thought havin' a baby was such a hard thing, or I mebbe wouldn't have done it. Hope she's gonna be all right.

"I can't hardly believe those white folks attacking the school like that. Can you, Charles? Jist seems plumb crazy they'd go to such lengths on account of a few gals wantin' to get some learning. I'm glad my Sarah got done with her education."

Charles was deep in thought as they rode. "I wonder what she'll do now. Miss Crandall, I mean. I feel a whole lot responsible for what's happened, because of Sarah being my sister and Marcy and me begging for Miss Crandall to let Sarah in the school. That's how the whole mess started."

"That don't make sense, Charles Harris, and you know it. How can it be yore fault if a mob of white good-for-nothings acts like a bunch of devils? Quit blamin' yourself, and concentrate on finding Mr. Philleo. It seems Miss Prudence sets quite a store by him, and she's more worried about him than--"

"What in tarnation is that thing over by those trees? See it? It looks like it might be a horse."

"It *is* a horse. But he ain't movin' -- just standin' in that thicket. *Oh, Lordy.* There's someone -- or something -- hangin' on to that critter for dear life."

*****

Prudence paced the floor of the Fayerweather's small parlor, tension in every muscle of her body. She could hear Sarah's groans coming from the bedroom, and Sally's soothing words. She prayed the baby would come soon, for Sarah sounded exhausted with the long labor. "First babies take the longest," Marcy had informed her, although she was uncertain how Marcy, who had never had a baby, knew so much.

She herself felt useless. "Maybe I ought to ride back to the church," she said to Marcy. "I am so worried about Almy and the rest. I hope and pray they will be safe. I wouldn't even put it past that mob to try to break into the meeting house itself. You won't believe it, Marcy, when you see the damage to our house. It makes me sick to think of it."

"I'se so sorry Charles and me wasn't there," Marcy lamented. "I know my Charles woulda done his best to chase them away and protect us all."

"I know he would have tried," Prudence said, "but there were so many of them, I fear he would have been harmed. I am just grateful he and George were willing to try to find Calvin." She burst into tears. "Oh, I wish I had gone with them. I can't bear this waiting and not knowing what has happened. If he has been hurt because of me, I don't know what I will do. He is the best... the most wonderful... the most unselfish man I have ever known. I love him, Marcy, and I have never told him how I feel."

Marcy wrapped her arms tightly around Prudence's trembling shoulders. "You'll have a chance yet, Miss Prudence. They'll find him. You'll see him again and make everything right."

Though she knew Marcy's promises were well meant, she could not stop crying. All the emotions she had held in check for the past months had been loosed by the tragic events of this horrible night. She threw herself onto the sofa and sobbed her heart out into the patchwork pillows.

"Marcy!" Sally called urgently from the bedroom. "We need you! Come here!"

Marcy darted from the parlor, leaving Prudence alone. Her prayers were a tangle of entreaties to the Almighty, first praying for Sarah, then for the girls back at the meeting house, and over and over for Calvin.

Sarah's cries grew more intense, and she could hear Sally Harris coaching her daughter. "Push, honey. That's right, Sarah. You're a strong woman, and you're gonna have a lovely baby any time now. Take a deep breath and push. One more. Don't you quit now, my girl -- hear?"

Prudence had never before been this close to the drama of birth, but she knew childbirth was dangerous. She had sad memories of her own dear mother dying when Almira was just a toddler. The little brother they longed for had died along with his mother, leaving them and their father bereft. But their mother had been weak and ill ever since Almy's birth, not young and strong as Sarah was. Prudence pushed the reminiscence from her mind and prayed again for Sarah.

"You're doin' jist fine, honey. Hang on to my hands and breathe. Like this, darlin'. Tha's right. Another push, here we go..."

In spite of everything else that had happened that night, Prudence was drawn into the wonder of a new life coming into the world. She found herself holding her breath along with Sarah each time her mother commanded her to push. No words could describe the awe she felt when at long last she heard Marcy cry in delight, "It's a girl." Then the miraculous wail of the newborn baby filled the night with joy and hope.

Marcy emerged from the bedroom with a huge smile on her face. "Mother Harris is getting her all cleaned up, and in a little minute you can come see the baby. Oh, she's a purty one. Looks jist like her mama." She scurried off to the kitchen for more hot water.

"What a relief. I don't think I could ever be as strong as Sarah. I'm worn out just listening to all the goings-on in there."

Prudence suddenly became aware of her own untidy condition. In her anxiety, she had not thought to wash the horse smell away or put on the clean clothes Marcy had given her. "Where can I get washed up, Marcy?" She pattered into the kitchen behind the happy "Auntie" Marcy.

A few minutes later, the faint violet promise of a new day was just rippling across the earth when Prudence took the infant girl in her arms. Inhaling its sweetness, she held the baby's warm cheek against her own and kissed her head. "Maybe Dawn would be a good name for her," she suggested. "Or Violet."

"Oh, no, we already have her name picked out, but I can't tell you 'til George comes back." Sarah's face was wreathed in smiles. "Oh, her daddy is going to be so proud. She's a real beauty, isn't she, Miss Prudence? I hope he gets here soon." She paused, and her face grew serious. "I heard just a little about the trouble at the school tonight. I'm so sorry, and I do hope they find Mr. Philleo."

Prudence willed her voice to be calm. "I believe they will, Sarah. God has promised never to leave us, and I believe that is true. He watched over you while you had this beautiful baby, and He will watch over Calvin, too."

No sooner had she said the words than Sally, who had gone to the parlor for a rest, poked her beaming face in the room. "I heard horses on the road and took a peep through the curtains. You'll want to see who it is, Miss Prudence."

Prudence wasted no time in running to meet them. Her heart leapt when she saw the early morning mist swirling around the flanks of three horses. The third horse was Jackson, and on his back he bore the drooping form of his master. "Calvin!" she cried out. "My dear Calvin!"

The exhausted brothers-in-law helped Calvin from his horse, brought him into the house, and laid him on the sofa.

"How is Sarah?" George's concern was all for his young wife.

"You're a daddy," his mother-in-law informed him. "You have a great baby girl."

With a shout of delight, he vanished at once into the bedroom.

"I'd better see to those horses," Charles said. "They've had a hard night's work, too."

"Lucky I still got lots of boilin' water," Marcy observed, as she went to gather the supplies needed to wash Calvin's wounds.

Prudence took Calvin's hands in her own and bent to kiss his face.

Her tears fell on blood-stained cheeks, and she examined his swollen eye and jaw. He shivered.

"Marcy," she called," bring a blanket, too. Is there black salve in the cupboard?" With trembling fingers she began to unbutton his blood-spattered shirt.

"I'm all right," he insisted through gritted teeth. "It's my rib that hurts the worst. I think it's broken."

"Don't talk now," Prudence whispered. "Just try to rest. Oh, Calvin, I was so afraid for thee. Thank the Lord thee is alive. I am never letting thee out of my sight again."

Wincing, he managed a feeble grin. "Is that a promise? If so, I'm glad to hear it." He reached up and touched her hair. The neat braid had long since come undone, and her hair flowed in golden waves past her shoulders. "You look beautiful with your hair all hanging down like that. Like an angel."

After Calvin was made as comfortable as possible on the sofa, Sally called the others into the kitchen. She had sliced some bread and cheese and gave them each a mug of tea.

Charles took a sip of the scalding liquid and helped himself to a bit of cheese.

"Don't keep us a-wonderin' son," admonished Sally. "What happened?"

"Well, we woulda been lost without Bruno's nose, but the dog took us way down by the river. There's a tangle of trees and brush down there, but we finally found Mr. Philleo. He was leaning on his horse -- barely enough strength to stand up -- and we could see he'd taken an awful beating.

"He caught one of the vandals, all right, but then he got himself caught by two more. He thinks the first one was just a thug from another town, but he did find out someone -- probably Judson -- was paying for men to join in the attack at your house. He's almost sure the two who beat him up are from Canterbury, and says he'd recognize them in a minute."

"Lucky we got there when we did." George had rejoined them, leaving Sarah sleeping with the baby. "He's pretty bad hurt, and layin' on the cold ground didn't do him any good neither."

"It wasn't luck," Prudence said thoughtfully. "It was the Providence of God, and the kindness of you two good Samaritans going to his rescue."

*****

Somehow everyone managed to find a spot to take a few hours' rest, but by eight o'clock, after an affectionate farewell to her new namesake, Prudence Crandall Fayerweather, Prudence was on her way home, anxious to find out how Almira and the others had fared through the long night.

As she approached the Green, she spied Andrew Judson standing near the edge of his property, gazing across the way at her house. She shouted out his name and urged the horse forward to cut off retreat to his house.

"Ah, Miss Crandall."He gestured weakly toward the bleak prospect of her yard. "Your beautiful home... I had nothing to do with it... regrettable... most regrettable..."

She stopped him with her upraised palm. "Save your breath, Judson, and spare me your hypocrisy." She spit out the words. "Whether or not your hand threw the stones, I know you are delighted my school is demolished. Do not think victory is yours. Truth may be crushed, but it will ever rise again. What happened here last night will not be forgotten. It may take one year, or it may take one hundred years, but the doors of education will open to every man, woman, and child in America regardless of skin color. You cannot win." With a sharp flick of the reins, she cantered across the Green, leaving the dumbfounded man staring after her.

By the time she reached the house, all the girls were there, shuffling through the rooms with cries of dismay and trying to clean up the rubble which filled their home.

Splintered wood framed the once-gleaming windows which were now reduced to thousands of shattered pieces. More than ninety windows had been destroyed by iron bars and huge stones flung at the house. The damage to the barn was minimal, thanks to the swift response of the Olneys, but the charred boards were yet another witness of the hatred of the Canterbury citizens and the continuing danger to Prudence and her students.

Almira came running when she saw her sister at the door. "Oh, Prudy. Thank God thee is all right. Where has thee been? What happened to Calvin?"

"All good news," Prudence answered. "Sarah and George are the happy parents of a darling baby girl. She was born just a few hours ago, and I was there when it happened. They named her after me. Isn't that wonderful? So much has happened, Almy." She proceeded to tell her sister all that had taken place in the hours since she had last seen her.

"Providence watched over us through it all," Almira sighed. "We'll never know what a dreadful fate we could have suffered without God's care. Even this cut could have been much worse." She lifted her hair and touched the inexpertly bandaged wound by her eye.

"*Oh, my dear*," exclaimed Prudence.

"Nothing to worry about," Almira soothed. "It has stopped bleeding, and it isn't very wide. It shouldn't leave much of a scar.

"Mr. Hobbes and his wife were so kind to us all," she went on, "and this morning they set out first thing to contact Samuel May and tell him of our tragedy."

"What about Father and Reuben? Someone should let them know we are all right. They may have already heard news of the attack."

"Mr. Olney sent a messenger already," Almira assured her. "They will probably be here shortly."

"Before they arrive," Prudence answered gravely, "we need to talk. Let's find a place where we won't be disturbed."

Their bedroom proved to be the best place for a serious conversation.

"How are the girls doing, Almy? Besides the injuries they suffered, how are they holding up?"

"Most of them are still terrified," Almira answered frankly. "They want to go back to their homes, and seeing the condition of our house and school, I don't see how we have any other choice."

Prudence reluctantly agreed. "The rooms are unlivable, especially the downstairs, and with the rains coming on in a few weeks, we'll have no protection from the elements. It will take a long time and a huge sum of money for repairs, and even if we could afford them, what assurance do we have we would be safe from another attack? I can't put these girls' lives in danger for any cause."

Almira sighed, crossed the room, and looked out at the grounds below. The once carefully-tended yard was a mass of ruts, mud, and debris, every late-blooming flower was trampled, and even the gate hung askew on the fence. Pain etched her young face with sorrow.

"So this is it. Judson has won."

Tears streamed unheeded down Prudence's cheeks. "Oh, Almy, I don't know if that's true. All we have done cannot be a loss. I thought my success in this venture was the most important thing, but perhaps I was wrong. Maybe obedience is the highest good. I did what my conscience told me was right, and thee did, too. Now we must leave the results to God and to the ages. Perhaps we were called 'for such a time as this,' to bring the nation's attention to the plight of our colored friends. The eyes and ears of our countrymen are opening and a fresh wind of freedom is blowing. We had the privilege of being part of that awakening."

Almira nodded in understanding. "'Act well thy part. There all the honour lies.' Isn't that what Alexander Pope said? Truly, Prudy, thee did thy part well."

"So did thee. Oh, sister, I have no regrets. Thee reminded me yesterday there is 'a time to every purpose,' and thee and I served our purpose and served our Creator. What greater success is there in life?"

They descended the stairs just as their friend Samuel May arrived at the house. His firm jaw sagged and his usually genial countenance was full of remorse. He hugged both sisters in a rare display of feelings and wiped tears from his eyes when he saw the devastation surrounding them. "I never dreamed it would go this far," he exclaimed, folding his handkerchief into a neat white square and tucking it into his pocket. "I am so sorry. I knew Judson was a hateful man, but I would not have believed even him to be capable of this."

"He is not entirely to blame," Prudence pointed out. "This is not the work of one man. The whole community bears the stain of this crime."

"Where are the girls now? What do you intend to do, Miss Prudence?"

"I have little hope of justice being done here," she answered, "since town authorities themselves are the ones responsible. I see no other course for me than to close the school and send the pupils home as speedily as possible. There is no way to guarantee their safety here."

She then shared with him the decision she and Almira had reached, and he was forced to agree with their view of the whole matter.

"I dread telling the girls," she said. "I don't think I can get through a speech to them without completely breaking down. Dear Samuel, would you be willing to talk with them? Almy and I will gather them to the schoolroom, where you can explain it all."

The girls were sequestered behind the closed door of the schoolroom while the sisters waited in the parlor. Hearing the melodic rise and fall of Mr. May's patient voice and occasional sobs from the girls, Prudence and Almira stared grimly at each other. Of all the trials they had suffered, it was the hardest moment of all. They were relieved to hear Pardon and Reuben's voices in the hallway and rushed into their open arms.

Mr. Burleigh was next to arrive on the scene. He had expected to begin a new term of teaching today, but news had reached him early of the catastrophe at the school. Relieved Prudence was unharmed, he turned his attentions to Almira. Shocked at her bandaged face and the pallor of her cheeks, he insisted she sit down and allow him to bring her tea. Prudence looked up sharply when Burleigh sat beside her young sister and tenderly clasped her hand. *Hmm. My little Almy has been keeping secrets from me. I always knew she was the romantic one.*

At last the schoolroom door opened, and a sad and bewildered set of young ladies filed from the meeting. Wordlessly they passed the parlor and made their way to their rooms. Mr. May, looking pale and shaken, nodded to the group huddled in the middle of the drafty parlor.

"Well, I told them," he said tersely. "The words nearly blistered my lips, but I told them.

"Mr. Crandall, I ask your forgiveness for my part in putting your daughters in harm's way. I had no idea it would come to this, but still, I have asked too much of them. They are the bravest, most true-hearted women alive. I know you Quakers consider pride wrong, but I think God would understand if you were proud of your daughters.

"I can feel no pride today. To have to tell twenty-some harmless, well-behaved girls, whose only offense is they want to gain useful knowledge and moral culture, they must go away because the house they live in will not be protected by the so-called officers of justice... Yes, it bows me to shame. I feel ashamed of my fellow countrymen, ashamed of Connecticut, and ashamed of my color.

"I shall spend this day arranging safe transportation for your young ladies to return to their families. Miss Crandall. Mr. Burleigh. Mr. Crandall. Reuben." He nodded to the people assembled in the room, placed his hat upon his head, and departed, his head bowed in dejection.

Later in the afternoon, Levi Kneeland's carriage pulled into the yard. Hearing what had happened to his friend, he had gone to the Fayerweather home and ever so carefully transported Calvin back to Canterbury.

"This fellow won't be going on a journey anytime soon," Levi declared as he assisted Calvin into the house, his arm bound snugly by his side to protect the broken rib. "Deborah and I intend to send for Elizabeth. She'll help us oversee her father's recovery. I'm taking him with me to Packerville, but he wanted to stop here for a few minutes."

"My, what a shambles. Like the toppling of Jericho." He led Calvin through the rooms, shaking his head in dismay over the wreckage. Eventually, he left Calvin with Prudence in the back parlor, which was the least damaged of all the rooms.

"Are you going to be all right, Prudence?" Calvin twined his fingers through hers.

"What a question," she answered. "You are the one who is hurt."

"My wounds will heal in a matter of time, but you have a far greater loss. I heard Almira and Burleigh talking about the closing of the school. I can only imagine the pain that must cause you after all your work and sacrifice. I am deeply, deeply sorry. Will those responsible for this crime be brought to justice or made to pay for their actions?"

She shook her head. "I doubt it. Who would call them to account, since all the authorities in town are in conspiracy against me? My only solace is in knowing that in the end, it is God who will be their judge, and then, I would rather be in my shoes than theirs."

He nodded. "I am tired, Prudy, and I know you must be even more so. Levi is taking me home with him until I am better. Soon, we need to talk. I remember little of what happened after George and Charles found me, but I do recall a certain moment at the Fayerweather cottage when you gave me hope that perhaps we have a future together after all."

"Oh, Calvin, I know now you are my future. I prayed last night -- it seems so long ago now -- that God would show me His will. I never expected such a sudden and dramatic answer, but what happened last night made it clear my work here has come to an end. I can't risk my girls' safety for any reason. The school is closed, and Mr. May is arranging to send them home."

Softly, Calvin stroked her hair. "Are you certain this is what you want?"

This time, she would pay no attention to whether she was blushing. It was time to speak plainly to the man she loved. "I want nothing more than to be your wife."

Even with only one good arm and a swollen lip, Calvin did not let the long-awaited moment slip by. He gathered her close to his side and kissed her tear-smudged face.

"I hear it takes about six weeks for broken ribs to heal. Will that be enough time for you, Prudy, to plan a wedding?"

Her happiness was like a rosebud unfolding in the sun. "That will be plenty of time. I already know what I am going to say... I, Prudence, take thee, Calvin, to be my friend, my soul mate, and my beloved forever..." Softly, she laid her lips upon his. Whatever trials tomorrow brought, there was no question they would meet them together.

Epilogue

July 26, 1876
Elk Falls, Kansas

Dear Sarah,

Thank you so much for writing again. You do not know how I value every word you write. I had not heard of the death of your husband until your letter came. What a good man George was, and how bravely he served his people those years your home in Kingston was a stop along the Underground Railroad. Your children must be a source of great comfort to you in your loss. I think it is wonderful they are giving their lives to do good to others. I am sure it is especially gratifying to you that two of your daughters became teachers. Think how we struggled those years ago in Canterbury for colored girls to have the right to learn! Little did we know that scarcely four years after the school closed and Calvin and I moved away, the state legislature would repeal the hateful Black Law.

I learned recently of the death of our dear old friend, Samuel May. He was one of the best persons I ever knew, and he has gone to that Heaven where soul responds to soul, and love and affection never die. The debt of gratitude I owe to him I can never pay.

It has been two years since my dear Calvin passed away. He was in ill health for several years, and we had to sell our property and stock. I was not able to manage the farm on my own. I am now residing here in Elk Falls with my brother and doing tolerably well. I keep a school for a few of my great-nephews, who are dear children and apt learners. I suppose I will always be a teacher at heart. I am glad Calvin encouraged me to keep a school when we lived in Illinois. He once teased me about starting a school for the Indian tribes. I am contemplating doing just that here in Kansas!

Just think, Sarah, I am now seventy-three years old. I have lived to see emancipation become a reality and also have had the honor of being part of the movement for women's suffrage and the temperance cause. What a magnificent time to be alive and part of the greatness of our country. Now, with the coming of the railroad and settling of the West, our destiny as a nation is glorious. I pray we have learned the painful lessons of the War and will never again allow the repression of any race or creed to blot our fame.

My dear friend, there is no one on earth I would be more rejoiced to see than yourself. Should our age and circumstances make that impossible, know I always remain,

Faithfully and truly,
Your friend,
Prudence Crandall Philleo

The End

Afterword

PRUDENCE CRANDALL (1803-1890)

The idea for this book took shape in my mind after seeing a picture of Prudence Crandall's Canterbury home featured in an architectural magazine. The description of this remarkable woman triggered a search to learn all I could about Prudence Crandall's life and inspired me to write *The Canterbury Question*. She established the first school of its kind, an academy for black females, in the United States.

Although the vicious attack on her home forced the closing of the school, the arguments used at her trials were reintroduced in the 1954 landmark case for desegregation of schools, Brown versus the Topeka Board of Education.

She also started a school serving American Indians in Elk Falls, Kansas, in 1877.

After the Civil War, Mark Twain became one of her admirers, and largely due to his influence, in 1886, the Connecticut legislature granted her an apology and a lifetime annuity. She was chosen the official heroine of Connecticut in 1995, and her home still stands today in Canterbury, a memorial to her courageous stand for civil rights in the early 1800's.

SARAH HARRIS FAYERWEATHER (1812-1878)

Daughter of William and Sally Harris, Sarah's desire for an education was the catalyst for the conflict surrounding the Canterbury school. However, instead of becoming a teacher, Sarah became active in the cause of abolition. After she and George moved to Rhode Island, they became conductors on the Underground Railroad. Two of Sarah's children (Prudence and Mary) became teachers. Sarah and Prudence remained close friends and corresponded for many years. Sarah journeyed west to visit Prudence one last time in 1877.

ANDREW T. JUDSON (1784-1853)

Besides being the person chiefly responsible for closing down Prudence Crandall's school (1834), he is best known as the presiding judge of the district court trial of the Amistad Case in 1840. (The *Amistad* was a slave ship with a cargo of kidnapped Africans, that had turned up in a harbor within Judson's jurisdiction.) It may be hard to understand why, as a racist, he ruled the Mendes were "born free" and "still of right are free and not slaves," but since he believed slaves were property, he based his decision on the fact that Ruiz and Montes could not show a title verifying their ownership of the Africans.

Judson died in Canterbury and is buried in Hyde Cemetery.

SAMUEL J. MAY (1797-1871)

A well-known Unitarian Minister and friend of William Lloyd Garrison, May was a tireless reformer whose support of women's rights, abolition, and temperance earned him the dubious honor of being burned in effigy by his enemies. After leaving Connecticut, he became pastor of a Unitarian church in Syracuse, New York, and also served as president of Syracuse Public Schools. He donated a large body of his own reform writings (over 10,000 titles) to Cornell University's library. His account of Prudence Crandall's trials was a helpful source in my research. (Samuel J. May. Some recollections of our antislavery conflict, 1869. http://yale,edu/glc/crandall/03.htm.)

May's sister, Abba May Alcott, was the mother of Louisa May Alcott, author of the famous classic, *Little Women.*

CALVIN PHILLEO (1787-1874)

Calvin Philleo of Ithaca, New York, was an abolitionist and a widowed Baptist preacher who had an evangelistic calling and enthusiastic style of preaching. He used his vivid imagination and descriptive powers to bring many souls to Christ. He had three children by his first wife, Elizabeth Wheeler, before marrying Prudence. He was sixteen years older than Prudence, and he died January 5, 1874, in Illinois.

JULIA WILLIAMS (1811-1870)

Julia was born in Charleston, South Carolina, but moved with her family to Boston when she was a child. After the closing of the Canterbury school, she studied at the Noyes Academy in New Canaan, New Hampshire. She married Henry Garnett, who was a fugitive slave minister, and together they became missionaries to Jamaica. After her death in 1870, Henry went on to become U.S. Minister to Liberia.

Almost all of the other characters in the novel played an actual part in the historical events; though, of course, the details are embellished. (Although there was a dead cat hung on Prudence's fence, I cannot say for certain his name was Whittington.)

2

About Jerilyn J. Tyner

Jerilyn Tyner's lifelong love of language and literature began when she was a preschooler, memorizing her Little Golden Books and continued through more than two decades of freelance writing and teaching high school English. Her first novel, *The Canterbury* Question, reflects her enjoyment of a good story as well as admiration for teachers whose faith and vision have helped shape our country. Jerilyn and her husband live in beautiful Washington state. They have four grown sons, four daughters-in-law, five grandsons, two granddaughters, and a playful Papillon named Anouk.

98517675R00119

Made in the USA
Columbia, SC
30 June 2018